What readers are saying:

"School has just finished. Life stretches before us. Do you move out or stay home? **I really really connected to this topic** because I'm always deciding and re-deciding what I want to do with my life. For some people it's easy but for Alba, IT'S HARD."
Cait Grace, *Goodreads*

"Alba is brilliant. [...] She's what teen girls should be portrayed as. Young adult authors take note, this is how you create a **quirky and off beat young adult contemporary** that no doubt readers will fall in love with."
Kelly, *Diva Booknerd Blog*

"**Five stars to Melissa Keil** for not writing a love triangle and for bringing a small albeit real and cute romance element to the story gradually. I was particularly fond of Grady and I loved his relationship with Alba."
Rebecca, *Goodreads*

"**I loved the way Keil has captured those uncertainties you have about the future**, which are especially prevalent when you're a teenager. There are so many choices Alba and her friends have to make, all of which will affect the balance of their friendship. I think we've all been in situations where change is on the horizon and you dread the inevitability of things being different and friends drifting apart, so you cling on desperately to the present where things are happy and comfortable."
Sarah, *Total Teen Fiction Blog*

"Each and every single one of these characters had a lot of depth and personality [...] **it's like they're all your BEST FRIENDS**."
Melanie, *Goodreads*

"**Alba ... is awesome**. YAY FOR GIRLS WITH GREAT BODY IMAGE. Alba's not your typical kind of beautiful, but she rocks what she's got anyway, because screw conventional beauty."
Emily Mead, *Loony Teen Writer Blog*

"Wow. WOW [...] I read this in one sitting and all I have to say is that **the moment you can get your hands on this, grab it**."
Mary Robinette Kowal, *Goodreads*

"*The Incredible Adventures of Cinnamon Girl* has cemented Melissa Keil onto my favourite author list [...] **The characters are wonderful** and I wish I lived in Eden Valley so I could know them, spend time with them, be friends with them."
Lily Reads Books Blog

"**I hereby declare that I am in love with Alba** [...] A refreshing read full of friendship, comics, holding onto the past, bakery products and also, the forthcoming end of the world."
Tara, *Goodreads*

"The brilliant thing about *The Incredible Adventures of Cinnamon Girl* was its originality. Alba was a fun, unique protagonist. **It's such a wonderful feeling when you find a character who you understand so well**."
Cat, *Between the Pages of Books Blog*

"A classic coming of age story, told in wry and amusing language by Alba, a girl on the cusp of adulthood... This is an **exceptionally engrossing, well told story** of a clever teen girl and her group of friends working out what they want from life, friendship and love."
Read Plus

STRIPES PUBLISHING
An imprint of Little Tiger Press
1 The Coda Centre, 189 Munster Road,
London SW6 6AW

www.littletiger.co.uk

Originally published in Australia by Hardie Grant Egmont
in 2014

First published in Great Britain by Stripes Publishing in 2016

ISBN: 978-1-84715-683-9

A CIP catalogue record for this book is available
from the British Library.

Printed and bound in the UK.

10 9 8 7 6 5 4 3 2 1

THE INCREDIBLE ADVENTURES OF CINNAMON GIRL

stripes

If I drew my life right at this moment, I'd want it to look something like this brilliant comic-book panel from *Wonder Woman: Spirit of Truth.* Wonder Woman is kneeling on the lush hills way above her island home, her eyes closed, all steadfast and resolute. The colour and tone in the art is phenomenal; wicked purple cloud streaks in a wide, pale sky, lashed with warm yellows as the sun sinks on the horizon. With the light glinting off her tiara, and the half-smile on her lips, Wonder Woman is so alive I swear you can see her breathing. The panel is a perfect, paused moment in time – it could be from the end or the beginning of her story. She's kicked all sorts of arse beforehand, and has much more nonsense to face. But this one moment is her reprieve. In this one moment she is content, and home.

It takes wicked skills to capture so much in a single quiet image; a story that's both frozen and full of potential. Only truly great comic-book artists can pull off that kind of storytelling.

I think I'm sort of rubbish at telling stories. It's weird, cos I can talk a lot – a *lot* a lot – but when it comes to my pencils and inks, my stories have this tendency to lose their way. Grady says it's natural with an illustrator's brain; I see imagery in eye-bursting colour, not 'linear narratives', as he once put it. I dunno. I think, in truth, I'm just sucky at piecing together the right details.

If I were to start this story with the most important detail of all? It would probably be something about the end of the world. But honestly, at this point, the apocalypse and whatnot is just a passing footnote.

My story – my perfect, paused moment – begins much earlier than that.

It begins with a house.

And it begins with two boys.

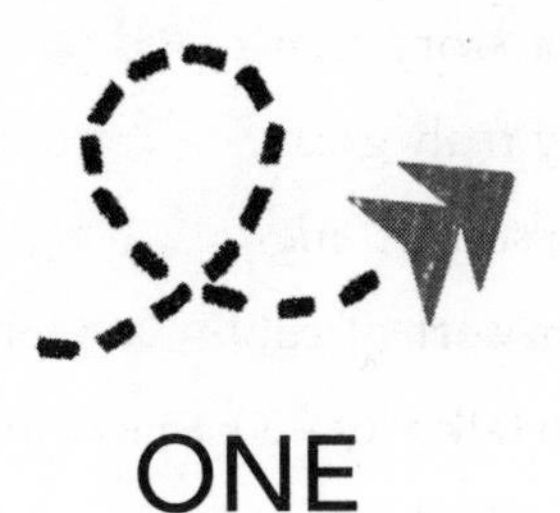

ONE

The house is a single-storey, chipped white weatherboard, and stands on the edge of a dusty road. It's set on stilts, unusual for around here, with a rickety staircase leading to the doors. French windows open on to a verandah, dappled by eucalypts and crammed with tables. In my sketchpad, I've always managed to make the house look adorable, in an *Oklahoma!* meets *Smallville* sort of way. In reality? It kinda looks like it should be harbouring survivalists hoarding Spam and toilet paper and stuff.

But it's beautiful. And it's my favourite place in the universe.

A neon sign, hung above the trellising, reads *Albany's.* That Albany refers to my mum, Angela, but I am an Albany also. On my many school participation awards I'm officially Sarah Jane Albany, though everyone in Eden Valley – almost all three-hundredish of them – has called me Alba since I was old enough to crawl.

And if I have been Alba since before I could walk, Domenic Grady has been my best friend since eons before then.

No telling if this story would be possible without a boy. Or, in my case, two. But I promise – it isn't what you think.

Grady is beautiful, in that way only a certain type of boy can be. He'd be pissed if he heard me saying this, cos I promised him I'd stop – but he's just so *pretty.* He has peachy skin and big doe-eyes, and the softest curls I've ever seen on a boy. Grady is kind of relevant to this story. I'll get to him in a minute.

Albany's is my mum's bakery. We bake cakes and bread and the most wicked apple strudel this side of Melbourne. Technically the house belongs to Grady's mum, Cleo, but ever since Mr Grady took off when Grady and I were five, Cleo handed the keys over and left us to it. Cleo is Mum's best friend. Hence why Grady was destined to be my bestie since we were, like, foetusi. Behind the converted kitchen is the living space that faces the Palmers' dairy farm, which has been my home since forever.

Now – before you start thinking that this is the story of some waify, sun-kissed country girl – get this straight. I am so *not* that girl. I have dark hair, and darker eyes, and did you hear me mention that I live in a bakery? Like, literally. I sleep in a fog of cinnamon and vanilla, and spend most mornings elbow-deep in pastries and pie.

And, um – I tend to eat a lot of it. I am OK with this. I've never glued my face on a supermodel's body while weeping into a tub of ice-cream. I have curves, and boobs, and no one I know has a problem with either. There were fourteen people in my year-twelve class, and believe me, if boobs of any kind were waved in their direction, it'd be cause for joy and celebration. Well, for the boys at least. Maybe one of the girls. My boobs are kind of irrelevant to this story.

I'm drifting. I should decide on a relevant detail.

OK. Best friend. Apocalypse.

Stories can have a multitude of false starts. In comic books, the first frames can take you any place, via anyone in the stories' universe. But I guess most stories only start when you place yourself in them, right? Well, mine starts when Domenic Grady bursts into Albany's one sweltering Sunday, waving his iPad in his hand, and says, "Alba! Have you seen this?"

He weaves through our sweaty customers and hoists himself on a counter stool, dropping his sports bag and grabbing a biscotti from one of the cake stands. Grady has forever been all arms and buzziness and the desire to do five bazillion things at once. If he were a comic-book character, he'd need his own signature entrance sound-effect, like a *Bazoing!* or *Bamf!* or something.

Today he's in his standard uniform: grey jeans, Vans and a navy Threadless T-shirt that says *Zombie Outbreak Response Team* on it. Grady plays basketball on Sundays, catching the bus to Merindale Creek, our closest town, almost a two-hour round trip away. Which means his hair is freshly washed, which means his dark curls would be extra soft atop his lanky frame, if they weren't shoved under a baseball cap.

I'm making Mr and Mrs Palmer their Sunday cappuccinos, and Grady's flusteriness has almost made me upend coffee all over my new swing dress. I hand the coffees to Paulette, our waitress, and I cross my arms and attempt a frown.

"Good morning, Grady. Was there something

you wanted to share?"

"I thought I established that with my dramatic entrance," he says through a mouthful of biscotti. "And don't look at me like that, Alba. You can't pull off cross-face."

I stick my tongue out at him, and he sticks his right back, then he plants his iPad on the counter. "Check this out."

"Grady, is it porn? I've told you I'm not interested in drawing that. No matter how much the Japanese'll pay for it."

Grady snorts. "Please, woman, if I was looking for porn, I think my brother's laptop would rival anything on the interwebs. Except, knowing Anthony, there's probably some home-made stuff on there, too."

Grady shudders. My eyes kinda glaze over at the thought of Anthony's lithe mechanic's body engaging in a badly lit sexcapade, until Grady leans across the countertop and swats my arm.

"Alba! Can you focus? This is potentially very cool. And weird. Check it out." He flicks his long fingers over the screen, and his New York screensaver disappears. A paused YouTube clip is waiting underneath.

Mum bursts through the kitchen doors. She slips a tray on to the counter and shakes a dusting of flour from her ponytail.

"Angie!" Grady says cheerfully, momentarily distracted by scone deliciousness. "You survived dinner last night? I had my doubts."

Mum grimaces. "Barely. If your mum suggests Asian Cooking Month again, maybe steer her in a less ... salmonella-esque direction?"

I slide the tray beneath the counter, ignoring the scone-starved customers trying to catch my eye. "Don't be so mean to poor Cleo. It wasn't *that* bad."

Grady laughs. "Sure it wasn't. After a handful of antacid and some Imodium."

The Christmas decorations above the door tinkle as Tommy Ridley enters with a wave. The bakery is buzzing this Sunday, as it always is on weekends before the pubs open. The string of bells bobs in the breeze as Tommy natters to Mr Wasileski in the doorway, and my eyes are drawn to the swirls of colour in the sky outside.

"So you're organising dessert?" I hear Mum say. "Don't let Cleo make anything with ingredients she has to find on the net."

Grady nods, grabby hands reaching for one of my lemon slices. "I'd like to not spend Christmas Day on a stomach pump, if I can help it." He takes a ginormous bite of mooshy lemon. "I have it covered. Don't stress, Angie."

"Stress is my middle name, Domenic," Mum says with a smile. Then the bells tinkle again, and Mum hurries off to hustle Mr Grey on to the verandah before he catches sight of Mr Bridgeman, and their obligatory smackdown over boutique beer ensues. Our two tetchy pub owners do not get along.

Through the open windows, the sky stretches beyond the Wasileskis' service station and my endless fields, the colour of breadcrumbs and sunlight. Summer skies are mind-blowing tones, almost impossible to capture—

"Alba? Now can I *please* show you this important thing I have here on my iPad?"

Maybe acrylic would work, or gouache—

Grady thumps his hands over mine. "*Sarah!* Woman, pay attention! This is potentially earth-shattering stuff here." He waves his fingers in front of my face, the hypno-thing he does whenever I'm being particularly spacey.

I know I'm in trouble. I have been first-named.

I hitch my dishcloth into my apron and flash him my best sparkly smile, which I know works a treat since his frown disappears instantly. "OK, OK! I'm focusing! Very important stuff. Go."

Grady blinks at me. Then he shoves aside a plate of croissants and hauls his butt on to the counter, angling sideways so that we're facing the same direction. He swipes at the iPad again.

The screen fills with the image of a bald guy with one of those glossy black Fu Manchu moustaches. He's sitting on a cheap set, with a nondescript guy beside him. Stuck behind them is a sign in what I think is Comic Sans. The sign reads: *The Original Ned Zebidiah. Prognosticator. Seer. Diviner of Ancient Mysteries.*

And below that in tiny letters: *And Frank.*

"Have you seen this guy?" Grady says. "He has a show on Channel 31. It's on at, like, two in the morning. I watch him when I can't sleep, and he's usually good for a laugh, but this – is beyond cool."

I choose not to comment on the return of Grady's insomnia. It's not something he wants to talk about, and besides, he says it's nothing to worry about. Though, ever since we were five and he managed to break his arm playing minigolf, worrying about Grady has been kinda routine.

"The Original? Is there more than one?"

Grady snorts. "Yeah, it's a pretty dodge moniker. But seriously, Alba. Watch."

He turns the volume up over the chatter and the *White Christmas* soundtrack burbling through the bakery. The clip has forty-five views and a bunch of comments I can't read because Grady's big hand is clutching the screen like he's crazy Mrs Garabaldi from the hardware store, and his iPad is the last cherry slice at the end of cherry season. He touches the screen, and the clip starts to roll.

Original Ned peers at the camera, his Fu Manchu wiggling as he swallows uncomfortably. "Welcome, friends," he says, his voice oddly high-pitched for a guy who looks like an *X-Men* villain. "It's, uh, another Friday, and, uh, the universe is once again speaking to those with the power to, uh, listen..."

He glances at the guy next to him, a skinny, wide-eyed dude. Presumably the *And Frank*.

"Grady, does anyone actually watch this?"

Grady points at the screen. "At least forty-five people on YouTube. Though I'm guessing that's forty-four views from Ned, and one from Frank's mum. Hang on … I'll skip the boring stuff…"

Grady's finger trails across the screen. Original Ned is somewhat stressed-looking now, beads of sweat dribbling down his forehead.

"… some call it the Rapture," he mumbles. "But I have seen it, friends. Ned Zebidiah understands the planetary alignments and the … ancient codes of Revelation and the … uh … Aztecs…"

"Jeez. This sounds credible."

Grady laughs. "I know. Talk about covering all your bases. But keep watching."

Ned straightens. "I have peered through the veil and … stuff. But now, the universe has chosen to speak to Ned Zebidiah." And then he leans toward the camera. "The End of Days," Ned whispers. "I have seen it. And, friends – I have seen the salvation."

I giggle as Ned's eyes roll back and his body shakes like he's trapped in a giant blender. Skinny guy shuffles his chair away with a start. And then Ned rattles off a list of numbers. Frank frantically scribbles in a notebook.

I can see Rosie Addler waving from the booth where she's parked with her poodle, Mr Frankenstein. I reach for a plate of donuts. "So what? He's predicting Powerball?"

Grady leans precariously toward me, his long legs holding him in place. "Nope," he says with excited eyes. "The comments say they're map coordinates."

"I have seen through the illusions!" Ned bellows, causing Frank to almost fall out of his chair. "The calendar will end with the turn of the New Year." Ned flops backwards. "And I have seen those who will be saved," he says in this portentous whisper. "Pray to whatever gods you believe in, friends. The end is upon us. And only the chosen ones will be spared."

Grady pauses the clip. "The rest is pretty boring. People call in for advice on, like, speaking to their dead cats. And then Frank sings. It's not exactly HBO."

He leaps down from the counter and leans over it again. I push back the brim of his baseball cap, cos I know his mischievous eyes are twinkling beneath it.

"Fascinating, Grady, but I gotta get back to work—"

"So get this," he says. "Those numbers he gave? The map coordinates?" He lowers his voice to a conspiratorial whisper. "They're here."

I brush my hands on my apron. They're suddenly all weird and tingly. "You mean—"

"Right. Here. Apparently, when the crap goes down, Eden Valley is the only place on the planet that's going to survive. We are the Ark, Alba. The – what's the name of the last city on Earth from that weird-arse comic you like?"

I giggle. "Pythonopolis. But you're not serious. Is this guy for real?"

"I googled him. His real name is Alvin Smith, and he used to work in real estate." Grady flashes his cheeky grin at me. "I would say his information is possibly suspect. But then again, Alba, if you can't trust a community-TV prophet…?"

I can't help but laugh. "So the end of the world is nigh in what, seventeen days – and little ol' Eden Valley is gonna be the last outpost? Very cool."

Grady grimaces. He flicks a glance over his shoulder at the dusty, empty span of Main Street. "Jesus. Can you think of anything more depressing than that?"

I busy myself rearranging the macarons I'd

painstakingly sandwiched with Christmas-coloured ganache this morning. "It's not *depressing*," I say eventually. "There'd be worse places to spend eternity. We'll have everyone we love in the one spot ... but, OK, it means we'll have to repopulate the planet. I suppose that might be inconvenient."

When I glance up, Grady seems to be focusing on a cloud of sugar on the countertop. And then he picks up one of my menus. He grabs a napkin and swipes at a jammy smudge. "People have no respect," he mutters.

I flick his arm with my dishcloth. "They're supposed to be used. Utilitarian, remember?"

"It's not Pizza Hut," he says, his eyes on the menu. "It's art – not that anyone in this town would know the difference."

My latest menu is a new style I've been experimenting with, sort of the wicked inventive layouts of the last *X-23* meets the linework of Faith Erin Hicks, but with a palette of old-school Marvel colours, all reds and blues and limey greens. I'm trying out a new character in this one as well. Her hair is styled a bit like mine, with a thick eye-sweeping fringe, but instead of my longish brown boringness I've given her masses of red curls streaked with blue. I'd played around with different outfits before settling on a style that I currently love, a scarlet gingham rockabilly dress with navy stockings and giant red heels. She's not *supposed* to be me, even though she dresses like me and has my height and, OK, maybe my solid thighs. I think she looks pretty kick-arse. In honour of her hair Grady dubbed her Cinnamon Girl, and I guess his name stuck. Our menu is embedded in the comic's panels, in the lettering and word balloons that litter her little streets. I'm sort of proud of this one.

Grady drops the menu. He peers at me from beneath his cap, hitting me with the full force of his stubborn Bambi eyes. Instinctively, I feel myself bristle.

"Alba … I don't know why you've suddenly become subject-change girl, but – you know, you've barely told me anything about your interview. Did they like your folio? Of course they liked your folio, your stuff is bloody brilliant …"

He tugs his cap down and gives me a bright smile. "We're a few short weeks away from getting the hell out of this dump, and I am *kinda* counting on the fact that the rest of the world will still be standing—"

"*You* are a few weeks," I say, my eyes on the macarons. "I'm not sure ... I mean, I don't know now..."

Grady picks up his lemon slice and devours the rest in one theatrical bite. "Seriously," he says, dabbing a smiley on the back of my hand with his icing-y fingers, "I cannot witness the results of Eden Valley inbreeding without seeing New York at least once."

I shuffle in front of the counter and nudge his hip with mine. Subject-change girl I may be, but I suspect that neither of us is in the mood for this conversation right now. "Grady, I think you're probably safe. Hasn't the end of the world been predicted, like, a thousand times? What is the plural of apocalypse anyway? Apocali?"

"Apocalypseses?" he says, nudging me back with a grin. "And picture this – if we do turn out to be the last people on the planet, someone we know will actually face the prospect of breeding with Eddie."

"Eww ... poor Eddie," I say with a laugh. "I'm not sure Judgement Day will be calamitous enough to snag him a girlfriend. He *may* be the first one sacrificed when we're forced to turn to human-burgers for sustenance."

But Grady's eyes are back on his iPad, and he doesn't seem to be listening. "Huh."

"What?"

He shakes his head, left hand kneading the back of his neck like he always does when he's thinking. "Nothing. Just, well – look at this."

He turns the iPad around and points at the view counter.

The view counter reads eighty-nine.

I peer at the screen. "Maybe Ned has more fans than country-boy insomniacs and Frank's mum?"

"Maybe." Grady snaps his iPad shut. "Anyway. You almost done?"

"Need to help with the rush. Another hour?"

"Cool. I promised Mr Grey I'd help fix that dodgy table at the pub, but I'm gonna pass out if I don't find proper lunch first. Unless you want to get some drawing done?"

"Nah. Food's good," I say, my mouth watering at the thought of the Nguyens' Sunday calamari special.

Grady picks up his sports bag in one hand, and reaches over with the other to adjust the flower I've stuck in my braid. "Kay. I'll wait."

He weaves through the tables, waving at various

people, and settles in his usual booth with a slice of banana bread. He buries his head in a John Grisham novel, his iPad propped in front of him, presumably with some random video playing.

Then Paulette drops a tray of forks with an almighty *clang*, and I'm distracted by serving Rosie Addler her third pink-iced donut, so two seconds later I promptly forget all about YouTube and Original Ned and that view counter that seems to have ticked over a little too fast for a clip from a dodgy nobody television prophet.

OK, I know I said that I am rubbish at remembering details.

In hindsight? That was one detail I should probably have paid attention to.

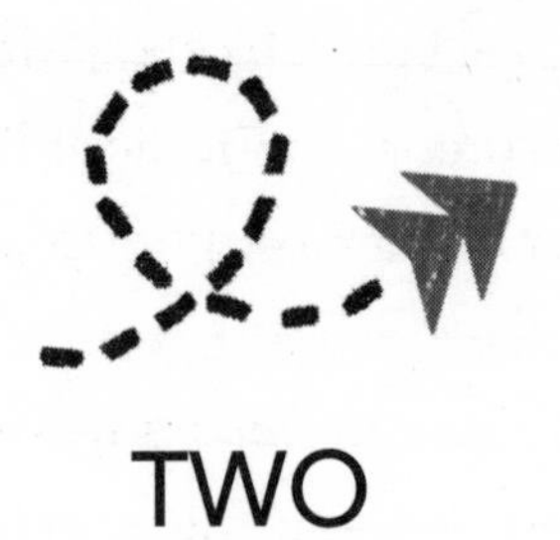

TWO

So remember I said my story would not be tell-able without two boys? Bear with me, I am coming to that part. My boys may be indispensible to my origin story, but nothing – apocalypse or otherwise – will make any sense without some prefacey panels of my other *Smallville* sidekicks.

On any normal school-year Monday, my friends will shuffle into Albany's for breakfast, school uniforms all skew-whiff, before we walk down the road to catch the bus we share with the primary school. But school-year Mondays ended for the very last time weeks ago, and so, for our last summer holidays – and as long as everyone is still here – I insist we meet as normal like every other Monday.

Tia barges through the side gate pulling a yawning Caroline by the hand, just as I'm laying a picnic mat on the springy fake grass.

"Happy no-school Monday, Alba!" Tia chirps. "Nice pink shirt. Is that ModCloth?"

I half-spin in my best pin-up girl pose. "Yup. Like it?"

"*Love* it!" Tia says. She nudges Caroline. "See? There are more styles in the world than jeans and stuff from Jetty Surf."

"I'll remember that when I get my Oscar invite." Caroline drops on to the mat and folds her long legs beneath her. "Christ, it's hot. I feel like my eyeballs are sweating. Does someone actually want us to burn in this hell?"

I hand her a croissant and snap a sneaky photo with my phone before she can flip me the bird. "Oh boo, Caroline. The sky is clear, the birds are singing – I think it's a small improvement on homeroom and that cloud of Mr Baxter's pit-sweat."

Tia sits, her floaty dress pooling on the picnic mat. "Besides, it's only eight sleeps till Christmas, and we'll never have to sit through another Monday assembly on drugs or, like, the dangers of tractor joyriding again..."

Tia grimaces. She glances at me. For a befuddled

second, I find myself wondering why she's not in her stripy school uniform. I think I can live without Principal Bairnsworth's eager Monday pep talks, or her one-woman sex-ed puppet shows. And yet, the mental flash of our teeny school quad, empty in the summer sunshine, fills me with a fleeting, throat-squeezy sadness.

Caroline squints up at the almost-midday sun. She shoots us a grin. "If the two of you burst into song, someone is gonna get punched."

Tia gives me a weak smile. Tia's real name is Tiahnah, cos her mum is – well, let's just say that Mrs Holbrook is a big fan of the reality-TV school of child-naming, giving her daughters the uber-classy monikers of Tiahnah, Brihannah and Khahliah.

I kid you not.

Brihannah scarpered to the city years ago, and Khahliah dropped out of school and moved to Perth to hook up with a guy she met on the internet. But Tia is ace, and reminds me of Josie from Dad's Archie comics, except, you know, with chestnut hair and way better fashion sense.

Grady stumbles in a few minutes later, his Labrador, Clouseau, trailing wheezily behind.

"You're late," I say as I give Clouseau a cuddle. "We had plans, Grady! Big plans! I've been sitting by my phone, worried sick, while you've been gallivanting around town with your no-good pals and that floozy from the hairdresser—"

"Hey, woman!" he says in his old-timey movie voice. "You're not the boss of me. Guess I'm just not a one-gal sorta guy." Caroline snorts as Grady gives her and Tia a wave. "And yeah, I promised Rosie I'd fix the gate on her chook pen, but I spent most of the morning stopping her mutt from humping Clouseau's head. Totally not worth twenty bucks. I'm starved."

I've laid out food on one of the tiny ornate tables that dot the yard. He reaches for a cupcake, but I slap his hand away. "Can't. Strawberry."

He drops the cupcake like it's a live landmine. "I knew it. You *are* trying to kill me. I don't even get a warning?"

I spin the plate and point to the giant pink post-it stuck right in front. It reads: *STRAWBERRY BIOHAZARD. HANDS OFF D.G.*

"Sorry, Mr Everson donated a box and Mum didn't want to waste them. But, see, I drew you a picture. It has your hair, and look, even a teeny chalk outline, right here."

Grady wrinkles his nose. "You couldn't have used them for compost? Why didn't you just draw him convulsing in anaphylactic shock?"

But I don't have a chance to respond, because a hulking arm grabs Grady around the neck from behind, while its meat-mallet counterpart punches him in the ribs.

"Yo, butt-face. How goes it, G-man?"

Grady grimaces. "Eddie, get off me, man," he growls.

"Aw, not in the mood for shenanigans, Domenic? Not what you said last night—"

Grady throws a cupcake at Eddie's head. "Ed, I know you can't keep your hands off me, but could you at least try when we're in public?"

"Will do my best. I can't help it that you're so fecking cute." Eddie grins at me. "Aloha, gorgeous," he says in his rumbly baritone. "You are looking especially hot today. Remind me again why we never went out?"

I hand him a Danish and a coffee, four sugars, his usual beverage for his usual conversation.

"Thanks, Ed! And I never went out with you because, well, a) you never asked and, b) I love you, but you're kind of an arsebag."

"Fair enough," Eddie says as he polishes off half the Danish with one bite.

If he were a character from an American movie, Eddie would be that meathead linebacker with a name like Biff or Chud. If he were a comic-book character, he'd most likely be surrounded by minions, or swanning around seeking indiscriminate revenge with half his freckly face melted off. But since he was born and raised in Eden Valley, Francis Edwin Palmer is neither a supervillain nor – despite what he would have us believe – a total meathead. If the universe worked the way it's supposed to, then Ed should be hanging with the thick-necked boys from Merindale football team, or the workers from his parents' farm. But deep down, Eddie is a sweetheart, and he's been our friend forever. He *does* tend to use the f-word a lot – but since I am telling this story, and I really don't want to drop it every seven seconds – I'm gonna use 'feck' instead.

"Fecking hell, it's hot as feck," Eddie says as he slumps on the ground. He glances at Caroline with a start. “And what the feck have you done to your hair, Gresham?”

Caroline smoothes a hand over the awesome violet streaks in her blond hair. “Shut it, Ed. I’m finally free from twelve years of uniform hell – the only reason I haven’t got my tongue pierced is cos Dad threatened to use Gran’s graduation money to redo the driveway if I did. Anyway, I didn’t ask for your approval. And I didn’t ask for your opinion.”

“Maybe you should’ve asked for a mirror?” Eddie says, ducking away before she can punch him.

“Well, I like it!” I say, stretching out on my banana lounge next to Grady, who is devouring a cinnamon scroll. He shuffles over to make room. “Add some spandex and you’d look just like a character from *X-Men*.”

“Who’s wearing spandex?”

Pete pushes through the gate with his bike in hand. He drops it with a thud and heads straight for the food.

Eddie gives him a two-fingered wave. “Petey! So Mum was watching *Water for Elephants* on TV last night. It was fecking shithouse, but it made me think of you. Circus tents, acrobats – isn’t that, like, porn to your people?"

Pete's face turns scarlet. "Eddie, are you ever gonna let that go?" he whines. "And can we *please* stop talking about it in front of my girlfriend?"

Eddie bursts into howly laughter. Even Grady fails to hide a chuckle. "Sorry, man," Eddie says with a dismissive wave. "Just trying to support your lifestyle choices."

Grady and I had always half-suspected that Peter Nguyen was gay, until the summer after year nine when Pete tagged along with Ed and his brothers on a camping weekend. Which happened to coincide with a certain circus-training weekend at the same campsite. Apparently, as Grady informed me, Pete was caught – ahem – *entertaining* himself after watching the girls' juggling. Needless to say, I've never been able to look at Cirque du Soleil in quite the same way again.

"Don't listen to him, Petey," I say, flashing him my sweetest smile. "You can't help how you were born."

"Dude, the love between man and clown is nothing to be ashamed of," Caroline adds innocently.

"I hate you all," Pete mumbles as he grabs a muffin and slumps besides Tia.

Nothing much grows here. The only living things are the eucalypts, and the plum trees Dad planted along the wire fence that separates our yard from Ed's farm. The real grass is gold and crunchy like straw, impossible to sit on with bare legs. But a couple of years ago Mum and I saw this picture in a magazine, some city bar decked with fake grass and plastic palm trees. So we decided to replicate it, even adding some pink flamingos on sticks and strings of little lanterns between the verandah trellising. I know people around here think it's tacky, but I love it – sort of a kitschy, tropical Secret Garden.

"So get this," Eddie says as he slurps coffee. "Guess who showed up at my door last night?"

Pete groans. "Eddie, is this one of your bogus sex stories—"

"Naw, unfortunately your mum was busy," Eddie says with a wink. "No – Baxter came to see me."

I pick up my sketchpad from the grass. "Mr Baxter? Ed, maybe you should give the poor guy a break. Let him have a summer of peace before you make him cry again."

Eddie looks out over his farm. "Yeah, well, that's what he wanted to talk about. I'm not going next year.

To year twelve. I've been thinking about it and … yeah. Thought of being stuck in class for another year makes me break out in hives. So I'm leaving."

Grady bolts upright. "Eddie. You cannot be serious?"

Eddie shrugs. "Why not? It's not like I'm heading to Mensa. Feck, thought Baxter'd be the first one throwing a party."

"Mensa isn't a place, Ed," Grady says carefully. "And come on. Year Twelve Eddie! Only one more year of high school and then you're done. The rest of us managed it – how can you think about quitting?"

"Yeah, well, not all of us are gonna be brainiac lawyers. And 'sides, there's plenty of work on the farm and … it's not like I was ever gonna go anywhere else. Right?"

Pete looks curiously at Eddie. Tia looks uncertainly at Pete. Grady and Caroline stare, horrified, at Ed. I drop my eyes to my sketchpad.

"Francis Edwin," Caroline says slowly. She picks up a stray branch and jabs him in the arm. "Are you seriously saying you're contemplating a future in Eden Valley? You're *really* thinking of becoming one of those morons we've made fun of for years?

You planning on losing your hair and your teeth and spending every Saturday for the rest of your life at the Junction Pub?"

Grady leaps out of the banana lounge. "Yes, thank you, Caroline! Eddie, I'm sorry, but this is so stupid! Even Caroline's made it through year twelve, and she only punched two people during exams—"

"Three if you count that cardboard Jamie Oliver at the grocery store," Caroline says flatly. "Smug tool. What the hell is a courgette—"

Grady glares at her. "The *point*, Eddie, is that you're smart enough to graduate. Then who knows, there's uni and Melbourne and—"

"What, we're all gonna move to the city and live in one house and throw dinner parties or whatever like some shite sitcom? Dude. You've met me, right?" Eddie glances out over his parched farmland. "Anyway. Only reason I stuck it out this long was cos of you losers ..." He clears his throat. And then he throws a stick at Grady with a grin. "Bit pointless now. Isn't it?"

Grady sits heavily on the edge of the banana lounge. "Alba! Help me out here!"

I focus on my sketchpad. Pete's been trying to

get me to draw him for ages, though I'm not sure I have the skills to do what he wants. I'm taking some inspiration from Sara Pichelli's Spider-Man, but honestly? It might take abilities beyond mine to transform scrawny Petey into a 'kick-arse ninja warrior', as was requested.

From the corner of my eye, I can see that Grady is still looking at me. Though I'm not sure why he thinks I'd have anything useful to say. Once upon a time, all Eddie wanted to be was a pilot. When we were kids he even had a whole mess of model planes hanging from his bedroom roof, though the planes are long gone now. But once upon a time, Tia wanted to be an astronaut, and Caroline dreamed of having her own show on the Disney Channel. I think Pete still dreams about being a DJ, or a ninja – though since his less-than-stellar results came in, he just mumbles "business or something" whenever anyone asks about his future plans, and then changes the subject.

And me? Apart from abandoning my pubescent ambition of becoming Wonder Woman, my dreams have always been solid, and unshakable. Until recently anyways.

"Eddie can do what he wants. Not everyone is destined to go to uni," I say as I run my pencil over the page. My fingers suddenly feel stiff. A finished action figure is only as good as the structure beneath it, and right now my skeleton of action-Pete looks like it's in the middle of a largish stroke. I tear out the page and scrunch it into a ball.

"Mr Baxter won't know what to do without you, Ed. You're the only person on the planet who can make his face turn that shade of burgundy." I glance at Grady, who is glaring at me. "But, Eddie, if that's what you want to do, then that's what you should do," I say firmly.

Tia picks at the fake grass. "Alba's right. People are allowed to change their mind about their plans—"

Grady scowls. "Right, because you're going to be a famous designer here in the Valley? Hey, if you're lucky, the guys from Anthony's garage might let you design their overalls—"

"Easy, Grady," Tia says lightly as Pete reaches for her hand. "Don't take your issues out on me."

Grady looks desperately from her to Pete. "Sorry, Tia – but, Petey, come on, man! Tell Eddie he cannot drop out of school to work his parents' farm. If for no other reason than he can't be such a dodge cliché."

Pete snorts. "Dude, you're talking to the Asian kid whose parents own the fish-and-chip shop. No comment."

I drop my sketchpad. "Grady, leave it." I give him the other half of my cinnamon scroll. "It's a beautiful day, and I'd rather not spend it watching you and Ed go at it. You know Eddie'll beat you to a bloody pulp."

Eddie grins. "You know it, gorgeous."

Grady slumps on to the grass and gives his snoozing dog a rough pat. "Fine. Whatever. Do what you want."

Caroline scowls. "Even if what you want is retarded, Eddie." She and Grady share a look, but thankfully neither of them says anything more.

No one on the planet is as well acquainted with Grady's stubbornness as me; the last thing I need is for him to be fixating on this all summer. And sue me, but I hate this conversation; who's staying and who's going and who's doing what when. Not least because it makes my stupid hands feel all seized up and icy cold.

The only sounds in my backyard are the familiar warble of magpie song, and the munching of my friends who are all finding the distant hills and empty sky fascinating. From somewhere in the ether, a lone cow moos.

Just to break the silence, I'm about to launch into the story of the time when Tia and I watched *The Sound of Music* and then tried to redesign Caroline's wardrobe using her mum's curtains, when we're rudely interrupted by the boom of a backfiring engine. Foghorn honks echo through the air from a car that I don't recognize.

"Feck was that?" Eddie mutters as he heaves himself to his feet.

I haul myself up and push through the gate, my friends and Clouseau trailing behind.

A few locals are dotted on Albany's verandah, pots of tea and pastries in front of them. Mrs Garabaldi is hunched in her corner table with a slice of toast halfway to her mouth. Everyone seems to be peering suspiciously down at Main Street.

An orange-and-blue VW Kombi van is parked in front of our bluestone path. Its back windows are covered by fraying purple curtains, and a couple of surfboards are strapped to the roof.

The driver sticks his head through the window.

He has one of those arrow bolts through the middle of his nose, and a bunch of neck tattoos that look pretty cool, though I can't make out the art under the beard that's covering half his face.

"Hello?" he calls out. "Can you tell us how to get to Eden Valley?"

"Dude. You're in it," Pete replies from behind me.

The guy leans out the window and squints down the empty road. "Really? This is it?"

Grady heads over, hands in the pockets of his jeans. "Yeah. I have that same reaction every morning. You looking for something in particular?" he says shyly.

"Think your GPS is off," Eddie mutters, his eyes on the surfboards. "Beach is about a thousand kilometres thataway—"

The curtains at the back of the van stir, and another sweaty face appears. A girl with a knot of ash-blond dreads peers sleepily out at us. A long row of piercings line one ear. She's also wearing the teeniest yellow bikini I think I've ever seen in real life.

Eddie's face turns the colour of raspberry jam. He drops his eyes to his feet, his feet shuffling up clouds of dirt. He makes this sound effect that's something like *garmurwedgie*, and I know that this is the last we will hear from Eddie Palmer for the foreseeable future.

"Hey there," I say with a wave. "Can we help you?"

The girl waves back. "Heya. You guys know if there's a campsite or something round here?"

Pete shoves past me, skinny arms gesturing to the paddocks behind the bakery. "That's the Palmers' farm. We don't get many visitors, I mean, from outside the Shire, and you know, sometimes a few arsebags from Merindale – but the Palmers did let some backpackers hire a bit of field once before. Keep going straight, then take the road on the left, just past the post office – that's the building with the red tin roof. You can't miss it. The Palmers' house looks like it's been dropped out of a tornado."

Tia, somewhat pointedly, grabs Pete's hand. "So ... you guys just passing through? Merindale's about an hour away, and they have an actual campsite..."

Driver-guy snorts. "You're kidding, right? No, man, we're right where we want to be." And then he guns the ear-splitting engine again. "Thanks – catch ya!"

Caroline frowns at the retreating Kombi's dust cloud. "That was weird?"

"Naw," Grady says wistfully. "Hippies out to discover the 'real Australia'. Guaranteed they've stocked that van with nothing but patchouli and a whole heap of weed."

The six of us stare at the Kombi as it disappears in a bitumen-heat haze past the Garabaldis' store. Caroline clears her throat. "Probably. Still weird though."

Hindsight is a beautiful thing. It's one of the things I love about comics; if you overlook something you should have noticed, you can always flip back and take a second look at the detail.

We head to my yard again, me prattling about this time when Mum and Cleo piled us into Mum's car on a whim and drove for two days just to see the Big Banana, and pretty soon the mysterious Kombi is all but forgotten.

THREE

Right. The other boy. I'm getting there soon, I swear. Thing is, since the beginning of time, it's always been Grady and me. But it wasn't always *just* Grady and me. Seriously though – it really isn't what you think.

If the heatwave sticks, summer will soon involve nothing more than crashing at someone's house with a pile of DVDs, but for now we amble down Main Street, shuffling aside when Lucy Albington from the post office drives past with a wave. In the afternoon, Grady helps Mr Garabaldi install a plastic Santa on the hardware-store roof, while I hover nervously beneath the ladder. And then we amble up the hill to hang at Grady's brother's garage. Anthony and Eddie have been helping fix this rust-bucket ute, Caroline's prized possession, though they still haven't managed to get the thing to run. I watch from my perch on a workbench as Caroline runs a hand longingly over the cracked steering wheel. I think I might be the worst friend in the world, but as always, when the engine splutters and dies, I can't help but be shamefully relieved. We stay till Grady can no longer take the ribbing from his brother, and then we shuffle into the sun again, leaving Ed and his giant freckly shoulders crammed beneath the ute and Clouseau snoring under a workbench.

Then Caroline heads to her shift at the grocery store, and Petey and Tia disappear, presumably for some awkward smooching, and Grady and I lumber back to my place.

"Grab food if you're hungry," I say as we push through the verandah door into the aircon coolness of my bedroom. I plop down at my desk. "You're not going home, are you?"

Grady collapses on to my bed and pulls a new novel out of his messenger bag. It's one of those classic detective things he loves, where the women are icy and evil, and the men wear fedoras and get shot at the end. "Nah. Will hang out here."

I wrap my hair in one of my scarves. "Cool. Just wanna finish one bit. Won't be long."

"Uh-huh," he says as he settles on to my pillow and cracks open his book.

My Mac springs to life with a chime. In front of it is my Wacom, a birthday present from Mum last year, completely amazing in its awesomeness. I still prefer drawing my lines in pencil, then scanning them and adding colour digitally. But it's given me heaps of freedom to play with my comics, and it's sort of revolutionized my art.

I open the piece I've been working on – three vertical panels with a background that links the segments of the scene. I'm calling it *The Further Adventures of Cinnamon Girl*, though I'm not really sure where this one is going. I've storyboarded her an apartment, a very cool warehouse with industrial furniture and ginormous arch windows. I have her outfits down, but I'm struggling a bit with her movement. It doesn't help that I keep changing my mind about what sort of story I'm making. I mean, I've always planned on creating my own superhero, a kick-arse heroine in a multi-dimensional world and whatnot – but lately, I've really been getting into these indie comics that are pencilled and inked by the same person, and these online zines that are made up of simple monochromatic panels and – anyways. For now, Cinnamon Girl is just hanging in her apartment until I can come up with an adventure worthy of her.

I zoom in on the middle panel and focus on nailing the foreshortening in her legs …

I sit up with a start. The light has changed to watery orange, and my back is knotted in a giant cheese twist. I stretch my arms with a yawn and push away from my desk.

Grady is stomach-down on the old couch in front of my window. He's flicking lazily through one of my new *Captain Marvel*s, his novel on the floor beside him. "Welcome back," he says with a smile.

"I zoned out," I say sheepishly. "Again. Sorry 'bout that."

Grady swings himself up, the floorboards creaking beneath his feet. "Your hands were moving and you were humming, so I figured I didn't need to check you were still breathing. Really? *South Pacific*?"

I flick a pencil at him, which he catches midair. "Don't knock the show tunes, man!" I say with another yawn. "You know they help me focus."

I hear the crack of bone as Grady rolls his neck. He leans over my shoulder. "Wow. That is … awesome. But it looks different to your other stuff. What are you doing with the background?"

I flex my fingers. "Dunno. I thought I'd experiment with muting the colour palette? Not sure all those shades of brown is really me though. You like?"

"Very much," he says. "It's sort of, um, like that one you showed me online … *Hinges*? But, you know. More you."

I spin my chair. Grady shoves *Captain Marvel* into the bookshelf behind my desk that's bowing under the weight of my bazillion comics and graphic novels and longboxes that belonged to Dad. "I like this character a lot, Alba," he says as his eyes linger on my screen. "Not really a superhero, but not an ordinary girl either."

"Well, I'm just messing around with her style for now. I have a couple of ideas, but … I'm sort of stuck on her story."

Grady leans down so we're eye to eye, his stubborn baby browns peering into mine. "Either way, she deserves a life bigger than a bakery menu," he says firmly.

I resist the urge to stick out my tongue. "So what time is it?"

He glances at his watch with a sigh. "Nine fifteen. Dunno where everyone else is –"

Right on cue, Ed's voice booms from my lounge. "Put your clothes on, kids! G-man, I'm coming in, and I hope to Christ I'm not gonna catch you with your tackle out."

"God, Eddie, do you have to be so disgusting!" I yell back, trying not to laugh at the very fetching Hellboy red that has flooded Grady's face.

I skip into the lounge, where a grease-covered Eddie is grinning like an imbecile. He dumps an armful of pizza boxes on to the coffee table and blows a kiss at Grady.

"You're such a butt-monkey, *Francis*," Grady grumbles.

Caroline collapses in front of the sparkly Christmas tree, hands wrestling open a box of Cheezels. She's changed out of her work uniform, and is back in denim shorts and her T-shirt that says *Angry Fembot Army*. "This is news to you?" she says through a mouthful of Cheezel. "Grady, meet Eddie."

Eddie sticks out a hand. "Nice to meet you, dude."

"Shut up, arsebag," Grady mumbles as he flops on to the couch.

I take the seat next to him and give his hand a sympathy pat. Pete has squished into Dad's lumpy armchair, while Tia dumps packs of Red Bulls and a bunch of shot glasses on to the table. She beams at me as I click on the TV.

Regardless of what is happening in our various lives, I have declared Monday nights for the past eight months to be a standing event that *no one* is allowed to miss.

OK. Deep breath. That other boy? He's barging into my story right about now.

"Kay, new rule," I say. "Apparently the guy who plays Dr Mac Macleod is in rehab. But they can't kill him off, cos everyone knows he's going to turn out to be Bianca's dad. So anyone wanna guess how they'll write him out? And remember, you guess right ..." Tia waves a jam jar in the air. "You get to scull the Cup-of-Death!"

Caroline wipes her Cheezel-y finger on her shorts and grabs a shot glass. "He's visiting a sick friend in Sydney."

I reach for a slice of Hawaiian. "He's on a training

course. In Darwin. If they need him to disappear for longer, they can just lose him in the desert."

Eddie grabs a pizza box and throws himself into an armchair. "He's walking the dog. Feck, they can keep that going for a year."

Grady kicks his feet up on the coffee table, toppling one of our Santas in the process. "He's performing experimental surgery," he says as he sets the Santa upright. "Gives them a chance to have people hanging in the waiting-room set."

"Yeah, they might as well use it before the show's cancelled," Pete adds. "And—"

"OK, *shush*!" Tia yelps. The twangy ukulele music kicks in, and the screen fades into a sunset beach under a shaky title. The six of us down a customary shot of Red Bull, for no reason other than the sucky theme song has always seemed to warrant it.

It's this soap opera called *A Home Among the Gum Trees*, and, barring the episode of *Embarrassing Bodies* that Grady and I once watched, it is a candidate for the honour of being the worst TV show in the history of the universe. It's set in a surf-beach hospital, where all the doctors are blond and look about eighteen.

The storylines veer between car accidents, mysterious secret children showing up out of nowhere, and weddings that are interrupted by one of the above. Occasionally someone will fall down a mine shaft, though no one is ever able to explain why there are so many abandoned mines on the outskirts of a surf town. It's also just moved to 9.30 p.m. on a Monday, which guarantees it's one step away from being canned.

Tia squishes in next to Pete, accidentally kneeing him in the nuts in the process. Pete makes what looks like a heroic effort not to react. Tia and Petey hooked up months ago, but they haven't really figured out how they work as a pair yet. Their hand-holding is always self-conscious, and there's typically much confusion over who puts whose limbs where.

"Sorry," Tia mumbles. She clears her throat. "And remember everyone, basic rules – one drink every time Indigo's shirtless with no proper plot reason."

Pete drapes an arm around her shoulder. "One drink if his face freezes in that emo frown while the music plays into an ad break."

Eddie reaches for a Red Bull. "Two drinks if he does that fecking expression like someone is waving off-cheese under his nose."

I look sideways at Grady, who's already laughing. "And two drinks if Indigo uses the phrase, 'Damn it, Becky! I'm not a doctor yet!'" I say, slapping my hand on Grady's knee for emphasis.

Caroline groans as a nurse mumbles something about Dr Macleod visiting a sick friend, and Tia gleefully hands her the brim-full jam jar of Red Bull.

We have tried this with booze a couple of times, but that never ends well for any of us. Last time, Grady passed out in my bed after trying to draw a moustache on Clouseau and then asking me to marry him. Needless to say, no one has questioned the Red Bull drinking game since.

"Christ, does this fecking guy even own a shirt?" Eddie says as the screen fills with the muscular, tanned torso of Indigo Lazorio walking languidly down his drive. The six of us down a shot. Indigo brushes shiny hair from his eyes and frowns into the distance, as the actress who plays his love interest bleats her lines in a faltering monotone.

"But, Indy, I thought we had something *spe-cial*," she whines, her glossy lips frozen in a pout. Then Indigo stares into the distance again, his blue eyes narrowed, lips pursed, nose scrunched.

"Cheese-face! Feck yeah!" Eddie yells, as the six of us down another two shots.

"Ugh. If this is an Indigo episode, none of us are going to be sleeping," Grady says as I wipe a dribble of Red Bull from my chin.

I sigh. "Well, I just hope he gets to put his shirt back on. It's *totally* unfair they're exploiting the poor boy's perfect pecs, and his yummy tanned abs, you know?" Caroline winks at me.

Grady props one long leg up on the coffee table. "The abs, the abs, always with the abs." He grins. "You know they're probably CGI, right? He's swanning around on set in a unitard, meanwhile, some poor sucker in a computer lab has the job of painting on a six-pack, one pixel at a time."

"Gah, don't shatter the dream!" I close my eyes with another theatrical sigh. "Besides. In my head – those abs feel *plent-y* real enough."

"Amen," Caroline says, raising a shot glass at Grady. Tia dissolves into giggles.

Grady rolls his eyes. "Suppose *I* am the only one who remembers that he once used his own wee to make a moat in the sandpit?" He thuds his knee into my leg with another smile. "But, you know, whatever does it for you ...”

So, dodgy soap-opera drinking game is probably not the most constructive use of our time. Really, there is only one reason why we watch this crap.

Daniel Gordon.

I need to backtrack a little right about now.

My Last Will was written when I was nine years old. I remember I wrote it in magenta pencil in the back of my maths book, which Grady assures me would hold up in no court of law. But at the time, it seemed vital that I divide my stuff equally between my two best friends.

As I’ve mentioned, Grady and I have been besties since, like, before we were born. But Daniel was the first person ever who broke through the me-and-Grady bubble, that day in kindergarten when he leaped into the sandpit where I was poring over a *Fantastic Four* comic and asked who I thought would win in a fight – Wolverine or Mister Fantastic.

We bonded over Smarties and Spider-Man, and our shared honour of being the two chubbiest kids in class. OK, my face has always been more round than cheekboney, and my height and width didn’t really balance out till puberty. But Daniel was – well, he was really *large*. But my Daniel was funny and loud, and never got picked on cos his personality just didn't leave room for it.

And then, about a month before my tenth birthday, Daniel's mum got offered a job in the city and, just like that, he was gone.

We didn't hear from him again. That is, until eight months ago, when he snaffled a minor role on *A Home Among the Gum Trees*, and appeared on my TV in all his shirtless, cheese-sniffing glory.

When we were kids, Daniel was always larger than life – no pun intended – but his personality was big and bright, and it filled any room. But maybe the years have changed more than his body, cos on the small screen he barely seems to register. He has great hair, killer cheekbones, and about six facial expressions that he rotates between episodes. Still, Daniel Gordon is the biggest thing Eden Valley has ever produced.

I hadn't thought about him in a while. I do remember he gave me his prized Spider-Man PEZ dispenser and a tearful hug on Albany's verandah just before his parents drove out of town, and that I cried like a baby for weeks after. Though technically, he *did* leave around the time my dad died, so some of my hysterics were for that, too.

I know that Grady was just as sad when Daniel went away. I also know that he tried to friend him on Facebook once, but Daniel never responded.

Grady nudges my shoulder. "Earth to Alba. You missed one. Actually, you missed two – Indigo had another fight with his dad, and then they played that dramatic crisis-music while his abs scowled at a door."

I choke down another couple of shots. "Guys, does anyone think we're being a bit mean to poor Indigo? I mean, Daniel? It's not his fault he gets a sucky script."

"Naw, but it *is* his fault he's a shithouse actor," Eddie says. "And did anyone read that interview in *Woman's Day*? Apparently his favourite hobbies when he was a kid were running and surfing. Did anyone ever see that kid run? Except maybe for ice-cream. And where the feck did he learn to surf? Merindale pool?"

Pete grins. "Dude. What are you doing reading *Woman's Day*?"

Eddie's neck flushes. "Feck off, butt-face," he mumbles.

"And there ends another Monday that I will never have back again," Caroline says as the theme music twangs. "You realize *I* had better offers for my last weeks here, right?" She catches my eye, her expression sobering. And then she gives me a wry grin. "I mean, Jason Dylan and those guys were planning on a drive-by egging of Merindale High – so there's those intellectual hijinks I'm missing out on." She stretches with a yawn, though her eyes are kind of energy-drink buggy.

I stretch out on my couch with my bare feet in Grady's lap. Through the window I can see a tiny pinpoint of light from the Palmers' north paddock, a teeny dot of yellow in a cicada-chorus-filled black. Even with the aircon cranked, the night heat radiates through the window.

"Guess those guys found your place, Ed," I say. "Your folks OK with stragglers hanging around?"

Eddie shrugs. "Any extra cash is good, I s'pose. Dad'll have loved scaring the shit outta them with the full total-fire-ban rant, though. And he'll be deadbolting the tool shed."

Grady swivels his head and peers through the dark as well. The outline of the Kombi materializes in the shadows as my eyes adjust. "Wonder where they're heading?" he murmurs.

I nudge his belly with my foot. "Patchouli and weed, remember? Didn't think that was your thing, *Domenic*?"

He drags his eyes back to mine. "Don't first-name me, *Sarah*. I didn't say I was ashram-bound just yet." I can tell he's trying for casual, but there's something tense going on in his face. I swing my legs off him, just as Mum pushes through Albany's kitchen door. She's all sweaty hair and tired eyes, but since my mum is ace, she still gives us a bright smile.

"Hey, kids," she says, as she pulls up a seat at our little dining table. Her eyes are on her mobile, her fingers scrolling across the screen.

I skip over and perch on the edge of the table. "How's it going, Mama? Busy day?"

"We ran out of cheese muffins, again. Should probably double the batch tomorrow." She sucks distractedly at the tiny piercing in her bottom lip. "Good day, just a little … odd. You know, Patrick dropped by earlier. He said the Junction's just booked out. Apparently they had a run on room requests." Mum looks down at her phone again. "Is that strange?"

"The Junction only has, like, ten rooms, Mrs A,"

Pete says. "It's not that weird it'd fill over the holidays. Is it?"

Mum shrugs. "Maybe more people are coming back for Christmas than other years, but – whoa." Mum sits up straight, eyes suddenly alert. "Domenic – have you looked at Twitter today?"

Grady bounces to Mum's other side. "No, reception's been buggy. Why?" he says, peering at Mum's phone.

I don't really get the Twitter thing. I have enough trouble keeping my stories succinct in real life, but Mum and Grady are both obsessed with it, having long conversations about what's 'trending' – though mostly, from what I can tell, what's 'trending' is usually, like, photos of singers without knickers and stuff.

"Mum? Which celeb's done a drunk rant this time?"

"No, it's not that. It's … well, look."

Mum turns her phone around. Grady sucks in a sharp breath, but it takes me a moment longer to figure out what I'm looking at. It's a list of trending hashtags:

#EVendoftheworld

#Edenvalleyrapture

#hicktownsurvival

#ApocalypseAustralia

Grady catches my eye, his mouth opening.

I leap down from the table. "No way. It can't be. Original Ned...?"

"Original who now?" Pete says, stumbling out of the chair.

Grady dives for his messenger bag and pulls out his iPad. "I forgot all about this. I mean, I thought it was a bit of a joke, but..." He taps frantically at the screen, and then holds the iPad a foot away from his face. "Jesus," he whispers.

Caroline pushes herself to her feet. "What? *What is going on?*"

Grady turns the screen around to face us.

Original Ned's YouTube clip has eighteen thousand, four hundred and ninety-seven views.

"I don't get it," Caroline says. "Why are we freaking out over YouTube—"

Tia and Eddie are suddenly crowded around us as well. "Play it! *Play it!*" Tia squeals.

Six people cram their heads around Grady as Original Ned's voice wheezes through the speakers, while my brain tries – unsuccessfully – to play catch-up.

Tia's phone pings as Ned's first caller rings in

and my friends start talking all at the same time. Her bewildered face peers down at her phone. "Guys – I just got a message from Brihannah. Check this out!"

Tia turns her phone around, six sets of eyes glued to the tiny screen it like it's a first-issue *Action Comic*.

On her screen is a page from that free newspaper they hand out in the city. Half the page has a story about a footballer who was busted peeing in an ATM vestibule on Saturday night. The other half has a photo that I recognize, cos it hangs right near the entrance of the post office. It's this panoramic shot of Eden Valley taken from the top of Eden Hill. The headline above the photo reads: *APOCALYPSE NOW? DOOMSDAY HOAX OR SMALL-TOWN SALVATION?*

"You don't think it's true, do you?" Tia whispers. "The end of the world? Who are those bad guys with all the nukes? The Mongolians or whoever?"

Caroline blinks at her. "Tiahnah, dude, you really need to watch the news."

"Of course it's not true," Grady says. "If that guy is a psychic or prophet or whatever, then I am training to be a sumo wrestler. But it doesn't stop ... people talking about it. And people being interested in it. In us, I mean."

"But it's just a dumb story, right?" Pete says excitedly. "People will forget about it as soon as the next stupid thing pops up on the internet."

"Right," Caroline says as she frowns at Tia's phone. "It's this, or a new Kardashian sex tape. Are we really surprised that the human race is doomed?"

Eddie laughs. "How fecking cool is this – sorry, Angie – but, man, Eden Valley was never gonna make it on to anyone's radar. Unless one of the Albert boys did turn out to be a serial killer after all."

Mum grabs her keys from the sideboard. "You know, I think I might head to Cleo's for a bit. I'm sure it's ... nothing," she says uncertainly. "Right. Be back soon, bub." She kisses me on the head and hurries through the back door.

Grady plonks himself on a dining chair, still looking a little dazed.

"Well," Pete says, "if I've only got two weeks left, I am *so* going to start doing stuff. Bugger working at the fish-and-chip shop." He settles into the armchair and flicks open one of Dad's *Legend of Wonder Woman* comics I've left on the side table.

"I'm gonna take off," Eddie says, grabbing the last slice of pizza. "Think I need to have a conversation with our visitors right about now. Catch ya," he says with a wave as he disappears into the darkness.

Tia pockets her phone, her face icing-sugar white.

"Tia? Relax," Caroline says, moving so they're shoulder to shoulder. "It's not like you and Dina are going to be protecting your house from the ravenous hordes. Pretty sure no one's gonna want your collection of My Little Ponys and your mum's souvenir shot glasses."

I take Tia's other side and give her arm a squeeze. "Besides – we're the ones who are supposed to survive, remember? Don't worry. If Eden Valley does descend into tribal anarchy, at least you've got a big strong man defending your honour."

Pete flexes his arms with a grin, his non-existent biceps not doing much of anything, but I still give him a cheery thumbs-up.

Tia looks somewhat unconvinced. "Sure. OK. Petey, can you give me a ride home?"

Caroline sighs. "I'll come too. I'm working tomorrow morning. Might be an interesting shift if people are stocking up on provisions for Armageddon."

In a flurry of hand slaps and cheek pecks, Tia, Caroline and Pete disappear as well.

I stare through the window, that single point of brightness glinting at me in the dark. I can see shadows of rolling hills swooping over the horizon, and those few red gumtrees in the Palmers' field that stand like ghostly Sentinels. In my whole life, the dark and quiet has always been comforting; but for some reason, it suddenly feels just a wee bit too oppressive, a little more *empty* emptiness than normal.

I drop into the chair beside Grady. "Crashing here tonight?"

He nods distractedly as he taps at his iPad. "Kay, sure." His gaze flickers up to me. "Wild, huh? Out of all the towns in all the world?"

"Yeah, well, don't get too excited," I say, swallowing down a knot of nerviness. "I'm sure the next famous baby named after a fruit will push us right off the radar again."

Later, after showering and digging Grady's jammies out of the laundry, I'm stretched in bed in my purple

Peter Alexander nightie, and Grady is splayed on the couch in his T-shirt and boxers. His feet are tucked under a blanket, his face gleaming in the light of his iPad. I make a mental note to draw him like that tomorrow; the light on his smooth face is awesome, though I'm not sure it'll really be capturable.

"Not sleepy?" I say.

"Nah. Gonna read for a bit."

I curl up on my side and adjust the sleep mask over my forehead. "Hey, Grady?"

He looks up at me. "Yeah, Alba?"

"Is everything OK? You've been looking sort of tired since we got our results. But you kicked arse, you know you're gonna breeze into law ... there's, like, no chance you won't..." I swallow a couple of times. "So why the sleeplessness?"

He shoves a hand behind his neck, and stares out at the night sky through my window. "Yeah, I did OK. But it's still no guarantee ... and also ... well, Dad's been getting on my case. He's got this bright idea I should move early and stay at his till I find a place to live. He's having some New Year's Eve thing he wants me at – I think it's his half-arsed idea of bonding or something—"

I sit up quickly. "Grady, are you serious? That's only a couple of weeks—"

"I know, and no, I'm not thinking about it. I can't be bothered, and Anthony's refusing to help me move if I even contemplate bunking with Dad..." He glances sideways at me. And then he grins. "The end of the world is also a bit distracting. Apart from that? Everything's cool."

I sink back into my bed. The artwork I've stuck to my ceiling is starting to come loose in spots, the edges curling in the heat. The *Kingdom Come* print flapping lightly in the aircon makes me feel inexplicably panicked, like I'm gonna wake up one of these nights with it over my face, being suffocated to death by Power Woman's giant boobs.

I roll on to my side again. I know when Grady is dodging a question. My best friend is a hopeless liar. "Domenic—"

"Ugh, don't first-name me. Everything's fine." He turns away from me. "Night, Alba."

I consider calling him on his bullshit, until I settle on my pillow and my eyes involuntarily drift shut. Needless to say, insomnia and I have yet to become acquainted.

Normally I sleep like the dead. But tonight sleep feels fuzzy, like I'm drifting in that half-awake middle world, with vague dreams of Kombi vans, and a restless Cinnamon Girl staring anxiously through her warehouse windows, and mash-ups of every post-apocalyptic comic that I know.

And I can't be sure, but in between I think I dream about Grady's wide-awake brown eyes peering forlornly at me through the dark.

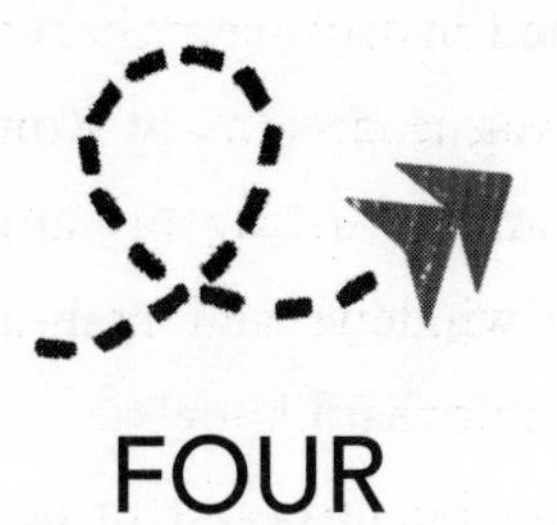

FOUR

The cars start arriving the next morning.

Gosh, that sounds dramatic. Like, it should be accompanied by crisis-music or something. But really, at first – despite Twitter and trending and thousands of people on YouTube – Tuesday morning begins no differently to any other.

As usual I'm wide awake and out of bed before six, leaving Grady face-planted on my green couch, one long leg dangling over the floorboards. I skip into the bakery in my jammies and kimono, my hair held back by my sleep mask.

The morning crew is already bustling as trays are piled in and out of ovens. Cleo is perched on a bench, eating cookie dough straight out of a bowl.

"Hey, Second Mama," I say, giving her a cuddle.

"Hey, miss," she says, hugging me back. "My son still sleeping?"

"Uh-huh. He really is a lazy no-good layabout. I blame the parents."

Cleo swats me with her spoon. "So I have Angie to blame for your mouth?"

Mum flings a wad of gingerbread dough on to the counter. "Not my fault. God only knows where she learned the sarcasm."

Cleo laughs. "It's a mystery. And our Modern Art tutor suffered a breakdown cos some *other* blue-haired chick kept hassling him about the lack of female artists on the syllabus?"

Mum narrows her eyes as Cleo serenely shoves more cookie dough into her mouth.

If I've inherited all my genes from my dad, then Grady is like a boy-clone of his mother. He has her chaotic dark curls and mischievous eyes, though Cleo is a head and shoulders shorter than both her sons. Today she's wearing the sensible slacks and soft grey shirt she's adopted for work at Doctor Lucas's office, with colourful strings of that chunky wooden jewellery she was all into making a few months back.

"Where'd you disappear to last night, Mum?"

I say as I nudge her out of the way and bury my hands in the dough. "Busy digging a fallout shelter?"

Mum catches Cleo's eye. "I wanted to debrief … Hey, I've seen *Armageddon*. Just checking that Mrs Garabaldi wasn't bunked on her roof with a shotgun."

Cleo pauses, mid-chew. "Bruce Willis was yummy in that movie," she says dreamily.

I work my fingers into the dough. "Please. Isn't he, like, seventy?"

Cleo bumps Mum with her foot. "And bald. Still though. Wouldn't say no."

"Gah! No old-man sex talk! Go away, both of you, before I yak into this perfectly delicious gingerbread dough."

Mum drags a giggling Cleo away by the arm as Mrs Doyle shoots me a disapproving glare, her papery hands swirling icing on to a tray of cupcakes.

As stories go, I'm fully aware that my world is probably not the most riveting of narratives. I could yammer for ages about the routine in the bakery, cos it's the story I've known for most of my life: the morning light that hits the pots hanging above the centre counter, the particular blend of smells and sounds I've loved ever since

I was big enough to hold a spoon. When I'm sifting and stirring, my hands can be on autopilot and my brain in whatever world I want to be. It's the only time – apart from when I'm drawing – that I can be right here, and a thousand other places all at once. It's the only place in the universe that's ever felt one hundred per cent like *me*.

Still. Comic-book worthy, Albany's is not. And besides, as I may have mentioned – there are far more interesting things afoot today than cupcakes.

So I help out, then skip back to the house. At some point Grady has crawled from the couch and into my bed, so I tiptoe around the lightly snoring Grady-mound as I throw on a tartan skirt and one of Dad's faded Bonds T-shirts. I twist my hair up in an animal-print scarf, chuck on boots and my favourite red lipstick, and skip back to the diner.

The first thing that catches my eye is beardy-man and bikini-girl, inhabitants of the mysterious Kombi. They're huddled in a booth, lips smooshed together like they're studying the terrain of each other's tonsils. At the counter, Tommy Ridley is gaping at them like they're one of those Amsterdam porn shows he insists he's going to see one day. I think PDAs are sweet, but still, it's disconcerting seeing strangers here; weird little cracks on the edge of my known universe.

The second thing that catches my eye is this: through the French windows, some unfamiliar cars are parked along Main Street. There's a battered Corolla, and a sedan I've never seen before. Across the road, the pump at the Wasileskis' service station has two cars backing up to it – a girl is leaning through a window to snap pictures of the *Eden Valley General Store* sign. The Wasileskis' shack is cute as, but I can't remember it seeing this much action since that time Merindale's truck stop shut for a week after poisoning people with dodgy sausage rolls.

Paulette hurries over just as Mum bustles in from the verandah. "Alba, have you seen what's going on outside?" Paulette says breathlessly. "There's, like, a dozen crazy hippies wandering around Main Street – some guy's even pitched a telescope in front of the Eversons' store." She tugs at her pigtails. "How stupid are people? What are they expecting is gonna happen *here* of all places?"

Mum glances through the window. "I'm not sure that's the point. People want to be where things are happening. Suppose it doesn't matter *what's* happening, does it? Or where..." Outside, Julian Ridley, our lone police officer, is scratching his head as he peers at the Corolla.

"Excuse me, kids," Mum murmurs, hurrying out the door again.

I haul myself on a stool. "Suppose some people just gravitate toward weirdness?" I say vaguely. "And a handful of tourists is no big deal. Didn't Merindale get a bunch of visitors when that stoner-guy said he saw a panther on the football field?"

Paulette laughs. "Yeah. Same guy who swears he saw the face of Jesus in a meat pie. Like I said, people are idiots. Look at them, Alba." I follow the direction of her hands. Some guy is posing for a selfie in front of our mailbox. "They look so cheerful," Paulette says with another laugh. "Like, hello, people? You're preparing for Judgement Day. Least you could do is be a bit sedate."

Paulette Barry graduated high school a few years ago, in the same class as Grady's big brother. I love her to bits, partly cos she's never felt the need to hook up with hot-but-somewhat-man-ho-ish Anthony. Paulette has vague plans to go to uni 'at some point', but right now, she's just happy hanging around home. She's super-fun and has zero angst about the future.

We should all be so lucky.

I peer at the street again. Scattered between the roses that line our path is the family of garden gnomes Dad and I had been collecting for years. Dad's favourite was the gnome he'd named 'Big Grant', a happy little guy in a bathing suit, giving a thumbs-up from a ceramic lilo. Every so often some drunk-arse local rearranges our gnomes in gross sex poses, but mostly, no one who knows me would dare touch them. The Kombi couple are sitting on the steps now, the girl nestled in beardy-man's lap. They're laughing at the gnome I've dubbed 'Frida', due to the gnomey monobrow I painted on her one day when I was bored. Haughty Frida is my favourite of all our gnomes. Right now, I think she's looking a little pissed at the attention. I resist the urge to run out and defend the poor girl's honour.

So I realize my capacity for dealing with reality may not be sound. Still, as I watch a few more unfamiliar faces making their way into the bakery, I can't help but think that, comic-book-wise, this whole episode would probably fill nothing but a couple of interlude frames; like that moment where a character has a sepia-tinted dream before crashing back into their real story.

"A few sightseers are no big deal," I repeat.

Paulette makes this *mhmhmm* sound, then wanders off to refill the sugar bowls.

Though I try to discount what's happening outside, our routine is rudely interrupted by the shenanigans. Caroline texts to say she's perving on a carload of boys near Anzac Park, and Eddie and Pete swing by to grab warm muffins before dashing down the road. Only Tia sticks to schedule, showing up with her sketchpad as planned.

Tia's fashion designs are pure awesomeness, but her bandy-legged stick figures are probably not going to get her a look-in at Chanel or wherever. I've been trying to help her for ages, but since I'm basically self-taught, I'm not sure I'm being much use.

"Hey, where're your pencils?" I say as Tia drifts into my backyard.

She sits on the grass next to my banana lounge.

"Had a crappy sleep last night, and I got woken up by Petey calling to tell me about – well, all this." She waves her hand nervously at the Palmers' fields, where the Kombi has been joined by a handful of other cars.

Tia shudders. "Mum's having a freak-out, too. She watched that Ned guy and then spent the night online buying camp stoves and blankets … I can't be bothered working anyway, Alba. I think I used up all my creative juices for my folio and … I'm just not feeling all that inspired lately."

"Oh?" I say carefully. I drag my eyes away from the farm and stick a eucalyptus bookmark in my copy of *Persepolis.* "That wouldn't have anything to do with a certain wannabe ninja, would it?"

Tia's eyes linger on the fields. "No. Maybe. I dunno." She sighs and kneads her temples. "I've never had a boyfriend before, Alba. I'm not sure what I'm supposed to do with one. But it's nice having Pete around, and he doesn't know what he's doing next year, so…"

"So now you're not sure what you're doing either?" I say gently. "But your folio was so ace … never thought you'd consider ditching design school for a guy who thinks detachable track pants are the world's greatest invention."

Tia rests her cheek against my chair, troubled grey eyes blinking up at me. "Is that really pathetic? It's really pathetic, isn't it. God, can you imagine what Caroline would say if she knew what I was thinking?"

As much as I know Caroline loves Tia, I also know she shares Grady's particular tunnel vision when it comes to this stuff. And I totally get where Tia is coming from. Why is it that we're supposed to just want to merrily zip away on the first bus out of here? Why is it that the second we graduate, people and history and *home* suddenly aren't supposed to matter any more?

I swing my legs off the lounge and plop on to the grass. "Nah. It's not pathetic," I say, giving her arm a squeeze. "Just, well ... isn't being in love supposed to make you *more* inspired? That's what I keep hearing in songs, anyway."

Tia grimaces. "I never said the L-word. But I like Petey a lot, and us getting together – it's changed things. That's supposed to happen. Right?" She stares out over the hills beyond the Palmers' farm and smooths her bob. "Am I still supposed to want to move to Paris and work for Isabel Marant if Pete wants to hang out here and, I dunno, invent the world's first hovercraft shoe or whatever?"

I'm not really sure what to say, except that this conversation is taking far too serious a turn for a sunny day. I push my sunglasses up my nose. "Well, if Peter achieves his goal of becoming a ninja, maybe you could design his costumes?"

Tia chuckles. "Right. Spandex undies. In boys' extra-small."

We're still laughing when Grady stumbles out of my room, bleary eyes blinking into the sun.

"Nice jammies," Tia says with another giggle.

Grady glances at his Christmas-elf boxers. "Don't diss the clothes," he croaks. "Alba bought me these."

Grady drops in front of me with a giant yawn. I drape my arms lazily around his neck, his skin too warm from sleep. "Aw, I think they're cute. Santa's little helpers – they reminded me of you, Grady."

Grady leans against me, his hair tickling my chin, his thumbs tapping at his mobile. I snatch the phone and squish my head over his shoulder, and I click a photo of us; partly cos I've become kind of obsessed with recording everything, but mostly cos I know Grady hates having his picture taken.

"You can't do that with your own phone?" he grumbles.

"Oh boo, Scrooge. One day, you'll be sorry there isn't more evidence of the time when you were so pretty." I've managed to cut off half of Grady's face and most of my forehead, but the photo's still cute. I message it to myself and then, for good measure, I set it as Grady's wallpaper.

Grady flicks the phone back from my hands. "So. Guess the word is out," he says cautiously. He flashes his phone at Tia. "Your boyfriend seems to be convinced that rumours of the world's demise are not at all exaggerated, judging by all the texts he's sent me. Any reason why Pete's so excited about the apocalypse?"

"I think Petey's just waiting for his chance to bust out the superhero moves," I say with a laugh. "I mean, that oil fire at the fish-and-chip shop doesn't count. Even though Pete was awesome. Apart from that unfortunate peeing-himself business..."

Grady tenses. My heart does a weird double-time before my brain takes in what I am hearing from the street out front. Something I hardly ever hear around Albany's.

The roar of a motorbike engine.

OK, yes, people ride the stupid things. But not often around me. Not Eddie's brothers, who stick to the top of the south paddocks with their dirt bikes, or the guys from Anthony's garage, who salivate over pictures in Harley mags when they think I'm not paying attention, or Lucy Albington, who traded her Ducati for a battered Honda Civic seven years and four months ago now.

Grady spins around on his knees to face me. He glances over his shoulder at Tia and gestures with a curt nod of his head. Tia stands and hurries out the side gate. A few moments later, the rumble of the bike engine splutters, before disappearing into the distance again.

I clear my throat. "Sorry. I'm fine." The growl of the bike echoes in my head, until Grady gently squeezes my arms. I focus on him – my best friend in his *Where's Wally?* pyjama T-shirt and Christmas boxers, his sleep-hair curling in every direction, with a handful of people in the field behind him who are patiently waiting out the end of the world – and involuntarily, I giggle.

Grady's grip on my arms relaxes. "OK?"

"Yeah. OK. Well, I'm a little concerned about the toilet situation on the Palmers' farm, and, you know, someone is definitely gonna get punched by a kangaroo, but—"

"Alba..." he says softly.

I leap up. "Hey, Grady? For once, something might actually be happening in Eden Valley. Isn't this what you've been waiting for? What are you doing sitting here in your jammies?"

I hold out a hand. He grabs it and lets me pull him to his feet. "Should probably put on clothes, I guess," he says, running a hand across the back of his neck. His dark eyebrows are still knotted. "Are you sure you're all right, though?"

I smile. "You know me. I'm always fine. No need for an intervention."

He smiles back. "Course you are. I'll be back soon. I wanna fix that loose rail on your verandah as well. It's been driving me crazy. Save me some breakfast before you're cleaned out of scones?"

"Verandah. Breakfast. Righto. See you soon."

Grady scarpers up the verandah stairs as Tia emerges through the gate. She pulls me down on the fake grass again, nattering about the Dean Quinn collection she's seen online. Tia knows better than to comment on my little episode, and I love her all the more for it.

The motorbike thing? Not part of my story that I want to talk about right now.

By Wednesday, things have gone from slightly strange to downright bizarro-world. With only a week to go till Christmas, I undertake a heroic effort at maintaining normal: working in the bakery, tinkering with my comic, and trying to corral my friends who are scattered all over town, annoyingly distracted by the commotion. The cars keep coming as if a beacon is flashing over the Valley like some demented Bat Signal, drawing every moonchild and hippy and stoner toward it.

But by Thursday? I am forced to admit that this episode might be *slightly* more significant than a singular panel in the story of my life. The reality smack is impelled by two events.

The first is that Mr Palmer, in what Eddie describes as "my dad's retarded Woodstock fantasy", sticks up a sign at the entrance to the farm, announcing,

Everyone Welcome! Best View of the Apocalypse Inside! Within days, half their north paddock is dotted with cars and tents, and the scene from my window shifts from a bucolic Fred McCubbin painting to something out of a Vertigo comic.

The second is that the national media, in what has got to be the slowest news week in the history of the universe, pick up the Eden Valley story and devote an inexplicable amount of airtime to us. My friends and I watch from my suddenly too-teeny living room as newsreaders chuckle at each other while using phrases like, "Well, at least the post-apocalyptic world won't run out of cowboy hats," and other condescending stuff. Countdown clocks appear on screens; one station even does this montagey history of the Valley, obtaining a pic of Mrs Garabaldi in her nightgown, waving a broom at the camera like a frenzied yeti. Alvin Smith, aka Original Ned, finds himself at the centre of the stupidest story in the history of everything, his bald head and Fu Manchu suddenly ever-present every time I look online.

And then, the news crews start arriving.

The six of us wander through town in a daze as our peaceful streets become jammed and chaotic. The

Garabaldis inexplicably snub the boom in business and hastily board up their store, but at the other end of town, Mr Bridgeman throws open the Corner Arms with gleeful enthusiasm and a new, goat's-cheese-heavy 'End of the World' menu. Cops are shipped in from Merindale, blustering about like they're from S.H.I.E.L.D. or something, but honestly? I don't think they quite know what to do with a bunch of people whose only goals seem to be pitching wonky tents and getting drunk as quickly as possible.

On Saturday, I haul arse out of bed to find Mum and Mrs Doyle in the kitchen frantically googling recipes for vegan muffins. Grady is in his blue booth in the diner, picking at a plate of yesterday's apple strudel. He's staring wide-eyed through the windows at the line of people forming on the verandah.

"Stealing food again? I *told* Mum we need to start padlocking the fridge."

Grady shoves the last of the strudel into his mouth as I squish in beside him. "I'm a growing boy, Alba. And I would've eaten at mine, but I just couldn't decide what to make with a jar of tahini and Cleo's homemade mustard. Her mustard tastes like socks. I love my mum, but there is a line."

His T-shirt this morning is a soft cocoa with *I Survived the Zombie Apocalypse & All I Got Was This T-shirt* on it. I jab him in the chest and he looks down with a grin. "Forgot I owned this. Seems appropriate though, right?"

I peer blearily at the verandah. It takes me a second to register the sound that's been buzzing in my head since I woke – a low hum of voices like the gabble of warbling geese. The familiar actual-bird-and-cattle song is all but drowned out by the clamour.

Grady hands me his mug. "Had to get up early anyway – the Eversons got a heap of extra veggies trucked in and they needed help hauling boxes. And anyway, as if I could sleep. Jesus, Alba. You don't find this even a bit exciting?"

I take a sip of coffee. "You have a weird definition of exciting. Exciting is ... a new *Best American Comics.* Whenever school closed on account of bushfires. Maybe a really perfect salted caramel slice. Not sure *exciting* is how I would describe this ... instalment."

Grady nudges my arm. "Don't be such a party pooper."

"Hey! Have you forgotten *why* we've become as

popular as scuba gear on the *Titanic*? You really want me to be excited that the planet might only have a week and a bit left?"

Grady waggles his eyebrows playfully, but even through my sleep-haze I can see the challenge in his eyes.

"Well, suppose that depends on what you think you're going to miss out on. Never seeing New York or Paris or that giant ball of twine in Kansas… Never trekking through Nepal or driving a Kombi across Romania—"

"Your dreams, not mine." I'm starting to regret getting out of bed this morning.

"Everyone dreams of seeing Paris," he replies with his stubborn-face. "You used to."

I squish down the sick feeling building in my belly. "Aw, Domenic, I thought we had something *spe-cial*," I whine in my best soap-opera bimbo voice. "Here I am, hopelessly devoted to you, and all you wanna do is skip town and leave me all by my lonesome—"

"Don't say that," he snaps.

I flinch. "I was kidding. Jeez … lighten up."

"Well, just … stop saying that." He grabs the mug and finishes the coffee in one gulp. "You keep doing that, Alba – giving me crap about leaving – but I'm not the one who seems happy to just wave goodbye. I'm not the one who's refusing to talk about it, or acknowledge what it'll mean. I'm not the one who's so … indifferent."

I bristle. "That's what you think? Wow, so nice to know that my best friend in the world thinks I'm a callous cow—"

Grady rounds on me in the suddenly too-small booth. "I never said that, Sarah. Don't put words in my mouth."

"Yeah, well, you don't put them in mine! And don't first-name me, either! Gah, why do all our conversations lately feel like they're stuck in the same boring groove?" I lean forwards and grab his ears, shaking his head like I used to do when we were kids and he was being a complete pest. Grady grimaces as I tug him by the ears until his nose is right up against mine. "Stop being a pain in the arse, Domenic. I'm here. You're here. The Rapture might be here, but at least we'll have strudel. All is right with the world, at least for a little while longer. I just want to enjoy my summer, Grady, and if the sun gets devoured by a giant evil space monster, then this conversation is gonna be pointless, so can we *please* just … forget about the other stuff for now?"

Grady unhooks my fingers from his ears. For the briefest moment, he holds my hands on the sides of his face. I don't think he's shaved this morning; the barest scratch of stubble is rough beneath my palms. Surprising, though I can't exactly place why. Grady's eyes flicker between mine. Maybe he thinks if he looks hard enough, he can find all those answers that seem to have deserted me.

And then he flips my hand around and thumps my palm against my forehead. "Fine," he says with a laugh. "All is right with the world. Even if there *is* a guy outside wearing a fez." He gestures over my shoulder, where a guy is, indeed, peering into the diner with a fez perched lopsidedly on his head.

"Man. Does it not bother you that these people might turn out to be the sole survivors of Armageddon? Cos *I* am not feeling all that hopeful about the future of humanity."

The slap of the kitchen doors ricochets through the diner, and I turn around to see Eddie and Pete making their way over.

"You were saying?" Grady whispers with a chuckle.

"What the feck is in these muffins?" Eddie growls, frowning at the dung-brown lump in his hand.

"We've had a run on requests for vegan stuff," I reply, untangling my fingers from Grady's. "Not sure it's really Mum's strong suit though."

"They taste like dog's balls," Eddie says definitively.

Pete shoves him in the arm. "Ed, how would you know what—"

"Argh! Too early for dog's balls!" Grady barks. "Can you two tone it down?"

I clear my throat pointedly. "Boys, please, it's never a good time for dog's balls. And Petey, where's Tia?"

Pete scoots into the other side of the booth, his thumbs tapping out a text. "Family stuff. Her mum booted me out cos Tia's sister's back. She came up on the bus last night with a bunch of her friends. Apparently, and I quote, Brihannah didn't want to miss 'the only awesome party the Valley is ever gonna throw', unquote."

Eddie glares outside. "Jesus. Tommy said that a bunch of guys from his year level have shown up as well. So much for getting the feck out and never looking back." He leans against the counter. "We had to come in through your house, Alba. Might wanna consider locking up from now on. These losers are gonna riot if they don't get their soy lattes or whatever..."

Eddie drops his eyes. Paulette elbows through the crowds, slamming the door behind her. She braces her back against the glass and gives us a feeble wave.

"Hey, Paulette," Eddie says, his eyes on his boots.

"Hey all," she says, smoothing down her pigtails. "Alba, ah, you might want to stick your head outside. There's a bit of a ... situation that I'm not sure how to handle."

"Jeez. What now?" I leap out of the booth and push through the waiting people on the verandah.

Eddie comes to a dead stop beside me, and Pete crashes into him from behind. "Feck is that?" Eddie says.

"Whoa," I reply. "Have I fallen through a worm hole into an HG Wells novel?"

"Huh," Grady says, appearing on my other side. "Where exactly does one ... procure a penny-farthing these days?"

A bronze contraption that looks like something from a freaksville sideshow is parked amid the people on our bluestone path. The back wheels of the bike – if that's what you call it – are only a little bigger than normal pushbike wheels. The other humungous, oversized wheel holds the seat and the rider, and is currently blocking Albany's staircase.

"Hello?" I call as I shade my hands against the sun. "Are you looking for somewhere to park that thing? You're kind of on our path."

Bike-man peers impassively down at me. He's wearing a Fanta-orange cord suit, and a serene, bovine expression. "Property is relative," he says dreamily. "We are all children of the universe. We need to share our spaces, yeah?"

I cross my arms. I'm generally pretty easy-going, but penny-farthing bozo is gazing at me with glassy-eyed apathy, and the conversation with Grady is still buzzing in my head, and my hands are doing that stupid pins-and-needles thing again, and all I want is to close my eyes and blink my normal summer back into existence. My capacity for dealing with this hippy rubbish? Right now, it's sitting on nil.

"Children of the universe we might be, dude, but you still need to move. We have customers."

Bike-man looks at me as if he's seeing me for the first time. "I don't think so, little lady," he says mildly. "There are no confines to human experience. Besides, the view from here is awesome. And it smells nice." He dings his bell and looks at me with a raised eyebrow.

"Hey, arsebag!" I snap. "You know this isn't the city, right? We have, like, shotguns and stuff and—"

"Jesus Christ," Eddie growls, his eyes down Main Street. "Tell me that's not who I think it is. Bloody hell!" He hauls himself over the verandah railing with one hand and bolts down the road.

Grady grabs my arm. I shoot Penny-Farthing Man a scowl before clambering under the railing and hurrying after Ed.

Mr Palmer is standing in front of a milling crowd and some news cameras, a cowboy hat on his head and an expression on his face like he's just won that Nigerian lottery.

I stand on my tiptoes and squint through the mobs. "Eddie ... is your dad..."

Pete bursts out laughing. "Dude. Is he wearing make-up?"

Eddie covers his face with his hands. "Dude, shut up! Dad's gone fecking nuts."

Mr Palmer smiles brightly at a pretty reporter. He tips his hat, and a thick smudge of cover-up cracks over his cheek. Beside me, Eddie groans.

"As I mentioned," Mr Palmer says, in the same boomy gravel-voice as Eddie's, "times have been tough round here, especially for us farmers. Now, I don't know about any of this end-of-the-world malarkey, but anything that brings you folks out to our corner of the world is a good thing in my book. As long as people need a patch to crash on, everyone's welcome at the Palmers'. Best butter in the state, by the way," he says with a wink at the pretty reporter.

Grady rounds on Eddie. "What are people supposed to do for food? And water?"

Eddie shrugs. "Maybe drink their own piss? Like those dumb-arse tourists who get stuck in the desert?"

"Be good preparation for the apocalyptic wasteland," Pete says cheerfully.

"Ed, this is crazy!" I say, as a station wagon crammed with a bazillion people does a donut in front of the Garabaldis' store. "The police aren't going to just let your dad turn the farm into his very own Burning Man."

Eddie shakes his head. "Julian Ridley can't even stop those Merindale losers from burning rubber on the football field. You think he's gonna be able to deal with all this? Jesus. Like anyone knows how to deal with this."

I spin around, taking in the crowds and cars and the riot of more colours than I think I'd ever have inks for. I can't see the clear horizon; Main Street is broken up by the heads of way too many people, as if someone has pinched together the edges of the world, tipping everyone into my tiny wedge of space. And it's so goddamned *noisy* here, the sky crackling with the static of a hundred speakers all turned up to a hundred.

Grady grabs my elbow. "Alba, are you OK? You're looking white as a—"

But he doesn't have a chance to finish, cos he's interrupted by Caroline and Tia pushing their way frantically through the crowds.

"Guess who's back?" Caroline says as she skids to a stop. Her voice is octaves higher than normal, which is more excitement than Caroline ever willingly displays.

Tia suppresses a little squee.

"I'm telling this story," Caroline yelps.

"I saw him first!" Tia bleats back.

"You. Saw. Who?" I say, resisting the urge to stomp my foot.

Caroline spins around, her hands planted triumphantly on her hips. "Daniel. Fecking. Gordon," she says breathlessly. "We saw his family pull into town. According to Lucy Albington, they're staying in one of the rentals up on the hill. Can you believe it?"

"Bloody hell," Eddie says with a whistle. "Cheese-face himself. Maybe I won't have to stick to just punching Indigo in my dreams."

"Daniel?" I manage to say. I may be one very teeny step away from complete mental overload.

"Alba, pay attention!" Caroline yells. "I saw him myself. Guess we should have expected the Valley's most famous expat to make an appearance. Man, he looks nice though. Even though I only saw the side of his face through a car window."

"Boy does have one very nice side-of-face," Tia murmurs.

I lock eyes with Grady. Grady stares back at me.

Since I am, as mentioned, rubbish at storytelling, I may have telegraphed the above from a bazillion miles away.

But honestly – at the time – who could've seen him coming?

FIVE

Once, when I was eight, I fell off the monkey bars in the school playground and landed with an ungracious *thwack* on my head. I woke up with Grady and Daniel peering down at me; Grady frantically barking at everyone not to touch me, and Daniel giggling like an idiot while trying to haul me to my feet. Even though that whole instalment is kinda concussion-foggy, the thing I remember most clearly is this: Grady's firm hands holding me steady, and Daniel's bluster pulling me upwards, while I sprawled between them with a headache and blossoming arse-bruise.

Ugh. How symbolic. Believe me, I am aware.

Grady gives my elbow a shake. "Alba!" His frown is replaced by a smile, slow and wide. "It's *Daniel.* Here. What do you think we should do?"

I glance at the Garabaldis' store. Someone has

drawn a giant penis on one of the wooden boards, complete with a jolly tuft of curls, like some weird alien cauliflower. In the gravel post-office parking lot is one of those ice-cream vans I've seen on telly, only, this van has been converted into something called a Taco Truck. Muzak wafts in my direction as a line of people appear out of nowhere.

I rarely feel uneasy. I mean, it's not like I've ever had much call to. But as I stand amid the noise and colour, for the first time in my whole life, I feel way, *way* out of my depth.

Grady is still staring at me expectantly. So I detach my elbow from his hand, and I give him a giant, hopefully not-as-fake-as-it-feels smile. "Well then. What else are we supposed to do? Let's go say hello!"

I take off past the tinsel-decked stores on Main Street with my friends trailing behind. We hurry up the hill, through the scattered houses on Warrick Road, and the shoe-box bungalow that Mum and Dad and I lived in before the bakery; all the while my hands are becoming sweaty, and the bits of my brain that are devoted to sensible thinking shut themselves off, one at a time, like Christmas lights with a faulty fuse.

Caroline veers us into a street. The view of the Valley

is awesome from up here; on weekends, half our high school hangs out at the tree-lined dirt road on the top of the hill, with the farms stretching around us, and the few lights of town twinkling below. For a moment, I have this crazy urge to see our new Valley from up here at night. I bet the camp-lights and colourful tents look awesome in the dark.

Tia pinches my side with a squeal as we skid to a stop at the edge of a gravel drive.

Grady takes a couple of steps in front of me. Caroline stops and shoves me in front of her. I hear Eddie's low whistle from behind, and a reverential "*Feeeeeeck*", no doubt as his eyes land on the shiny BMW parked in front of the house.

I take another floaty step forwards.

And there he is.

He's unloading a rucksack from the car, a pile of bags at his feet. I catch a glimpse of a woman with a neat auburn bob disappearing into the house. Daniel's mum was always pretty set in her ways; dunno why I'm surprised she has the same hairstyle almost a decade after I saw her last.

Grady glances over his shoulder at me. Then he faces forwards and clears his throat.

Daniel turns, gold aviators glinting in the sun. He gives us a look that's part exasperated, part benign resignation. He blows his hair off his face with a puff.

"Hey, look, we've been on the road since hell-time this morning, and I've just stepped out of the car – and I really need to pee – happy to sign some autographs, but give us a minute, would you?" And though his voice is a few shades deeper than the last time I spoke to him, and though the only words I've heard it speak recently are cheesy lines, I would know that voice – languid, but with laughter bubbling behind it – anywhere.

Grady's Vans scuff at the gravel. "No, we're not here for an autograph. Um, sorry to bother you, but ... do you know who I am?"

Daniel looks at him blankly. And then, ever so slowly, he takes off his sunglasses. He blinks at Grady like he's trying to focus a mirage.

"No. Freaking. Way," he whispers. He steps tentatively toward him. "Domenic? It's you? You're ... still here?" Daniel swallows. The tips of his ears turn fiery scarlet. My brain may have short-circuited, but I'm failing to grasp why his expression suggests he's just been wedgied by the Ghost of Christmas Past.

And then he seems to shake himself out of whatever trance he was in, and he covers the space between us in a few theatrical bounds. "Hey!" he yelps, grabbing Grady in one of those boy hugs that's all back-slap and no below-the-chest contact. "I can't believe this. I can't believe you're still here – I thought for sure your mum would have moved on ages ago." He clasps his hands around Grady's arms, and he beams at him with his blinding Indigo smile. "Jesus, Grady – you got *tall*, man. What the hell happened?"

Grady grins, giving his arms a thump back. "Puberty. Still convinced this place might be built on a radioactive alien crash-site. Nice to see you again, too, Dan. You … look good, dude. I mean, we've seen you on TV, but, yeah. You … changed. Nice hair." Grady clears his throat again. "Well done on that."

But Daniel doesn't appear to be listening. His brow is furrowed, his familiar too-blue eyes zeroed in on me, and suddenly I'm ten years old again, watching as he waves goodbye through the back window of his parents' car, a Spider-man PEZ dispenser in my hand and a medley of Mum's sad-arse Lisa Loeb music in my heart.

"That – is not possible," Daniel says quietly, his

frowny forehead trained on me. "Sarah Jane ... *Alba*?"

Eddie drapes one arm firmly around my shoulders. It's like being hit across the back with a piece of two-by-four, but it also momentarily clears the brain-freeze. I wiggle out from his grip. "Heya, Daniel. It's me. Jeez. It's ... been a while."

"Hey ... yourself," he says as his arms – nice, nice muscly arms – envelop me in a giant hug. My arms snake around him, too, but it feels a little like I'm hugging an apparition. All I can think is that the surrealness of the potential apocalypse has got nothing on this. I hug him back, noting hazily through his T-shirt abs that are most definitely not CGI, and half-expecting Indigo's fish-lipped love interest to appear from off-screen and punch me in the face.

Daniel pulls away and holds me at arm's length. He looks me up and down, his eyebrows climbing skywards. I'm wearing my favourite cherry-red sailor dress and black Chucks, an outfit that even on an ordinary day turns more than one head in the Valley. I suppose I should be a bit self-conscious that he's blatantly checking me out, but hey, what can I say? I look kick-arse in this dress.

"Wow," he says. "You look..." His eyes are on me,

but somehow they seem to be focusing elsewhere. And then he smiles, all cheek and cheer, and it's so freaking familiar the TV-Daniel fizzes. Standing in his place is the person who was once one of my best friends in the universe, albeit he's taller and shapelier and has shiny auburn boy-band hair replacing the crop his mum used to give him with her sewing scissors. "I could never picture you as anything other than a shortarse in overalls and that Harvey Birdman jumper, Alba." He grins. "You grew up nice, girl. Good job!"

I give him a sweeping bow. Funny how going toe-to-toe with Daniel's bluster is just like riding a bike. "I did my best. You look great yourself, though you know, you're not nearly as tall in real life."

Daniel laughs. "Yeah, I get that a lot. Forget about the camera adding ten pounds – in my case, it also adds, like, two feet. But, man, it's so good to see you guys again." He beams at Grady and me, and now I'm six years old again, giggling in the back of the classroom as Daniel attempts to break the Guinness record for the number of pencils shoved up a single human nostril.

Eddie bumps me out of the way, his hulking shoulder suddenly in front of mine.

Daniel's eyes travel upwards. He takes the tiniest of steps backwards. "Hey man. I don't think I remember you?"

Eddie snorts. "Yeah, you wouldn't. You didn't spend a whole lotta time in the special class, or detention, as I recall."

I shuffle in front of Ed. "Daniel, this is Eddie. Eddie Palmer? He wasn't in our year level, but you remember his parents from the dairy farm?"

Daniel looks blankly at Eddie, but he holds a hand out anyway. "Sorry, I'm not always good with faces. But yeah, hey, nice to see you again?"

Eddie doesn't say anything, but he does clasp Daniel's hand while eyeballing him with the intimidating stare-out he likes to use on new guys, until Pete pokes him in the side and pushes him out of the way.

"This is wild, huh?" Pete says. "Have you ever seen anything like this? You've probably seen heaps of cool stuff, parties and whatever, but this is awesome, right?"

Daniel frowns at Petey. "Have we met?"

"Nope, no, I moved here a couple of years ago, you were before my time, but –" he sticks out a hand

– "It's Pete. Peter, but everyone just calls me Pete. Or Petey. But, yeah, Pete is fine. Or Petey. Whatever."

"My boyfriend loves your show," Tia says nervously. "Peter is a big fan."

Caroline snorts. "Yeah, you don't own a tightrope outfit by any chance?"

"So, this is insane," I say, hastily introducing Tia and Caroline, who were only on the margins of our little group before Daniel left. "I don't think Eden Valley's seen this much excitement since that time the Ridleys' goat shed burned down. Is all this why you're back?"

Daniel's ears turn red again. I'd totally forgotten that he blushes from the ears whenever he's embarrassed. It's the weirdest thing to remember, like a tiny fragment of his picture I'd erased from my memory has drawn itself back in the frame.

"Yeah," he says sheepishly. "It was my manager's idea. The publicity and everything. Being my home town and all, he figured it might be good to, you know … cash in on that a bit." He shrugs. "It was either this or spending Christmas doing *Carols by Candlelight*. No one seems to care that I can't sing for shit."

Grady sticks his hands in the pockets of his jeans. "Don't ever remember that stopping you before?" he says shyly.

Daniel laughs. "But a gig in front of a couple of million people is a little different to Miss Beale's grade-three talent show. Not sure my 'Daydream Believer' would've really cut it on live TV. I think this whole thing is pretty stupid, but it's a weird business. Any publicity is good, right?"

The six of us nod sagely, like we know exactly what he's talking about.

Daniel flicks his sunglasses out of the pocket of his jeans and pushes them on to his head in one smooth move. I'm sort of distracted by pondering whether those cheekbones were always hiding under his pumpkin cheeks, or if they're those implants I've heard celebs like to stick in their faces, so it takes me a few seconds to process that my friends are awkward and silent, and Daniel is still talking.

"God, you guys – it's so awesome to see you," he says, his eyes darting between me and Grady. "I didn't think I'd ever set foot in this arse-end-of-nowhere place again, but –" He smiles at me.

"This might turn out to be a fun few weeks after all. Assuming the planet doesn't explode."

I glance over my shoulder. From up here, the crowds look almost motionless, like weird multi-coloured livestock milling in the russet fields. "Daniel, we're still not exactly sure what's happening. But no one seriously believes any of this ... right?"

Daniel shrugs. "Most people seem to think this Ned guy is taking the piss, but, you know – it's an excuse for a party. Guess Judgement Day is as good an excuse as any, right? Though I still can't believe that this many people have bothered. I could barely believe Eden Valley was still on a map. In my mind I always just picture a couple of tin sheds and tumbleweeds."

"Yeah, suppose the Ark might've been more crowded if Noah was on Twitter," I respond. I don't know why, but his tumbleweeds comment makes me bristle ever so slightly.

Daniel glances at his watch. "So I need to unpack, and I think I have an interview or something lined up, but – when can I see you guys again?"

"Tonight," Pete yelps. "The Junction – you remember it, right? I work there. I DJ—"

Caroline grunts. "Does hitting shuffle on the

soundtrack of *Good Morning, Vietnam* count as DJ-ing?"

"But there's a dance floor," Tia adds, giving Caroline a sharp nudge with her hip. "It's fun. For the Valley ..."

Grady steps beside me. "You should come, Dan. Granted, you probably have more stories than we do, but we should catch up. If you're not busy."

Daniel flicks his sunglasses back on to his face. "Not busy. And I've never been to a hoedown. Should I have bought a fiddle?"

Behind me, I can practically feel the waves of disdain rolling off Caroline and Eddie. My friends may heap a lot of crap on the Valley, but it's totally different for an outsider to chime in as well. It hits me suddenly that Daniel Gordon – with his designer jeans and great hair – is about as outsider-ish as it gets.

"A fiddle could probably be rustled up," I say lightly. "But mostly, we just hang out, and dance a bit. Don't eat the peanuts, cos they've been sitting on the bar for the last century. You in?"

"Sounds fun," he says with that easy laugh. "Can't wait, Alba," he adds, and it's so sincere that for a moment I forget about outsider-Daniel, this person who should be as unfamiliar as any of the strangers wandering around town. For a moment, the edges of Daniel seem to shimmer, till all I can see is my funny, overconfident best friend. For a moment, it's like he never left. I grin back at him.

As we amble home, I can't help but think that the universe may be freaking bizarro, but Daniel's return has to be some sort of sign. Cos it feels just right that he's here, one of the pages ripped from my story, slotted back exactly where it's supposed to be.

Grady and I hang behind the others. He's talking a thousand miles an hour about our weekend sleepovers and prepubescent Daniel's attempts to get himself into the *Guinness Book of Records*, and I find myself laughing along with him, swept up in his infectious, if uncharacteristic, nostalgia.

"You know, Grady," I say as we push through the mobs on Main Street. "If the rest of the world is obliterated, it might turn out to be not be so bad after all. Everyone is right where they're supposed to be. *Daniel* is home. It's like someone up there finally answered my prayer to rewind the clock. It's a Christmas miracle! Don't you think?"

In front of us, Caroline is tugging the others

toward the Taco Truck. Penny-Farthing Man peddles past with a couple of cheerful dings of his bell in my direction, and I resist the urge to flip him an equally cheerful bird back.

Ravenous, I follow the others, thinking that maybe I can get on board with this twist in my storyline after all. Hey, Daniel's return seems to have made even unsentimental Grady nostalgic – a Christmas miracle if ever there was one.

I'm so buzzed that I almost – *almost* – overlook the fact that Grady never actually answers me.

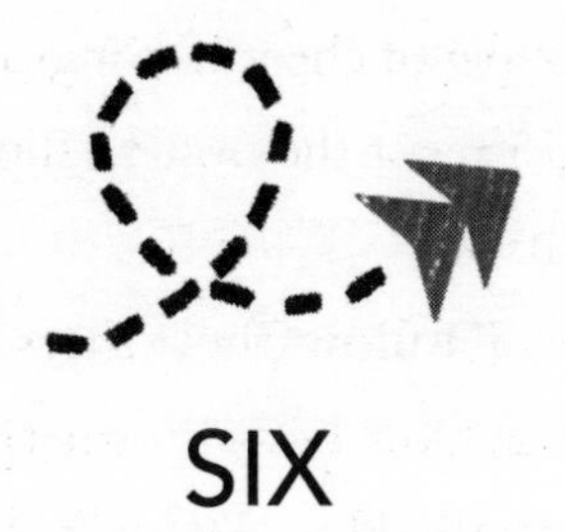

SIX

The afternoon passes in a blur. My friends scatter, and Grady and I grab nachos and head to the far edge of town, to our spot on the porch of the abandoned feed mill. We can't seem to stop swapping Daniel stories; it's like we both feel this need to yank his memory out of the past and into the present. Oddly, I'm a teeny bit nervy. Maybe cos the show-offy part of me *really* wants Daniel to remember that he used to love our life here. Or maybe I'm just not accustomed to hanging with a guy who I've faux-drooled over shirtless more times than is probably respectable.

When the worst of the biting sun has passed, I drag Grady up by the hand and we head to our homes to change.

A few hours later Tia bursts into my room just as

I'm finishing my hair. She's wearing a gorgeous silver dress and an unfamiliar pissy look.

"Heya," I say as I unwind a strand of hair from Mum's curling iron. "What's with the sour face? Is Caroline refusing to wear shoes again?"

Tia flings herself on to my bed. "I've barely had a chance to catch up with her, Alba. You know why? Cos I got woken at six this morning by Peter tapping on my window. He wrote a poem that he just couldn't wait for me to read. He only left when Mum threatened to torch his bike, otherwise he would've stayed for breakfast. And lunch. He probably would've written more poetry. It's like his *thing* now."

I giggle at her exasperated reflection in my mirror. "Petey wrote you a poem? You mean, he actually found something that rhymes with 'nunchuk'?"

"*Albaaaa!*" she wails. "It's not funny! I don't want to hurt his feelings, but *argh*! I turn around, and Pete's there. We hang out for hours, and then guess who texts me the minute I get home? And why does he always have to have an arm around me? You know how hard it is to walk glued to someone that skinny? It's like trying to do a three-legged race with a piece of plywood."

"Tia," I say through laughter that threatens to mess my make-up, "I know I'm not fluent in boyfriend, but aren't you supposed to be able to talk about this stuff with one?"

"Alba, you know Pete! He'd take it as a sign that I'm about to break up with him. It'll lead to tears. And probably more poetry. And it's not that I don't like spending time with him, cos I really do, just not every second of every day!"

I dig through my mini advice bank, but I'm really not sure what to say. The only permanent guy I have in my life is Grady, and I'm just used to him being as ever-present as a limb. I've never found that intrusive. Wonder why that is?

"Tia, you guys are still kinda new. OK, so Petey's probably trying a bit hard, but if you don't want to talk to him, then ... not sure I know what to tell you."

Tia sighs. "I know. I'm sorry I'm laying my relationship dumpage on you, but I just can't talk to Caroline about this stuff. Not without my eardrums exploding from a lecture, and – whoa," she breathes as I stand up. "Alba! You look amazing!"

I glance at my reflection. I'm squeezed into this dress that used to belong to Tia's gran, but that Tia tailored to a pattern she made from something we saw on *Mad Men*. It's sapphire blue, and looks like it belongs in a smoky cocktail lounge or *Sin City* comic.

Tia beams as she adjusts my neckline. Even when we were kids, with only church markets and a few stores in Merindale, Tia always managed to look like she'd fallen out of one of those fashion mags that are all bird-boned girls with no hips. I, on the other hand, look like I could be mounted on a sturdyish Viking ship. Still, I'm too tall to be inconspicuous, and I've never seen the point in being bashful with my looks. I've added some strokes of heavy eyeliner, and a touch of ruby lip-gloss. With my fringe brushing my eyes, I *think* I might pass for one of Grady's noir heroines.

"Thanks! You did an awesome job, Tia. You gonna add this one to your folio?"

Her clinical eyes sweep over the fabric. "Yeah. This satin was a real pain to work with, so I reckon I'll get bonus points for that. I have no idea what sort of stuff uni might be expecting next year..."

She swallows, her hand fiddling with the cluster of stars on her necklace. She gives me a watery smile. I give her an uncertain smile back.

"Hey, Tia? Let's not think about that tonight. You know, we're both gonna feel pretty stupid stressing about the future and whatnot when the only thing we might have to worry about is learning to weave loo paper out of corn."

She exhales. "Alba, is it strange that that almost makes me feel relieved?"

I glance through my window. From the edge of my yard I've been watching this one group who've been growing all week as they piece together a scrappy canopy over their camp. From this distance, it kinda looks like a demented Thunderdome. I don't understand how that many people can feel safe sleeping under a billowy gazebo that's mostly T-shirts and towels strung together with bungee cord. Though, I suppose it must be a little like being caught beneath a vivid fabric ocean.

My eye lands on the character studies of Cinnamon Girl that I've blu-tacked to my bookshelf. Lately, I can't seem to capture her face in anything other than an expression of impatience.

I grab my bag and nudge Tia outside, my eyes lingering on Cinnamon Girl until the verandah door slams shut behind me.

Lights glimmer in the windows as Tia and I make our way toward the Junction. We sweep past the crowds at the door with a wave at Tommy Ridley and Ed's brother Howard, who've been co-opted as makeshift bouncers. Howie ushers us in with rough pecks on the cheek and a smug look at the strangers lining up at the door. I'm not proud to admit it, but for a moment, I feel just a teeny bit smug myself.

I step through the foyer and into the dingy main room of the pub.

"Oh. Jeez. This is … different?" I manage to say. The wall of sound and sweat and music hits me like a sonic boom to the face. I grab hold of Tia, who huddles against me with a whimper.

Caroline elbows through the pulsating mass of bodies, a pint of tawny liquid sloshing over her hand. She scowls at a guy who's squishing into Tia, hip-and-shouldering him with a vicious glare that makes him scamper away quickly. Her face brightens. "You guys took your time," she yells over the music. "Have you ever seen this many people in your *life*? Bit different to last Saturday – Rosie and her glass of port, and

Anthony's dumb-arse friends trying to bullseye toilet paper on the Cascade sign." She looks me and Tia up and down. "Must have missed the memo that the Queen is popping by," she says with a grin.

"Caroline!" Tia hisses as her eyes skim over Caroline's purple-streaked ponytail and faded T-shirt. "You promised you were gonna make an effort! Did you forget the TV hottie we're supposed to be entertaining?"

Caroline wraps an arm around Tia. "Relax, Tiahnah. Indigo and I are old mates now. He dropped by the grocery store this arvo. Eddie almost wet himself when Daniel breezed in looking for quinoa. We had to look quinoa up on the internet. You wouldn't believe the dumb stuff celebs are into."

Tia squeals. "What did you say? What did he say? Why didn't you call me?"

Caroline rolls her eyes. "Indigo and I just had a bit of a ... chat." She winks at Tia. "Fill you in later. And Eddie didn't deck him, which was a bonus. I'm guessing Daniel's gonna be finding that last tub of fat-free yoghurt pretty unsatisfying though. I'd almost feel sorry for him. If he wasn't such a ponce," she says with a giggle.

"And I am guessing that *that* is not your first drink," I say, slipping the pint from her and taking a swig of beer. "You're way too smiley, Caroline. It's not natural."

"Hey, I was expecting to spend my last weeks in the Valley burning my school uniform, and maybe having a farewell snog with Lachlan Hurley. But look around, Alba! It's like, hot-boy buffet. Aren't I allowed to be in a good mood?" Her eyes linger on a pair of admittedly very nice jean-clad butt cheeks that are sauntering past. Their owner glances over his shoulder, taking in Caroline's tanned colt legs in their teeny old shorts. He waggles his eyebrows at her. Caroline throws him her nonchalant-face and grabs the beer from my hands. "Seriously, you guys look ace. Though Tia, I think your hottie may be a bit preoccupied. Check it out." She nods toward a bright spot in the pub.

Daniel is leaning casually against the wall of old road signs as a guy in a suit natters in his ear. A bevy of girls hover in his vicinity. Debra DeLuca is gazing at him all starry-eyed – the same Deb DeLuca who once refused to sit next to Daniel in music class cos she said he took up too much space on the recorder bench.

I snort. "Desperate much? You'd think people would have more important things to be distracted by. Like, you know – the end of the world and all that?"

Caroline sips at her beer. "Maybe they're thinking we'd better pair up now, in case the future turns out to be some nightmare where we, like, have to wear matching bonnets and share husbands." She nudges Tia. "Fancy being a sister-wife?"

Tia grimaces. "Gross. Anyway, what's wrong with not wanting Daniel to think we're small-town? Have you seen what they're saying about us on the news?"

"Yeah," I say with a sigh. "Pity they keep interviewing the Alberts. We're not *all* toothless doofuses who can't spell *apocalypse*."

I sweep my gaze over the Junction, trying to see it through outside eyes. The bow-legged table where the six of us eat dinner every Thai Thursday, the pissy-looking stuffed ducks mounted on the walls. The handful of lost-looking locals between the strangers, scowling or gaping at our visitors. I'm not embarrassed. Though, I am kinda wishing Mr Grey wore something other than his beer-gut-hugging Led Zeppelin T-shirt and eighties-awful acid-wash jeans.

Pete is squished in his DJ booth, his eyes scanning

the crowds. I can't help but notice that Tia's face lights up when Pete catches her eye. He waves her over, and she disappears with barely a backwards glance.

Eddie is huddled beside Pete. Poor Ed's eyes are kinda terrified as they roam over the unfamiliar girls jammed into the pub. I give him a wave, and he gives me a wave back before grabbing Tia and placing her bodily in front of him.

Caroline sighs as her gaze follows Tia. "Well. Suppose that's the last we'll see of her." She drains her beer. "And on that note, I need another drink."

Caroline pushes toward the bar, squishing in beside a stool where Grady is perched. He's wearing one of the two good shirts he owns, a chequered blue-and-orange thing that stretches across his broad shoulders. A girl in a trilby is sitting on his other side. She keeps sneaking glances at him, but Grady is deep in conversation with Mr Grey and doesn't seem to be paying attention. He'd get pissy with me for saying it, but in his good jeans and boots, Grady looks every inch the country boy. Even though I'm staring at his back, I can guess the moment trilby-girl catches his cute little-boy smile, cos she shuffles her stool closer and gives his hand a nudge. I'm just about to bound over when a Hugo-Boss-scented arm envelops me in a side hug.

"Alba!" Daniel says. "Thank God you're here. My manager was just going through the plan for the next few days. Who knew it was possible to sleep with your eyes open?" His eyes glide over me, and he whistles. "Girl, you look incredible. What the hell happened to the kid who used to sneak Smarties into PE?"

"Same goes for you, Daniel." I give him a once-over, his black T-shirt and jeans managing to be both casual and super-classy. "You know you're living every little kid's fantasy? Only thing that'd make you more of a Cinderella cliché is if you tell me you've been training at wizard school for the past eight years."

His eyes narrow mischievously. "Not sure if I should be offended or blushy, Alba."

We stare at each other for a weird beat before I grab his hand and tug him through the crowds to a table near the Christmas tree. When we were little, Daniel had this way of bouncing into a room and instantly owning it. Now, as we squish into the small table, he's looking at me like he's not sure what to say, and I feel suddenly, strangely shy. I focus on his blue eyes, the only part of his face that hasn't been touched by the superhero morphage.

"So … you're famous," I say with a nervous laugh.

Daniel smiles. "Don't get weird on me. *Gum Trees* isn't exactly the dream. It's one step above doing ads for haemorrhoid cream."

"Oh, but hey – you get to snog Aimee Smith? That's gotta be a big job perk?"

He snorts. "Please. She's got the personality of wet laundry, and besides, she hates my guts. You know, she purposely eats tuna sandwiches before we have to do our kissing scenes? Every single time. It's like pashing the fish that John West rejected."

I fall into a bout of snort-giggles. "Aw, but I thought she'd be just your type? The fifth runner-up in *Next Top Model*, and the guy voted 'number thirteen sexiest TV star you've never heard of' in that uni student web poll? It's like Romeo and Juliet. But, you know, with more fake tan."

Daniel's eyes widen. "Jesus. I see I'm gonna have to work hard to prove I'm not the walking himbo you seem to think I am, Alba." The Christmas lights bounce across his cheekbones. He's smiling, but his eyes give him away. I remember that look – that same one he used to get whenever his mum gently suggested he go on a diet. It's bluster, covering up a smidgen of hurt.

I shuffle my chair closer. "I'd never in a bazillion years call you a himbo, Daniel Gordon. Please. You are the person who gave me my first *Spawn* comic, remember? You are the person who tried for eight months to break the Guinness record for the world's tallest mohawk – not sure if that counts as genius, but still."

Daniel laughs. "A Japanese guy won that this year. It was over a metre high. Very cool."

Pete's music changes to some thuddy nineties REM thing, and a cheer erupts around the pub. The leapy crowds on the tiny dance floor double in a heartbeat.

Daniel drums his fingers on the table. "So you're still drawing? I saw some of your stuff hanging in the grocery store. You have mad skills, Alba. Your friends at the store couldn't stop gushing."

"Well, thanks. I've branched out a bit from my Wonder Woman obsession, but yeah. Still working on it."

He looks back at me. "And you and Grady are still tight? That's great."

I glance at the bar but Grady and trilby-girl are nowhere to be seen. "Course we are. You sound surprised."

He shakes his head. "No, not really, but I suppose I was just assuming—"

"Gah, OK, I can guess what you were assuming. And no. No no no. That's just ... not the thing with us." I feel my face flush, and probably a good slab of my neck as well. "Everyone knows that. No one even mentions it. Not since we were thirteen and our friends double-dared us to go on a Valentine's date. D'you know what happened? Grady was so panicked he fell out of Merindale bus and broke his collarbone, and I drank two blue-heaven milkshakes at the hospital and yakked in Cleo's car on the way home. It was weird and stupid and – no good can come from this conversation!"

He bursts out laughing. "No need to shout, Alba. OK, fine – new subject." He hangs an elbow over the back of his chair. "So what's your take on this? I mean, what sort of gods wait for us to finish school and *then* pull a Night of Eternal Darkness? You bummed the last city on Earth didn't turn out to be Berlin or Vegas or someplace cool?"

I take a deep breath, my still-flaming face warring with my tingly hands. "Well, this crazy is annoying, for sure. But I was thinking maybe I'd stay put anyway, for a bit. I love working at the bakery so it'll be cool to do that—"

Daniel baulks. "Really? You're planning on staying *here*?"

I glare at him. "Man, don't you start! I know you skipped out and never looked back, but not all of us think this place is a giant dump."

"No, that's not what I was going to say. I realized I probably sounded like a bit of an arse this morning, but I didn't mean I wasn't looking forward to coming back. I'd forgotten how much I missed the Valley."

"You did?"

"Sure. I missed heaps of things." He shuffles closer and clears his throat. "Alba, I never got to tell you … I was really sorry to hear about your dad. But I was ten, and wasn't big on emailing … and I'm a bit shit at that stuff. I didn't know what to say."

In the DJ booth, Pete is twirling haphazardly while Tia ducks around his arms and the CD cases they periodically send flying over the dance floor.

Caroline is in front of them, beer glass in hand as she sways to the music. For a moment I think I see Tia and Caroline's eyes locked in my direction, though when I blink again they're focusing on nothing but the music.

"It's OK, Daniel," I murmur. "It was sucky for ages and then … I guess it sucked a bit less. What can I say? Life went on. Though I really wished you'd kept in touch." I catch his eyes, only to find that he is staring at me pensively. "I really missed you."

"Hey. I missed you, too," he says quietly.

My eyes roam across the pub again. Involuntarily, they seek out Grady's curls, but there are way too many people here and I can't find him anywhere. I dunno why, but I feel strangely exposed.

I thump my hands on the table. "Ugh. This is getting maudlin. Quick – tell me something else about the wacky life of a celebrity. Do you have your own mini pig? I keep reading on the internet that they're popular among your people."

Daniel shakes his head. "Jesus, do you not remember Lucy Davidson's birthday party? A certain Merindale petting zoo, and a certain crotch-biting incident? I can't even watch *Babe* without breaking out in a sweat."

I laugh, and he laughs back, and just like that, I'm filled with that cosmic, universal rightness again. His boomy laugh is *exactly* the same. I relax into my wonky chair, surrounded by a cosy blanket of all my stories.

Daniel glances at the DJ booth. He smooths back his hair with both hands, but the shiny strands stubbornly fall back into his eyes. When he looks at me again, there's something odd about his demeanour. Something sort of … calculating. Last time that look was aimed at me, little Daniel was trying to badger me into sneaking on the bus, fuelled by rumours of the opening of a Merindale Wendys.

"What?" I ask.

"Well I was just wondering … why does everyone here still call you Alba?"

"I … dunno. No one calls me Sarah. Well, Grady when he's pissy, but…"

"But a nickname's only cute when you're a kid." He swings back on the rear legs of his chair. "And, *Sarah*, you haven't been a little girl in a really long time."

I narrow my eyes. "What's that supposed to mean?"

He considers me for a moment. "Well for starters, you wear a lot of make-up, don't you? I mean, someone who dresses like you obviously doesn't want people to think of them as a kid. Right?"

I draw myself up to my full height. "Daniel, this may surprise you, but I don't care what people think. I like how I dress. I like my name. Is that OK with you?"

The music changes to some croony Johnny Cash song. Daniel's eyes widen. He leans down so his lips are beside my ear. "All I meant was, I'm surprised you think you belong here. You aren't a small-town girl at heart. I knew that about you when we were six, and I wasn't the most perceptive kid in the world. I always thought you were awesome, and cool, but I'm finding you really … fascinating now. Is that OK?"

Maybe I am a tad dense, but it takes me a full five seconds to figure out that Daniel Gordon – who once ate a tub of neapolitan ice-cream on a Grady-inspired dare and then yakked in my sock drawer, and who used to have sleepovers at my house in *Toy Story* jammies – is actually attempting to *flirt* with me.

I blink away the mental flash of a golden six-pack. I shove my chair backwards and punch him in the arm. "Daniel, was that a *line*?" I say with a laugh. I gesture to the contingent of girls who are still staring at his back. "You already have a fan club.

Doesn't Indigo have a thing for blondes?"

He grins. "Yeah. But I've always preferred brunettes."

I roll my eyes, but thankfully I'm saved having to respond because I catch a hint of blue from the corner of my eye, and I turn around to see that Grady is right beside me.

Grady slips into a chair. "Hey guys," he says lightly, folding his legs under the table. "So … see you found the Junction, Dan. If this is the last pub at the end of the universe, then we are in serious trouble, right?"

Daniel shrugs. "I dunno. I sort of like the fact that nothing has changed since I left. And this place has character." He taps Grady's arm and points to Mr Grey, who is currently trying, unsuccessfully, to start a conga line near the door.

"Character?" Grady says with a grin. "Right. And that character would be a hobo in a questionable trench coat shouting obscenities on the street?"

I toss a coaster at Grady's head. "Domenic here already has one foot out of Eden Valley's door, Daniel. Check your car, cos you might have yourself a stowaway."

Daniel drapes an arm over the back of my chair.

"Grady, man, you haven't changed a bit," he says with a smile. "You were always tripping over your own feet to run forwards. Dude, can I give you some advice? Chill out. Look around. The rest of the world isn't going anyplace." He bursts out laughing. "Well, you know – theoretically."

To an outside observer, Grady's face would be expressionless, but I know that look of his – what I have dubbed his baby-lawyer face. I can tell he's sifting through the responses in his head, carefully picking his words before he lets himself speak.

"Sage advice." Grady says eventually. "But trust *me*, one week of listening to the guys at the post office talk about the price of cheese, and you'll be hoofing it out of here." He smiles. "And I remember you had big plans of your own, once upon a time. I think they had something to do with building the world's biggest Lego fort, but still. You can't tell me that you're not desperate to get back to your real life?"

Daniel blows his hair out of his eyes. "Maybe not. I don't have to be on set for another month – maybe I'll stick around. Assuming we're not attacked by Dark Elves or killer tomatoes or something." He tugs lightly at the end of my hair in that familiar, naughty way he used to do when we were little. "Whaddya think, Sarah? I promise I will be on my best behaviour. Not a single mini pig shall cross your eyeballs."

Grady looks at me with a raised eyebrow, but I see his confidence stumble. Man. How had I forgotten that Daniel could put Grady on the back foot like that?

"Well ... sure *Sarah* and I can rustle up some stuff to keep you entertained," Grady says. "Though it might involve navigating more cow poo than you're used to."

"Anyway, our holidays plans have gone out the window, what with the invasion of the moon people," I add. "Stay, Daniel. We'd love that. You can get to know our friends – I could even be talked into hosting an *X-Men* marathon and cookie-fest. It'll be just like old times. Except you've probably ditched the Buzz Lightyear jammies?"

He winks. "I'm strictly an undies-only guy now."

Grady grunts. "Nice mental image. Sure *Sarah* was desperate to hear about your jocks."

In my memory, my boys were always like Spider-Man and Superman to my Wonder Woman. I guess I'd forgotten that they were more like the duelling halves of Bruce Banner and the Hulk; sort of half in love, half one step away from poking each other's eyeballs out.

I stand. "Actually, Sarah would really like to dance. You guys coming?"

Daniel sits back. "Nah. Happy to hang here and admire the view."

I grab Grady's hand and drag him on to the swarming floor, ignoring his bewildered face. He swings me into his arms and loops one hand lightly around my middle.

"So … Dan seems to have slotted right back in. Then again, he never had a problem fitting in," he says as my feet move easily alongside his. Cleo did rope Grady into taking dance classes with her when she was going through her ballroom phase, but secretly – and he would die before admitting this – I think he loved it. Either way, my boy has *rhythm*.

"It's weird though," Grady says thoughtfully. "It's Dan, but not Dan." He smiles wryly. "I dunno, Alba. Abs or no abs – maybe this whole trip down memory lane thing is kinda pointless?"

I'm only half-listening, because now that Daniel's

twinkly eyes aren't focused on me, I'm replaying our conversation and my thoughts are getting all … jumbly.

"So what's wrong?" Grady says.

I look up at him with a start. "Nothing. Why?"

Grady taps his forefinger between my eyes. "You have frowny line. Which you only get when you're annoyed, or when you're doing algebra. And I'm guessing you're not puzzling out quadratic equations, so…?"

Through the crowd I catch a glimpse of myself in the mirror behind the bar. The feathery sweeps of eyeliner are visible even in the hazy reflection.

"Hey, Grady?"

"Yeah, Alba?" he says distractedly.

"Do you think I wear too much make-up?"

He frowns at me. "No. It's just your thing. Why?"

"Nothing," I say sheepishly. "You just never say anything about how I look. Was just wondering, is all."

His rhythm sputters slightly. "I never say anything about how you look because you always look great," he says carefully. "And I know you don't care what I think. Does that … bother you?" He clears his throat. "I mean, do you want me to tell you—"

I give his side a poke. "Relax. I'm not fishing for

compliments. You're just a closed book sometimes. You know, this chick was giving you all sorts of eyes earlier, but you didn't seem to notice. I'm just curious what goes on in that curly head of yours."

He shrugs. "Boobs, cars. The catastrophic destruction of humankind. And she was? You need to point these things out, Alba! You're a useless wingman otherwise."

"Right – suppose I should take my wing-person duties more seriously now that there are *real* girls in town."

He laughs. "And girls who haven't snogged my brother. That's a nice change."

Pete's song changes to something breathy and slow. I've finally noticed a theme to the music; pretty sure Petey has spent the last week crafting his very own end-of-the-world playlist. I forget about Daniel, and the itchiness in the back of my skull that our conversation stirred.

I glance up at Grady. "Maybe this is your chance to test some moves?" I nudge my head toward a crowded booth behind him, where trilby-girl is propped on a tabletop.

Grady glances over his shoulder, and she

smiles and waves at him. He gives her a shy wave back. "Ah. Yeah. That's Jess. We ... sort of met earlier. She's from Melbourne." He grins at me. "I oughta have more sense than to take chances with strangers, Veronica," he purrs in his husky old-movie voice.

"Aw, but I would've thought strangers would be just your bag, G. No mess, no fuss – no ol' ball-and-chain tying you down. You should talk to her. Say something smooth. Come on, man! You must have some moves. Practise on me if you like."

Grady stops moving. He squints at me. In the dim light, his eyes are vaguely amused, and mildly terrified. "Um ... I like your dress, Alba. It's very blue. And, ah ... shiny?"

"Man, you are *hopeless*," I say with a giggle. "I said be smooth, not be weird robot-guy."

He rolls his eyes. "Well, maybe I should be taking pointers from Daniel? He seems to have the smooth thing sorted."

"Please. Daniel is all talk. Or don't you remember that either?"

"Yeah, I don't know about that, *Sarah*. Pretty sure I was detecting some moves. Not that I'm judging.

I mean seriously, woman – he'd have to be blind not to notice you in that dress."

I slap his arm triumphantly. "See, *that* was a line. Aim some of that at hat-girl and you'll be set."

He shakes his head with another laugh, and he pulls me toward him again.

In the DJ booth, Pete is bleating something into his microphone that I think is supposed to be rousing, though he really doesn't need to pump up the crowd; the Junction already looks like a circus, and smells like an explosion in a BO factory.

Caroline shuffles across the floor, steering some random guy toward us. She gives me a thumbs-up behind his back. Random-guy is just Caroline's type, all muscle and slightly confused vacant eyes.

"Heya all," she says. "This is Raymond."

"Randal," random-guy says sullenly.

She gives his arm a pat. "Sorry. Randal's mates have driven all the way from Brisbane. And they've brought nothing but gas masks and Bear Grylls DVDs with 'em. How stupid is that?"

Eddie and Tia appear beside us, Tia dragging him into a rigid, half-hearted sway; in her silver dress she's what I imagine a fairy might look like trying to dance with an unwilling side of beef.

"Alba!" Tia yells. "How's Daniel? Is he having fun? Why isn't he dancing?"

"Maybe he's holding out for the stripper music," Eddie grumbles. "Bet he's busting to get his shirt off." He scowls at random-guy, who gives him a pained look back.

Caroline spins around so Randal is forced to shimmy on the outside of our circle. "OK, I'll say it. This apocalypse totally rocks! Is it wrong that I'm starting to look forward to it?"

Grady laughs. I'm still squished against him, and I feel his laughter rumbling right through me. "Don't get too excited, Caroline," he says. "It's still Eden Valley. The post-apocalyptic world is going to be less of a giant party, and more like a rotary lunch with a handful of stoners and a couple hundred confused cows."

Petey lands breathlessly on the dance floor, black hair clinging to his face in sweaty strands. "Guys, this is awesome!" Pete yells. "There are more than four people dancing! Some chick puked in the deep-fryer! It's the best night *ever*!"

He grabs Tia's hand and hauls her into his arms.

"Like, when we're ancient, it'll be *this* story that we bore our grandkids with!"

Tia giggles hesitantly. "Petey, maybe your grandkids will be more interested in hearing about life with electricity and, you know, deodorant and stuff."

Random Randal wanders off, and my friends close in on his space. I tug Grady's phone out from the back pocket of his jeans – only before I can snap a photo, out of nowhere, I'm enveloped by this sweeping sense of *ending* that makes my breath stick somewhere behind my tongue. Grady seems to realize that I am having a freak-out, cos the hand that's resting lightly on my waist tightens around me.

"Alba?" he whispers. "What's the matter?"

I look up at him and I try to smile, but I just know it comes out all wavy and wrong.

The first time the six of us hung out here together was just after year-eight graduation. Grady and I got totally sugar-highed on green jelly and spent the night making beer-coaster hats for all of Mr Grey's ducks on the walls. It was the first time Eddie worked up the courage to have more than a monosyllabic conversation with me. It was the first time Petey shyly asked Tia to dance, though it would take him years to make another move. It was the first time Caroline kissed a boy – I remember that she left him in the carpark as she pulled me and Tia aside to give us a report of how gross it was.

Maybe the earth will continue to spin, and the stars won't implode for a bazillion more years, but I know, with a certainty my stupid brain has done its best to ignore, that this moment – right here, with the people I love most – is not going to last.

My back is to the door, my cheek resting against Grady's arm. But I'm suddenly trapped in one of those tingly moments, like the hairs on the back of my neck know something the rest of my brain hasn't caught up on. The atmosphere in the pub has changed, too; there's a weird hushy hum beneath the babble.

"Oh. My. God," Caroline says. She grabs Grady's arm from my side and points both their hands in the direction of the door.

I spin around, and almost fall sideways off my heels.

The crowds near the entrance have parted, allowing a man into the pub. He's of mid-height and medium build, unremarkable except that all pairs of eyes near the door have glued themselves to him.

He's wearing pinstripe pants, and suspenders over a shirt the colour of rain-sky. He glances around, nonchalant, like he's just a regular who's popped in for a beer and burger. Then he saunters to the bar, seemingly unaware of the kerfuffle following in his wake. I can tell he's trying his best to appear nondescript.

But the bald head and Fu Manchu? He may as well have walked into the pub wearing a spandex onesie, or a Batsuit.

"I don't believe it," I whisper.

Daniel appears beside us. "Well. This is unexpected," he says cheerfully.

"Fecking. Hell," Eddie says. "It's Original fecking Ned."

SEVEN

The arrival of the psychic has the same effect on Eden Valley as the Joker setting up shop in Gotham. Someone starts a Twitter account for Ned's moustache, and by Sunday morning, it has twelve thousand followers. His moustache seems to be preoccupied with Beyoncé and *Doctor Who*. I decide to stay away from the internet for a while.

The news people, who seem to be springing forth like so many anonymous comic-book henchmen, forget about stalking us locals and begin stalking Ned Zebidiah instead. Though he's been all over the place since his dodge TV broadcast, Original Ned refuses to grant a single interview. He parks his caravan on the outskirts of the Valley and rarely appears in town. For a guy who should be relishing the attention, Ned looks put out by the fuss. I catch a glimpse of him

Monday morning as he's hurrying past the bakery, and I could swear he looks terrified.

I don't know what's going on with me. Since that night at the Junction, my thoughts are all slushy, and glummer than I ever allow myself to indulge. I stick on my brightest smiley face, but inside, everything is whirling. I spend my spare time hiding in the shade of Dad's plum trees while doodling Fiona Staples-style sketches of the distant scene. Half the Thunderdome has collapsed now, but shouty laughter still echoes from the remnants. I know my friends have all ventured out there. But from my yard it's like being on the outskirts of a giant, steamy monkey enclosure. And as curious as the wildlife is to watch, I'm just not game enough to get within poo-throwing distance.

I know some of this stuff should work its way into my comic. But every time I turn on my computer, I find myself staring at Cinnamon Girl's anxious, restless face, looking through her warehouse windows to a world that I can't seem to fill, and I'm overwhelmed by a throat-squeezy panic.

Luckily I don't have time to sink into a full pity-party, as spare moments are almost non-existent. The bakery is booming, with lines forming down the bluestone path from the time we open till we run out of food. It's as if Albany's has fallen through some bizarro dimensional crack, where Rosie Addler and the mouth-breathing Albert boys have been replaced by their alternate-universe doppelgangers – an old woman in a see-through fishnet vest, and a bunch of frowny emo kids who look like the end can't come soon enough. I try to channel my boldest She-Hulk as I bustle around the packed diner, but I still feel besieged, smaller in my space than I ever have before. Mum is chuffed by the booming business, but I suspect that a teeny part of her subconscious might be mulling over the possibility that the end is indeed nigh, cos she spends an awful lot more time hanging with Cleo in the diner after-hours, swapping giggly stories of their university-day shenanigans.

And still, the people keep coming. The Palmers' farm looks like the last campground at the end of the universe, with tents and cars and manky furniture swallowing up the dry fields. Surprisingly, the mood among our visitors is generally chilled; our bewildered cops don't have a lot to do, other than rescuing Rosie Addler's poodle, Mr Frankenstein, from the back of a pot-smoke-filled van, where he'd been co-opted as a mascot. Kites are flown, hacky sacks are tossed, and a spontaneous nudie run through the fields transpires, guaranteeing that wobbly sunburnt flesh will be seared on my brain for the rest of my days. Poor Eddie just about has an aneurysm. I suspect he may never be able to look another girl in the face again.

Ed's dad is one of the few locals who is happily on board with the crazy. He welcomes this group of beardy English guys who show up in an RV, with a trailer of guitars and amps in tow. Mr Palmer hires a couple of generators and some cans of stage lights from Merindale's community theatre group, the Merri Men. After a bit of kerfuffle with the council – *boom* – just like that – the north paddock is transformed from a dusty cow-haven into the centre stage of Glastonbury.

Penny-Farthing Man seems determined to get his arse kicked by me, as he sets up his 'bike' as an 'installation' on our front lawn. I see him perched atop his stupid oversized wheel, and despite my most fearsome scowly faces, he does not budge. I take some comfort in the fact that as soon as I get Cinnamon Girl back on her feet, she *will* be destroying an obnoxious one-wheeled mutant with a cascade of lava from her eyeballs.

I'm too busy to catch up with my friends, but it doesn't matter since everyone else is flat out as well. The Eversons practically beg Grady for full-time help at the fruit-and-veg; I see him for about twelve seconds on Monday as he sweeps by to drop off some boxes, though we spend the rest of the day swapping texts on the various weirdos who bustle through our doors.

I do, however, manage to spend some time with Daniel. In between photo ops, he installs himself at Albany's, playing catch-up with Mum and flirting with Paulette. Talking to him after all these years is the strangest thing; as if I'm flicking through a favourite comic, only since the last time I looked at it, all of the panels have been redrawn by someone new. Seeing him here – on the same stool he used to sit when he was little – is just too weird. Not least because his nose wrinkles in repulsion at our baked deliciousness. He even refuses to be tempted by Mum's salted caramel slices, his favourite snack in the universe when we were kids. I remember Grady's observation – it's Daniel, but not Daniel. I can't really name it, but reliving my stories with him doesn't make me as buzzy as I first thought it would. And my stomach seems to knot whenever his curious blue eyes fix on mine.

Daniel seems to be taking the apocalypse business in his stride. The only moment I see his confidence falter is when I drag him inside to give him a tour. He glances at the artwork stuck on my walls and ceiling, and makes some predictably dodgy comments on the underwear scattered over my floor. But when his eyes land on my bookshelf, where his Spider-Man PEZ dispenser lies nestled between volumes of *Birds of Prey*, his ears turn red, and his smile becomes less smug and sort of charmingly shy. It only serves to make my wobbly thoughts even wobblier.

Christmas feels like a millennium away. But before I know it, I wake up on Tuesday to find the Palmers' red gum trees draped with toilet paper and beer cans, and the bakery chirping with carols as the crew gets ready for Christmas Eve. By the time Paulette ushers a few strays out the door, my feet are achy and my back feels like it's been kicked by a horse. But it's almost time for our traditional Christmas Eve breakfast-at-dinner dinner, and for the first time in days, I feel a little of the old cheery me resurface.

I shower and change into a new dress I bought online, kind of as a joke for Grady; it's green and flared and dotted with teeny strawberries. I've just skipped into the diner with my picnic basket when Paulette bursts breathlessly back into Albany's.

"Alba, I'm so sorry! I was cleaning up outside … it's terrible, and I really don't want to be the one to tell you—"

I grab her arm. "Oh my God, Paulette! Are you OK? What's happened?"

She gives me a fierce hug, and then tugs me outside.

I follow her down Albany's steps. We're partway down the bluestone path when Paulette comes to a dead stop. She motions to the ground, at a flat spot of dry dirt right beneath Mum's favourite purple rose bush.

"No!" I gasp. "Not Frida!" I stare at the empty place where my beloved garden gnome lived.

"She was here earlier – I'm sure of it, cos she always gives me the heebies," Paulette says sympathetically. "It's the monobrow … she always looks so judgemental…"

I whirl around, frantically checking the rest of my gnome family. Prince Ferdinand is standing watch over the mailbox with his crown and sceptre, and Dead-eyed Derrick, the zombie gnome Dad found on Gumtree, is peeking his bloodied little face through the grass; Mooney Mac Mooneyeton with his naked backside pointing up in the air, and Herman the Gay Biker, in his leather chaps and gnome hat, are right where they're supposed to be. Big Grant is still chilling in his blue floatie, and I almost pluck him from his dandelion bed to give him a hug. I do a quick headcount, but the rest of my gnomes are all accounted for.

Penny-Farthing Man peddles his bike unhurriedly across the lawn.

"Did you see anything?" I call up at him.

"I've seen lots of things," he replies as he munches on a muffin. "I've seen the golden light of the divine—"

"Oh, shut it!" I yell. "You are *useless*! And hello, a penny-farthing's only supposed to have one back wheel – you're basically riding a giant tricycle."

He shrugs. "Little lady, perhaps after an age of being embedded in this one spot of earth, she decided to choose a journey of her own? Who are you to hinder her plans?"

Just as I'm visualizing myself soaring into the air with a backwards tumble and punching Penny-Farthing Man in the neck, Daniel appears through the crowds on the street. He peers at me over the top of his aviators.

"Sarah, you look ravishing. Though you also look like someone just flushed your goldfish. You all right?"

"Someone pinched my gnome!" I moan.

Daniel frowns. "Is that a … euphemism? It sounds kinky."

I stamp my foot and point, wordlessly, at our collection of little people, and then at the space where Frida used to be.

"Oh. *Oh.*" He looks at me with something like sympathy. "Was it a sentimental gnome?"

I sigh. "Sort of. Not really. We bought her from eBay … but she was *Frida.*"

"Well then," Daniel says as he pockets his glasses. "The world is a dangerous place for a garden ornament out on her own. Not everywhere works like the Valley, Sarah."

"Yeah, thanks for the mansplanation," I growl. "Any other lessons for this wide-eyed farm girl?"

Daniel grins. "Sorry. Didn't mean to lecture. But

you have to admit – you do have a bit of a naive streak."

I plant my hands on my hips. "Naive? Me? I seem to recall that *you* were the guy who refused to share a seat with a girl on the school bus for months, cos Deb DeLuca told you that that's how you make babies."

He laughs. "Yeah, all right, my bullshit radar was a bit off when I was seven." He takes a step toward me. "Though you know, Sarah, I've *totally* caught up on the whole baby-making process now."

I take a step toward him as well. "Are you trying to make me squirmy, Daniel? I'm not seven any more either. You should spend some time with Eddie – I'm immune to bad sex jokes."

He shakes his head, his eyes all mirthful. "I'm sorry, Alba. I guess I'd just forgotten how much fun it is to tease you. But OK, maybe naiive was the wrong word."

I take another step down the bluestone path, till there's nothing between us but a solitary rose bush and Herman the Gay Biker. "What would be the right word then?"

He is silent for a moment, his eyes on mine. "Oblivious," he says.

Penny-Farthing Man, whom I'd temporarily forgotten about, dings his bell. Paulette chuckles, and Daniel gives me that giant, silky grin. It's all I can do not to add them all to my brand-new list of people to be punched in the neck.

I grab my picnic basket. "Merry Christmas to you too," I say dryly. "Let's just go."

At the west end of town, where Main Street becomes dirt again, lies Grady's house. The yellow weatherboard and white-trim bungalow is snug between a thicket of beech trees, and has always reminded me of gingerbread and vanilla frosting. The farm fencing that divides their block from the Ridleys' canola fields is a bit saggy, but, in spring, the view from Grady's bedroom is an amazing swaying sea of yellows. His springtime bedroom view is one of my favourites in the whole world. Right now, the summery farmland is flat and empty.

Daniel pauses. "Wow. It's exactly the same. The basketball hoop, and his mum's crazy birdbaths... Jesus, Alba. This place. It's like the land that time forgot," he says wistfully.

I glance at the house as well. "Sometimes I think that in a bazillion years, when the spider monkeys have taken over, Eden Valley will still be standing exactly as is." I sigh. "Mrs Garabaldi might give those monkeys a run for their money, though. When marauding bandits are wandering the Earth and whatnot, she'll still be holed up in the hardware store in her dressing gown. It's kinda comforting, in a way."

Daniel seems to snap himself out of his daydream. That melancholy expression vanishes, replaced by his usual unreadable grin. "And will you still be serving coffee in your cute dresses? I suppose those monkeys might have some strudel needs. But, Sarah, I'm guessing the rest of the world might have moved on."

I let myself into Grady's without responding.

Music blasts my ears. Cleo's old aircon always struggles in summer, and inside it's thick and muggy. I squeeze between the boxes of craft supplies that line their tiny hallway. The sizzly smell of bacon wafts from the kitchen as I clomp inside.

Tia and Petey are bustling near the grill, matching reindeer hats on their heads. Tia's lobes flash with Christmas-light earrings, making her grey eyes sparkle with festive colour. I can't hear their conversation, but whatever joke they're sharing must be hilarious, cos Tia is doubled over in breathless giggles. When we were kids, *that* was a sure-fire sign she was one step away from peeing her pants.

Caroline has her bare feet kicked up on the table with Grady's laptop on her knees, lost in whatever she is looking at on-screen. Eddie is hunched at the stove, flipping misshaped orbs on to one of Cleo's good plates. I have a sneaking suspicion he is attempting to make boob-shaped pancakes.

Grady swings himself out of the fridge with a carton of juice in each hand. He's ditched his customary T-shirt for a short-sleeved button-down shirt, which must be new, since I've never seen it before. The dark blue fabric looks soft, and really nice on him. His curls even seem to be behaving; for a change, Grady's hair doesn't look like it's just lost a fight with a forest.

I stand back and let the sunspots fade from my eyes. Christmas Eve breakfast-at-dinner dinner originated a few summers ago, when Eddie had to have his tonsils out. It was, of all people's, Caroline's idea – since Ed's always been obsessed with breakfast food, she suggested that eggs and pancakes swimming in ice-cream would be a fair substitute for a proper Christmas Eve dinner. And, as Eddie said, when he eventually regained his voice, getting his tonsils "fecking scalpelled out" was almost worth it since it gave us an excuse for dinner pancakes.

And before I can rein in my woolly emotions, my eyes fill with tears. Damn it. I love Christmas. I don't cry at Christmas. I am the fricking *queen* of Christmas cheer.

"Hey! There you are!" Grady says as he dumps the juice on the table. I brush my hands over my face before my stupid tears can spill, but Grady is busy rearranging glasses and thankfully hasn't noticed my weirdness. He waves a flippant hand in my direction. "So she badgers and bullies us into preserving tradition, then she moseys in late while the rest of us toil in the kitchen like minions..." He grins at me. "I was about to send out a search party. Busy day?"

Daniel is hovering on the edge of the kitchen. "Sorry. Gnome-related crisis," he says distractedly.

I reach into my basket and pull out my Santa hat. "Yeah. Someone stole Frida," I say as I shove the hat sullenly on to my head.

Grady stops pottering and gapes at me. "Oh no! Really? Not Frida! Arsebags!"

"And *that* was the right reaction," I say, punching Daniel in the arm. Though I can't help but laugh a little bit too, the ridiculousness suddenly just too much for me and my jumbly brain.

Grady reaches for my picnic basket, a thick bandaid wrapped unevenly around his left hand. I grab his arm. "What did you do?"

He grimaces. "Um, tried chopping tomatoes without supervision? I know I'm banned from knife duty, but given that you also banned me from frypan duty, there wasn't much else for me to do. It's not bad. There may be some blood in the omelettes."

"Domenic! How many times do I have to tell you? Knives are not toys! Gah! No one wants a three-fingered lawyer."

"Yes, ma'am," Grady replies with a smile. "I will endeavour to make it through this Christmas without the need for stitches or surgery."

I tug out my phone, but Grady pokes his tongue at me before I can snap him in non-face-pulling mode.

"You guys are hilarious," Daniel says dryly. "Want me to take one with both of you?"

I pocket my phone again. "There's a reason I resort to sneak-attacks, Daniel. Unless you're talking mug shots or photos of a crime scene, Mr Hard-boiled here doesn't see the point in, and I quote, 'capturing every sneeze', unquote. His Facebook pic is a movie poster of *The Maltese Falcon*."

Daniel laughs. "Domenic! Dude, a bit of sentiment is mandatory at Christmas." He gives my hair a cheeky tug. "And how could you not want a photo of this girl?"

I nudge Daniel back. "Grady, if I'm abducted by an evil space-monster tomorrow, your only evidence of my existence would be some strudel crumbs on your bedroom floor."

Grady glances between Daniel and me. "I know what you look like," he says mildly.

Grady's Labrador lopes across the kitchen and sniffs at Daniel's feet. Daniel steps hurriedly backwards. "Jesus, is that ... Clouseau? Man, I thought that dog would have died years ago."

Grady cups his hands over Clouseau's ears. "*Easy*, dude! She has feelings."

Daniel laughs, but then he catches the look on Grady's face and quickly wrestles it into a spluttery cough. "Sorry. I didn't mean to … offend the dog. She looks good?"

"She's fine," Grady says firmly. "Her best years are still to come, aren't they, girl?"

I drag Daniel by the arm and shove him in a seat at the table as Grady launches into one of his in-depth conversations with his dog.

"Alba!" Tia chirps, waving tongs in the air. "OK, so we have bacon and eggs, sausages, hash browns – a feast of greasy goodness."

Pete giggles. "And possibly the breast pancakes in the universe. Right, Ed?"

Eddie spins around triumphantly with his plate of dodgy pancakes in hand. "Uh-huh. Fecking works of art right here on this plate." He picks up a floppy boob pancake with an off-centred nipple, and he waves it in Caroline's face. "Whaddya think, Gresham? Am I not, like, the Picasso of lady parts?"

"I suppose dickhead-shaped pancakes were too hard to make?" she says without looking up.

Grady pulls Tupperware from my basket. "Breakfast scones? Awesome. They *almost* make up for that dress, Alba. You look like a walking butt-rash."

I stand on my toes so my face is right up in his.

"Aw, you're such a sweet-talker. So explain to me again why you bombed out with hat-girl?"

Grady rolls his eyes. He tugs my Santa hat down over my face. "Woman, maybe normal girls are just immune to my charm."

Beside me, I hear Daniel snort. "The chick you snuck off with at the pub? Didn't look like anyone was bombing out. From where I was standing, hot chick looked totally into someone's 'charm'. Right, Domenic?"

I readjust my hat. Grady's innocent-face is fighting with his uncomfortable-face. He glares at Daniel before giving me a lopsided grin. "Maybe we had a chat while the rest of you were gawking at Ned... Anyway, that doesn't explain the dress, Alba. I can barely look at you without itching."

Daniel jabs me in the arm with a Christmas cracker. "What am I missing...?"

I swallow down an unfamiliar hunch that Grady is not being entirely upfront. "Grady's ... allergic to strawberries, remember?" Grady wrinkles up his nose at my dress in faux-disgust.

Daniel leans back in his chair. "Right – yeah, I remember that. Dude, you couldn't have picked a less-manly allergy? Really not what you want mentioned in your eulogy. It'd be, like, 'Here lies Domenic Grady – he was tall and brave, beloved by all, until he was felled by a torte'. Way not cool."

Grady installs himself on the other side of the table. "Guess I don't spend a lot of time worrying about how cool I'll look at my funeral, Dan," he says as he pours some juice.

Daniel swings precariously backwards. "You've never imagined the thousands of people gushing about how awesome your life was? The gorgeous blonde with just the right amount of funeral-appropriate cleavage weeping over your casket?"

Eddie grabs a tray from Pete and squeezes himself into a chair. "My funeral is gonna be like a cross between a NASCAR rally and a party at the Playboy mansion. Feck funeral-appropriate cleavage. The more boobs, the better. Right, G-man?"

Grady laughs as he hands me a juice. "Knowing my luck, my funeral will be more like Scrooge's. Just my cold, dead body, and a couple of people who've shown up for a free lunch. I think cleavage might be in short supply."

"Argh! Can we please stop talking about your

funerals?" I say. I pull up a chair at the end of the table. "Not only is it mega-depressing, but also, this obsession with cleavage is *really* disturbing."

Eddie looks at me blankly. "You prefer no cleavage? Feck. Talk about depressing."

Caroline groans. "Francis, if you ever find your way to a breast that doesn't belong to a cow, your eyeballs would explode from the trauma—"

"All right, *enough*!" I yelp as Daniel and Pete burst out laughing. "It is Christmas Eve – hence, we give thanks to the little baby Jesus, and we do *not* talk about funerals and boobs! Jeez. Breakfast-at-dinner dinner is supposed to be *classy*."

Pete and Tia settle at the table. "Sorry, Alba," Petey says sheepishly. "Even though, I would like to point out, I had nothing to do with the boob pancakes."

Daniel pours himself a glass of water, as relaxed as if he'd been part of our group a thousand Christmases before. "But what about you, Sarah? The End of Days are on everyone's mind. Surely you've been thinking about mortality and stuff as well?"

"Indigo? Surprisingly, I don't spend a lotta time contemplating my demise." I swallow a gulp of juice, my throat feeling dry and papery. "This girl is totally living in the moment," I say, with a smile I can't totally pull off.

Daniel's eyes linger on the bacon. He grabs an apple from the basket on the table. "I don't believe that for a second. Little you was always crazy ambitious. Didn't you want to run away to draw for Dark Horse, once upon a time? You banged on about it so much when we were kids it's pretty much imprinted on my brain. What the hell happened to the plan?"

I glance around the table, noting that my friends are busy piling their plates with food and are all, suspiciously, silent. Grady is the only one not distracted by the deliciousness. He's running his hand along the back of his neck, his eyes on me.

I fidget with my Santa napkin. "Maybe I did, once. But I don't want to walk around town in a Wonder Woman bra, or grow my own unicorn any more either. I … wanted those things, sure, but I don't know if I still do – and even if by some miracle I *do* get into uni, which, hey, who knows at this point … I mean, I'm not sure…"

"Dan, just let it go," Grady says quietly.

Daniel takes a ginormous bite of apple. "I'm just saying, Sarah, that maybe it'd pay to not *completely* ignore what's happening around you," he says through crunches. "Check it out. While the rest of the population is knocking things off their bucket lists and hooking up, you are baking cupcakes and doodling in your little sketchbook."

I grab a scone and slice it in half with one angry swipe of my butter knife. "So you're saying I should be 'hooking up' with some random stranger, just in case the world ends? Cos *that* will be the thing I'm going to most regret come the Rapture."

Daniel leans across the table. "Sarah, I don't believe I *ever* suggested a random stranger—"

"Hey, Daniel?" Grady growls. "Stop."

Grady and Daniel stare at each. Clouseau hefts herself off the ground and parks her face in Daniel's lap.

Daniel eyes Clouseau distastefully. "Dude. Your dog drooled on me."

"Dude. She has good taste," Grady replies.

Daniel looks at Grady with a raised eyebrow. Then he laughs, and somewhat pointedly swipes a hand at the doggy-drool wet spot on his crotch.

Petey smiles brightly at Tia. "Well. Merry Christmas everyone. Personally, I'd like to give thanks for these awesome eggs and the weirdly conspicuous tension—"

He yelps; my guess is as Tia kicks him in the shin under the table.

Tia raises her glass. "Happy Christmas, guys! Here's to surviving high school, and, um ... to new-old friends," she says shyly as she taps her glass against Daniel's.

I clink my glass with everyone else's. Petey cranks the music, and my friends drift back into conversation. I hear snippets of stuff about Mayan calendars and Large Hadron Colliders as I pile more scones on to my plate, but I'm only vaguely aware of what my hands are doing. A few minutes ago I was starving; now, my stomach feels like a big ball of bread dough on the inside, kneading itself into a knot.

Grady pushes a jar of peach jam toward me. I take it from him with a smile that falters the moment his dark eyes lock on mine. I know that look – his I'm-going-to-badger-you-until-you-tell-me-what's-wrong face.

I shuffle my chair closer to Caroline. "What were you doing, Caroline?" I say, nodding my head at Grady's laptop.

She shovels in a mouthful of pancake. "Grady's helping me fix my résumé. I started applying for jobs months ago, but so far no luck." She grins. "Personally, I reckon scooping manure on the Ark probably isn't gonna require references, but *someone* thinks that I'm getting 'waylaid by mob mentality'."

"Yeah, *I'm* the insane one," Grady says. "This from the person who has 'wee off Harbour Bridge' and 'obtain neck tattoo' on the top of her bucket list?"

"*Regardless*," she says, flicking a chunk of pancake at him, "apart from the grocery store, and that year-seven nativity play, my résumé is looking pathetic. D'ya think anyone is gonna care that I was 'second sheep in manger' when I was thirteen?"

Grady peers at her over his mound of scrambled eggs smothered in chilli sauce. "Which is why I think you should apply for some courses as a backup."

"Yeah, thanks but no thanks." She steeples her fingers behind her neck. "Anthony says it's gonna cost another couple of hundred bucks for the parts to finish my baby. But I *will* be riding off into the sunset. Even if I have to do it on one of the Ridleys' goats."

I abandon my scone on to my plate. "What ... sort of job do you think you want, Caroline?"

Caroline pauses, a piece of bacon halfway to her mouth. "I don't really care, Alba. An office job, or something in a cafe. Anywhere that's not here is fine with me. I just wanna try on a few things and see what fits." She drops the bacon and glances at Grady, but Eddie has him bailed up in a story about these topless frisbee-playing girls camped near the farm gates, and Grady is all wide-eyed and distracted. "Why d'you ask?" she says quietly. "I know you ... well, hate talking about this stuff."

I pick up her bacon and munch slowly. It's not like I've *never* thought about leaving Eden Valley. But visions of my fabulous adult life usually involved sharing a light-filled artist's loft with Ramona Fradon, or building my own Iron Man suit. I guess it's easy to dream about things that are abstract, or impossible.

"I can't believe we're done with school," I blurt. I lower my voice. "It's like ... my brain just glitches when I try to imagine not being there. How is that going to be a thing, Caroline? Don't you feel sad? Is it really going to be that easy for you to leave?"

For the briefest moment, Caroline glances at Tia, who is giggling with Petey over some story Daniel is gracing them with. Caroline drops her voice to a whisper. "Alba, you know, ever since we were kids, Tia and I had this plan to move away together? OK, when we were kids Tia also wanted to live in the planetarium ... but it was always supposed to be us. And now, pretty sure I'm gonna be out there alone." Colour rises in her cheeks. "And you guys ... it's gonna really ... suck saying goodbye." She takes a long swig of juice. "But the other option?" she says eventually. "It's not an option. I can't stay here. Even if the rest of the world is a zombie-infested wasteland, I still have to go see for myself. It's not going to be easy at all. But it is necessary."

I push back from the table. "I had no idea you were so adept at philosophization, Caroline," I say dryly. "You're, like, rocking the Zen-master thing."

She shrugs. "I have my moments. Clearly, fewer moments than you, but I've made my peace with it. What choice do I have?" She gestures surreptitiously around us. "It's not like things can stay the same as this."

"You don't know that."

She elbows me in the arm, her face just a wee bit too exasperated for my liking. "Yeah, I do. We're not a superhero team, Alba."

"What are you two whispering about?" Eddie barks through a mouthful of hash brown.

Caroline scowls. "Girls' stuff. Clothes and periods. You have something to add?"

Eddie blushes. "Feck that," he mumbles. "I'm eating."

I smother jam on to my scones as Caroline turns around to spar with Ed. Daniel continues to make vaguely rude comments, which do get a laugh out of Petey and Tia, but serve only to make Grady's cheeks turn deepening shades of red. I keep smiling, and my mouth keeps moving, cos when all else fails I can talk my way out of a paper bag. Part of me is grateful for my friends and their banter; part of me knows that the thing I need most right now is time to sort through the rubbish in my head.

I'm not sure that food is the solution to my problems. But I stare at the whirls of peach on my scones, wishing that – like the face of Jesus in a meat pie – the answers to my questions might miraculously materialize on my plate.

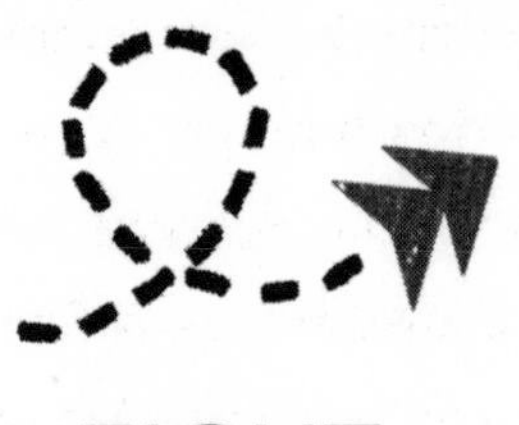

EIGHT

Later, sickly full, I park my protesting friends in Grady's lounge as festive sounds and music drift through the windows. Daniel is the only one not in a fidgety rush to be elsewhere. He has a thousand anecdotes about life as a D-list celeb, and my friends seem duly fascinated – admittedly, the boy knows how to tell a story. I can just picture him, with his chaotic, colourful life. And it's not exactly jealousy that stirs in my belly; more like this itchy, faltering curiosity.

The thing is – despite all the stories that the three of us share – my memories of Daniel are framed by those last few weeks before he went away. The misery that followed him like a cartoon raincloud; the playground lunchtimes with Grady and Daniel devising rubbishy ten-year-old boy plans to keep him in the Valley; and the last glimpse of Daniel's despondent face through the window of his parents' Volvo. Even seeing him on TV, with his new body and shiny smile – some part of me always believed that Daniel must be miserable away from here. Whatever the reason, Daniel's cheer makes me feel even more inexplicably confused and morose.

But then Daniel drags his feet to his manager's rental, and Grady whips us into a cleaning frenzy before everyone finally scarpers to the farm, and the two of us head back to my place. Yes, I am a sucker for tradition, but our time-honoured post-Christmas-Eve-breakfast-at-dinner dinner dessert-fest is just about the only thing that can rescue me from my bewildering funk.

Mum's gone all out this year, whipping up a spiced white chocolate and cherry cake that's like a piece of Christmassy heaven in my mouth. Grady has clearly forsaken his one job, as Cleo has attempted an American pumpkin pie, which tastes like she scraped the bottom of a roast-beef pan and then added cinnamon sugar. My poker face is ruined when Grady bursts out laughing, covering Mum's Santa statues with sprayed chunks of pie.

Then Anthony gives me a giant hug and Grady

an affectionate head slap before he hoofs it to the Palmers', and Grady and I leave our mums making cocktails in the bakery kitchen as we retreat to swap presents. I can't remember how this tradition started. I think it was that time Grady bought me these wicked earrings with dangly Legos on them – Wonder Woman for one ear, and Spider-Man for the other. For some reason he was way embarrassed for me to open them in front of our mums, and I guess our private gift-giving ritual just stuck.

We're sitting cross-legged on my bed, Grady grinning like a maniac as I hand him the box that I know he knows has been hiding on top of my wardrobe for months.

I've gone for a themed present this year, scouring online for the perfect collection of stuff. On top, I've sketched a shadowy Cinnamon Girl on the steps of 221B Baker Street. Individually wrapped inside is this boxset of the complete Sherlock Holmes stories with beautiful silhouetted covers, and a rubber ducky in a Sherlock Holmes outfit, and a T-shirt that says *Sherlock is my Holmesboy* on it, and a proper houndstooth deerstalker hat, which Grady unwraps with a delighted, albeit girly, squeal.

"This is brilliant! I've always wanted one, but it was way too dorky to buy myself. You are the best!"

"And you look like a tool," I say, laughing as I adjust the earflaps over his curls. "But it suits you. Very investigationy."

He sits back and gives the Sherlock ducky a couple of squeaks in my direction. "OK. Your turn." He reaches under my bed with one hand and emerges with his old Santa sack that I've been busting to get my hands on all evening.

"Oof. It's heavy!" I say as I haul the sack on to my lap. "Lemme guess, you've bought me that very special concrete slab I've always wanted?" I yank out a giant rectangle shrouded in glittery Christmas wrapping and tear frantically at the paper.

And then I freeze. Grady smiles shyly. The hefty present is Gil Kane's *The Amazing Spider-Man: Artist's Edition*, which I have been salivating over for years. It contains the original artwork of the infamous LSD issues, and the first Morbius storyline, and one of the most classic Spidey stories ever – *The Night Gwen Stacy Died*. It's amazing, and perfect, and it costs an absolute bucket-load.

"Grady, you are insane!" I say as I carefully peel

back the plastic. "We said we'd stick to a budget!"

"You don't like it?" he says innocently.

I leap across the bed and book and throw my arms around him. "It is the best present in the universe. You suck. How am I ever gonna top this?"

Grady gives me an awkward half-hug. I sneakily slip my phone from my side table and hold it in front of us before he can move away. Grady groans. Though, for a change, he doesn't pull a face or attempt to squirm away. When I look at the photo, even though half his face is buried in my hair, I can tell he's sort of smiling as well.

I shuffle backwards. Grady adjusts his hat. "The Eversons have pretty much given me a full-time job over summer, and all those odd jobs and tutoring at the primary school last year added up, and hey." He grins. "Who knows what the currency of the future might be, Alba? This might turn out to be our very last Christmas ever."

He seems to realize what he's said just as the words leave his mouth, because his smile disappears. He takes off the hat and runs a hand through his hair.

I glance through the window. The string of lantern lights is clouding the fields, giving the entire view a surreal glow. I can see shadows moving in the distance, but they're vague and indistinct, the tops of ghostly heads swarming in the darkness. I've stared, daydreaming, out this same window since I was five years old, and the only things that have ever changed are the height of Dad's plum trees and the formation of cows in the Palmers' paddock.

From my living room drifts the croony voice of one of those old guys that Mum likes, filled with snow and fireplaces and loneliness. I never understood why anyone would want to sing Christmas songs so melancholic. It's like, dude, the song's called 'Have Yourself a Merry Little Christmas' – cheer the hell up. Tonight, though, I think I know how glum-guy feels.

I drag my eyes back to Grady. He fidgets with my bedspread. "I do have something else for you, Alba." He fishes through the back pocket of his jeans and emerges with a crumpled envelope.

"What's this?"

"Well, it's two train tickets to Melbourne. I thought we could go after Christmas—"

"Oooh, to see that Vali Myers exhibition? I read there's a couple of unpublished drawings on display."

"Well, yeah, that, but also ... I thought maybe

we could check out some schools again as well? Melbourne Uni law faculty is having a summer session I'd like to go to, and I thought maybe you'd want to see the College of the Arts again? You zoomed out so quickly when you did your interview that I don't think we saw more than the reception and, you know, you should look around before..."

I drop the envelope, my hands doing that clammy thing again. "Why would I want to do that?" I say quietly. I flip to a random page in my Spider-Man book and stare blankly at a panel. In my peripheral vision, I see Grady cross his arms.

"Because, up until a few months ago, it was all you could talk about," he says, just as quietly. "Because whatever it is you're thinking about, it doesn't hurt to look, Alba."

When I glance up at him, he is staring at me with his stubborn-face, and though I don't get my back up often, I feel my spine straighten.

"Grady – stop pushing. It's really starting to get old. You know – gah, I can't even remember anything I said in that stupid interview, I was so freaking nervous! And you saw how many other people were there, all clutching their folios like hopeful morons...

I don't know why you just assume they're gonna want me. And why can't you understand... I don't get what's so wrong with being happy where you are. Why does everyone need to be in a super-mad rush to be somewhere else? I love it here, and I'm happy—"

Grady squares his shoulders. "You're scared," he says, in this decisive tone that pisses me right off. "You're afraid, and so you're hanging on to what you know because you are terrified of what comes next. OK, right now things are awesome as they are, but Alba, why can't you see that things could be even better?" He runs his hand over the back of his neck. And then he picks up his Sherlock hat and twirls it frantically. "I know it's not my place to tell you what to do—"

"It's really, really not, Domenic," I snap.

His eyes fly up to mine. "Don't first-name me, Sarah," he snaps back. "I'm trying to help you."

"And who says I need your help, or your advice? You are not my Alfred!"

Grady tosses the deerstalker on to the bed. "Don't know if you've noticed, *Batman*, but I am not your butler!"

"Then why are you acting like a know-it-all

grandpa!" I bark back. "You don't know everything! You don't know what I'm supposed to be, or where I'm supposed to go! You can't make me do something I don't want to do—"

Grady leaps off my bed. "So stay here!" he yells. "You'll end up marrying Eddie, since he'll be the only guy left. Your kids'll be born with five o'clock shadows and have, like, no necks, and you'll move into the flat behind his dad's milking shed and join the country women's knitting club or whatever, and you'll stop drawing and reading and smiling, and you won't be *you* any more. And you'll forget all about me."

I hunker against my wall, my blood not so much fizzing as boiling. "Cos they're my only options, right? And who says I need to marry *anyone*! Maybe I'll run the bakery with Mum! Maybe I'll open a shop with Tia and start making my own dresses! Maybe I'll build a studio and publish my comics right here in the Valley! Maybe I'll be the first person to rollerblade over the Tanami Desert! You don't know!"

Grady stops pacing and swings around again. "It really doesn't bother you at all, does it?" he says, glaring down at me. "I'm leaving, and you're staying, and you couldn't care less that *that* is going to be it. Because think about it, Sarah. Paulette isn't going anywhere. Eddie's brothers, and my brother, they aren't going anywhere. Half our class has already hightailed it, and we're probably never going to see them again. If you stay here, you're stuck, and if I leave—"

"You're not coming back." Those stupid tears that have been threatening all week finally well and spill over. Grady freezes. His face becomes stricken. I hardly ever cry, and he's never been able to stand it when I do.

"Alba, I'm sorry… It's all right. God, I'm an idiot. Don't listen to me."

"You can be a real arsebag sometimes, Grady." I throw myself on my bed and attempt to wipe my tears with a ream of Christmas paper.

The bed dips as Grady sits beside me. I can feel my whole body trembling with angry tears, but I take a couple of deep breaths. Grady and I don't fight. I *refuse* to accept that we are fighting.

"I'm really sorry, Alba," he whispers. "I'd rehearsed this speech in my head, and I'm pretty sure it sounded less … toolbag-ish in there. I know it's your call what you do. But you are *so* talented, and the thought of you wasting that…" He touches my back tentatively. "Alba? I don't get what's going on in your head. I don't know what's changed. And it's freaking me out because I've never not known before..."

I take another breath and haul myself up. I push my palms into my eyes, focusing on the sparks behind my lids. "Grady, listen to me. I don't know what I want. I know what I've always *said* I wanted, but I haven't had to properly think about any of it, and now that I do have to think about it, it's just all too ... big. Too much. Sometimes my head is so foggy with all the stuff I'm *supposed* to want, I can't pick the bits that are me talking and the bits that are everyone else. Sometimes I can't shut your voice out of my head, and it's like, I can't hear *me* over it. Does that make sense?"

I drop my hands. His cheeks are flushed, but I can tell that behind those stubborn eyes, he's trying his best to rein it in. "I didn't realize I was crowding you—"

"No, shut up for a sec. I'm trying to make a point. Grady, sometimes it feels like you have fired this starter pistol, and, what, I'm just supposed to start running behind you? Even though I'm basically comfortable hanging around the snack bar in my pyjamas, and I don't even know if I want to be on the track, and my shoes are somewhere underneath my bed, and hey, maybe swimming is more my thing—"

Grady shakes his head. "That ... is a terrible metaphor."

"Yeah, OK, my metaphors are rubbish, but the point is – I need to figure it out on my own. *My* decision." I swipe my hands on my dress, but the icky tinglyness remains. "I'm ... not your sidekick, Grady."

He nods, but his eyes stay locked on his hands. I lean into his shoulder, aiming for a confidence that seems to have left me somewhere around boob pancakes. "Domenic Miles Grady – do not panic. Look, I know you're scared." He snaps his head around. "But Grady, you are going to be brilliant. You'll be a big fancy lawyer, and you'll get to see all those places you've always wanted to. And whether I go or stay shouldn't make any difference."

He laughs, but there's zero humour in it. "Yeah. It shouldn't."

He stares at the floor, and I stare at the sweep of curls near his neck. And, for just a moment, I allow a tiny crack in the compartment in my head where I store all the stuff I haven't allowed myself to contemplate. For just a second, I imagine waking up in my bedroom, and looking out over the Valley, and realizing that Grady is not in his yellow house. He's not stretched out on my couch in his pyjamas, or waiting for me in his booth in the diner. He's not hanging with his brother at the garage, or hauling boxes at the Eversons'. He's not doodling stick men on my notebooks in our teeny classroom, long legs in his scratchy school uniform taking up too much space beneath our table. He's not about to burst through my verandah door with a story about something he's read on the internet. And then I slam a lid on the compartment, cos it feels pretty much exactly like someone is sitting on my chest.

"We can't do everything together forever. Maybe … we aren't supposed to?" I say, the words feeling wrong even as I'm saying them.

Grady's eyes linger on the collage of photos I've hung lopsidedly above my bookshelves. "I know," he says softly.

He collapses backwards on my bed with a sigh. And then he reaches up and tugs at my wrist, pulling me down beside him. We used to play this game when we were little, lying like this and mashing our knees together until someone caved and *owwed* and called stop. We haven't done that in a long time, though; Grady stopped wanting to play when his legs got big enough to leave a bruise.

I reach for his hand. His fingers twitch, before he links them tentatively through mine. For a long time, neither of us says a word. For the first time in my whole life, I have no idea of the right words to say to him. But it's *Grady.* We don't run out of things to talk about.

"Do you really want to rollerblade over the Tanami Desert?" he says eventually.

"Should probably learn to rollerblade first, right?"

"I'm guessing it would help, yes."

"And do you really think I'd marry Eddie? Our kids would have very giant heads."

He chuckles. "Naw. Can't see you ever being quite that desperate. Even if we are looking at a last-man-on-Earth-type scenario."

"Grady, you don't really think it's true, do you? I know it's impossible, but what if … the world has to end sometime, right? All those rogue nukes and tsunamis and ice caps melting, and we're just sitting here, and, I dunno…"

"What?"

"Well, maybe we should ... do something. You know. What would you do if you only had one day to live and all that?"

Grady pulls my hand on to his chest. "What would you do, Alba?"

"I dunno. I think – and I know you don't feel the same way – but I'd want to be right here. I'd want to be home, with you and Mum and Cleo and the guys..." With my hand on his chest, I can feel the solid, familiar *whump* of his heartbeat through my palm. "If I only had one day to live, then this is exactly where I'd want to be."

Grady is silent for ages. "And if you had more than one day?"

I untangle my fingers from his and roll on to my belly. "Well. Guess that's the question, isn't it?"

"I guess so," he says, his eyes on my ceiling. "But Alba, you're wrong about one thing. I want big things, you know that, and I can't imagine any of them happening here. I can't change that about me. But if I did only have one day to live, then this – right here – is exactly where I'd want to be."

I rest my chin in the crook of his elbow, and I smile at him until he drags his eyes to me. He smiles lopsidedly back, and just like that, I know this conversation is over.

"You're staying here tonight. Right?"

He sits up and swings his legs off my bed, and he sticks the deerstalker on his head. "Nah. Better go. I promised Mum I'd wrap the presents we bought Aunt Molly and I've got … other stuff on tomorrow. And I should probably not leave the house empty. You know, I caught some drunk guy drinking out of Clouseau's water bowl this morning? Seriously, this whole episode has put me off alcohol for life."

He grabs his Christmas box and heads outside. The gabble from the farm gusts into my room, and I try not to flinch as the jarring noise invades my space.

"Merry Christmas, Alba," he says softly as he steps on to the verandah.

"Hey, Grady?"

He turns around again, the lanterns and Sherlock hat throwing his face into shadow.

"Yeah, Alba?"

"You know, you don't ever have to worry about me forgetting you. Ever. You had very distinctive hair when we were little. I'll always remember you as that kid I once knew who looked like Beaker from *The Muppets*."

He hesitates. Then he leans down and gives me a fleeting kiss on the cheek. "Woman, has anyone told you that you can be extremely mean?"

I give him a dismissive wave, and he waves back as he disappears into the darkness.

I sit on the edge of my bed again. Now, depressed-guy in the lounge is whining about only being home for Christmas in his dreams, and I have this overwhelming urge to run out there and chuck Mum's iPod into the compost.

I lie down and shove a pillow over my head.

I'm not totally delusional. I know I can't stay in this room forever. I know I'm supposed to want to leave. And maybe I do, one day. I want to see MoMA and the Musée d'Orsay, and I want to check out the headquarters of Marvel and DC and Dark Horse. I want to go to art school, one day, though the thought of being just one of a bazillion wannabes makes me feel small and blue. I want to make plans. But I just don't know how to make myself jump on this arbitrary schedule the universe keeps trying to set for me.

Because honestly? Part of me knows that Grady is right. I'm just not brave enough for the things I want. Any of the things that I want.

My phone chimes. I drag the pillow away from my face and grab my mobile from the floor. On my screen, Daniel's blue eyes are staring at me with a selfie I took of us that night at the Junction. His expression is straight from *A Home Among the Gum Trees* – part-bedroom eyes, part-someone-has-just-given-me-an-enema face.

Merry Christmas, SJA. Hope Santa brought everything your little heart desired. Looking forward to catching up again – got a pres for you. xx Dan

I text him back my most articulate response – question mark, exclamation mark, smiley face. And then I toss my phone on the floor and change into my jammies. I crawl under my sheets, despite the heavy, oppressive heat, and make a tent with my Spider-Man book and lamp, just like I used to do with Dad's comics when I was a kid.

Sometime later I hear Mum and Cleo stumbling into the lounge. The god-awful Bing Crosby music is replaced with one of Angie's early-nineties mixes that will, inevitably, end with one of them standing on the coffee table while belting out a Nirvana song. No doubt to be followed by the digging out of Mum and Dad's wedding album, and a gush of cocktail-infused nostalgia-tears.

I switch off my lamp and pull the pillow over my head again.

I should be happy. Almost everyone I love is in the one place, and Grady bought me a brilliant present, and, despite a weird hiccup, we've had an awesome Christmas, as always, and Daniel is here, and the world is spinning the way it's supposed to, regardless of the ridiculousness happening outside.

But I can't shake this horrible feeling that – even discounting the end of the world – nothing at all in my universe is right.

NINE

I wake up on a sweltering Christmas Day with an unfamiliar sense of foreboding.

Normally, I'd be spending the morning schlepping in my jammies, reading Dad's Marvel holiday specials and watching *Double Indemnity* with Grady, as is tradition. But normally, if the universe worked the way it's supposed to, then Grady would've been snoozing on the other side of my room, waiting for me to pounce on him with Christmas Day cheer.

But Grady's couch is empty, and I can't sleep. My mental alarm pings at 5.30 a.m., and my eyes are instantly wide, my heart double-timing in bewildering panic mode.

I fall out of bed and click on my computer. The news is led by a bunch of jokey doomsday stories, each more nonsensical than the next. But there's other stuff, too; stuff that should make me giggle, but serves only to send a clammy trickle of sweat tumbling down my spine. There's a story about an outbreak of a bizarro tropical disease in Kenya. This weirdness at a Dutch zoo, where the entire troop of baboons freaked out and then fell silent, not eating or moving for days. Some dude in a village in France is convinced his goat gave birth to a rabbit. Though really, his proof seems to be an unfamiliar bunny hopping around his yard, and his goat appearing a little more chuffed than usual. Drunk goat-herders aside, the signs are, apparently, everywhere.

But honestly? I have zero interest in decoding these portents of impending doom; wondering if the sky is falling cos someone saw the horsemen of the apocalypse riding through their cornflakes or whatnot.

And besides. I know that the very worst things of all can sneak up behind you in the quiet and sunshine. And they don't often come with warnings.

I wander on to my verandah. The sun is creeping over the hills, and the horizon is a mishmash of smudgy pinks. A handful of people are moving in the fields, and many more are splayed on sleeping bags and car hoods. Stray paper Christmas hats and the odd bit of toilet paper tumble past. Apart from the faint song of the Palmers' cows, the farm is eerily silent.

In the distance, where the fields are broken by the line of red gum trees, my eyes fall on a motorbike parked beside a tent. The bike is huge, a black body glinting in the early sun – a classic retro cruiser, or it looks like that from here. If Dad got a glimpse of that beast, he'd probably be halfway across the field barefoot in his jocks, drawn to it like a zombie toward chrome-accented brains. Even from a distance, I can tell it's a beautiful bike. And it kinda makes me feel like yakking last night's pumpkin pie all over my plastic backyard.

I scamper back inside and draw my curtains tightly behind me.

I stand aimlessly in the middle of the room, staring at my tacked-up sketches. Cinnamon Girl seems wholly unimpressed by Christmas Day. I briefly consider adding a Santa hat to her rockabilly outfit, but she's becoming steadily more pissy-looking as her panels progress; messing with her could be a bad idea. I'm getting a little worried that one of these days she might jump out of the page and beat me to death in my sleep with one of her red stilettos.

Though it's barely passed six, I pick up my phone, and I call Grady. I have this flash of him face-planted in his pillow with his Sherlock hat on his head, and I can't help but smile. I don't know what I'm planning to say. I just feel this need to talk to him, like, right this second. I call twice. But Grady doesn't answer. I send him a Merry Christmas text, chock full of festive emoticons, but – though I know he sleeps with his phone under his pillow – I don't get anything back.

So instead I wake up Angie with a pot of Lady Grey tea and a tonally challenged 'Trolley Song' from *Meet Me in St Louis.* It feels like ages since I've properly hung out with Mum. Angie and I whip up breakfast in our PJs while mercifully chatting about everything other than the apocalypse, and then we swap our presents. Mum gives me her traditional awesome artists' bag with graphite pencils, pots of India ink and pads of Bristol board. Annoyingly, one of the art books I'd ordered for her still hasn't arrived. For a fleeting moment, I see myself on a busy street with more than a handful of crusty old shops. And the rows upon rows of comics patiently waiting on the shelves of city stores ...

Mum's added something extra to her present this year. As she whips cream in a bowl, I tear the paper off a small PVC folder. It's about the size of a paperback, with a very cool reproduction of Warhol's *Campbell's Soup Cans* printed under the plastic. I flip it over in my hands before it dawns on me that it is a passport holder.

"I don't even own a passport," I mutter.

Mum adjusts the Christmas cracker hat on her head. "Cleo found it on Etsy. You know how I feel about Warhol, but you dig his stuff. Hey, use it for storing recipes," she says casually. "Or whatever."

I slip the wallet into the pocket of my kimono, wondering vaguely whether there is such a thing as a PVC pop-art signal from the universe. "Thanks, Mama. I'm just grateful that you didn't go all survivalist-themed for your presents this year."

Mum grins. "Your chemical toilet might be in the mail." She glances at her phone. "Domenic still sleeping? You should give him a nudge before the scones get cold."

I gulp a mouthful of tea. "Nah. Grady's not here."

Mum frowns. "I thought Cleo's cook-fest would have kept him holed up in your room. Aren't you two supposed to be watching something black-and-white right about now?"

I shrug. "I think Grady wanted to check on Clouseau or something. You know, after what happened to poor Mr Frankenstein."

Mum grimaces. "Who would've thought Rosie and I would ever have to google 'how do you remove blue hair-dye from a poodle'? Is it really six whole days till New Year's? This whole bizzo can't be over quick enough for me."

I hoist my butt on to the counter, running my fingers over the familiar pattern of burns on the green laminate. And I can't help but laugh. "Mum, honestly, did you *ever* expect this kind of crazy in Eden Valley? I know you guys moved here for the fresh air and weed-growing potential, but this has got to be *way* beyond what you signed up for."

Mum rolls her eyes. "The weed-growing was strictly Grady's dad's vision. And Adam couldn't grow mould on bread." She gives me a faux stern look. "Anyway, there was no *weed* involved, Sarah Jane. It wasn't exactly a hippy fantasy that brought us here. More like … well, in my case, the need to avoid getting a job," she says with a laugh.

"Uh-huh. And that's how you sold the idea to everyone else?"

Mum settles into a chair. "It wasn't entirely my idea. But you know that. Your dad and I both wanted to try the small-town thing after uni—"

Mum's breath catches. And her eyes do that thing they still sometimes do when his name is mentioned: pinched at the edges like the world is just a bit too bright.

The ceiling fan bounces the pots suspended in the centre of the room. For a moment, the only sounds in the kitchen are pans against pots, like sad, ghostly windchimes.

"Hey, Mama? What do you think Dad would have thought about all this?"

Mum shakes her head. "Best guess? He would've vanished into the fields the second that first van showed up. We'd have found him in a tent somewhere making friends with a bunch of old guys with beards. And our car would have been given away to the first person he met with sad eyes and a sob story."

I shovel in some jammy scone, and blink until my eyes don't feel so blurry. "Yeah. I reckon he'd totally be partying like it's 1999." I take a ginormous swig of cold tea. Then I give Mum a cheery smile.

"So I sort of get why you and Dad schlepped out here, but what about Cleo? How did you talk your bestie into trading twenty-four-hour bars for, well – a bazillion cows and the Junction?"

Mum grins and surreptitiously swipes her eyes. "I didn't need to talk her into anything. Cleo would've moved to a yurt in Kathmandu if someone suggested it. And Adam and Cleo were joined at the hip … but you know, none of us were thinking too far ahead. I mean, Cleo had a *baby* – trust me, Anthony wasn't in anyone's plan. But then Domenic and you came along …" She frowns. "Bub, what are you asking?"

I leap down from the counter. "Nothing. Just idle Christmas chitchat, Mother. Aren't parents supposed to *want* to melt their kids' faces off with stories of their glory days?"

"Face-melting aside – you sure there isn't something in particular you're getting at?"

I toss my cup into the sink. Outside, morning sounds filter into the kitchen. There is a distinct cheerfulness to the gabble; the kind of optimism of people waking up in the summer sunshine and, I suppose, realising they're not dead just yet.

Mum hugs her knees into her chest. With her hair

hanging around her shoulders in blond waves, and her faded Pearl Jam T-shirt and red pyjama pants, I can just see her looking right at home among the masses; shoeless and happy.

I sit down beside her. "Mum ... what was the deal with Grady's dad? The few times Grady and I've visited, it's like, small-talk fest-o-rama, but Grady doesn't really know him. Anthony won't talk to him, and Cleo won't talk about him. I don't remember much, but ... was Adam always miserable here?"

Mum looks up. "Wow. Sarah, remind me to give you a lesson sometime on the rules of idle chitchat." She picks up a plastic Christmas cracker whistle and fiddles with it absently. "The answer is no. He wasn't always an arse. Not even Cleo would hold him to that. I'm not even sure he was all that miserable when he left."

"So then what was he?"

Mum is silent as she ponders her cup. "Restless," she says eventually. "Like Domenic." She takes another long sip of tea. "Like you."

I baulk. "Angie – I am so *not* restless. I'm, like, as unrestless as they come."

Mum shakes her head. She stands and brushes my fringe out of my eyes. "You'd better get dressed and rescue that boy of yours before Cleo puts him to work as her taste-tester. Last I heard, she was planning on a Christmas surf-and-turf." Mum giggles. "Christmas at Merindale Nursing Home is bad enough, but at least the food'll be erased from Aunt Molly's memory by tomorrow. Poor Domenic. No one should have to endure oysters on lamb."

I snap a couple of sweaty Christmas selfies of Mum and me, and then I wander back into the house. I get dressed slowly, twisting up my hair into a fancy knot and layering on some mascara. I gather up the Christmas paper and dirty clothes from my floor, and straighten the stacks of comics on my desk. I doodle a couple of pencil sketches on my pads of pink post-its, faint outlines of Cinnamon Girl with her floating face all disgruntled and testy. And then I check my phone.

I have a message from Grady.

Mrry xmas 2 u 2. Mum is alrdy in the kitchen. If I dnt make it out, tell my friends I'll miss em. Got lots on tday. Spk l8r?

I stare at my phone. Grady has an old-man disdain for text shorthand, and he never sends me *anything* less than a couple of rambling, but grammatically correct, paragraphs.

I think about tracking him down. And then I think about him training his baby-lawyer face on me; his stubborn certainty that he knows what's best for me, cos clearly, I'm not capable of making a call myself.

I grab my sketchpad and I stomp outside into the blazing early morning sun instead.

Daniel throws open his door about eight seconds after I text him from his porch. He's all sleepy-eyed, his hair cutely skew-whiff. His face brightens when he sees me. At least, that's what it does in my head. My eyes are locked on his naked chest, solid and buff and a handspan in front of my face. He's a bit less tanned than he seems on telly, but still, he's just so ... and really, just ... with those V-shaped boy-muscles trailing down his sides and disappearing beneath the band of his boxers—

"Morning, Alba," he croaks. "Forgot you were always up with the birds." I tear my eyes upward. Daniel envelops me in a hug. "Merry Christmas. I wasn't expecting to see you today."

"You're not gonna ask what I'm doing here at eight in the morning?" I mumble as I hug him back. Funny thing is, when Indigo's biceps aren't staring me in the face, it's easy to remember that he's just *Daniel.* Still overly huggy, just like he was all those years ago.

"Let me guess. The only times you ever showed up at my house this early is when you ran out of Coco Pops, or when the post office got your dad's *Fables* comics in..." He steps backwards, sobering. "I haven't had Coco Pops in years though."

I wave my sketchpad. "Was just looking for some quiet. Thought I'd see what you were up to."

"I was up to dreaming of beaches and girls in bikinis." He steps inside with a grin. "There may have been some stuff about trains and tunnels and launching rocket ships in there, too. You coming in?"

I follow him into the quiet house. It's one of those awful rentals that was decorated in, like, 1985, where everything is beige and brown and blah. On the walls are generic paintings of sunflowers, so lifeless they make me want to cry.

Daniel leads me into the kitchen. He throws on a thin grey hoodie that's draped over a chair and then yanks open the fridge. "So where's Grady?" he says as he rifles inside. "Thought an invisible umbilical cord kept you guys attached at the navel?"

I grab a bottle of diet juice from his hand and take a seat at the breakfast bar. "Grady's family do lunch with Cleo's great aunt, remember? And I have my own life. And don't get pissy, Daniel. It wasn't so long ago that you were showing up at Grady's ten times a week to play basketball and watch *Inspector Gadget*. Don't pretend you're too cool to remember that you two were joined at the hip as well, once upon a time."

He sits down next to me and rubs the sleep out of his eyes. "Maybe," he says with a yawn. "But I'm getting the impression that Domenic and I may have grown apart since we were ten. He's kinda serious these days, isn't he?"

Despite the fact that I'm still pissed with Grady, my best friend is *not* up for dissection. "Grady isn't 'serious'. He's just focused. Determined. He's worked his arse off this year, so this waiting limbo is stressing him out."

Daniel laughs. "You say focused. I say veering a bit close to self-important. And what's with the hair? Has the guy not heard of product—"

I slam the juice on to the counter. "Gah, Daniel – what's the matter with you? I refuse to believe you've turned into this mean-spirited doofus. Don't talk about Grady like that!"

His eyebrows shoot skyward. "I was just *teasing*, Sarah. You know I think Grady's cool. All I'm saying is, I don't know many guys our age who are so sure of what they want. He's been the same since we were kids. He's wanted the *exact same thing* since we were five years old." He looks at me impassively as he takes a sip of juice. "At the very least, you gotta admit that's rare. Right?"

I fish my pencil from my boot, and grab a blue pen from the counter. My brain is starting to hurt, like there's something it should be processing that I'm missing.

"I don't want to talk about Grady. What I want is to pretend for a moment that you haven't spent the last seven years morphing into a giant douchnozzle. Just talk to me. Like you. Like *my* Daniel."

He leans forwards suddenly and clasps his hands over mine. "I'm sorry, Alba. Being back here, finishing school … it's all kind of messing with my head. Like, yesterday, I'm walking past the grocery store, and all of a sudden I'm remembering that holiday when you and I made the bet that I could eat their whole stash of frozen donuts. Do you remember? I'm standing on the side of the road, and all of a sudden your voice is in my head … those pep talks you gave me … do you remember?"

Do I remember? I haven't been able to eat a jam donut since without invoking that memory of Daniel at Anzac Park in the thick winter fog, his head shoved under his green *Muppet Babies* beanie, giggly face crammed to bursting with sugary goodness.

"No one ever made it into the *Guinness Book of Records* by wussing out on a challenge," I say with a smile. "Still think I was right. Despite your projectile jammy vomit. I don't think your mum was impressed with me."

He laughs. "Especially since I couldn't fit into my school pants first day back." He gives my hands a squeeze. "Alba, I think I might be having a bit of … nostalgia overload or something. But I'm still me. Just new and improved. OK?"

I squeeze his hand back. "OK, Daniel. So, just talk to me." I grab my sketchpad. "Tell me something normal. Tell me about home."

He swings on the back legs of his stool. "What do you want to know?"

"I dunno. Anything. Where do you live? Do you still have that Princess Peach poster hanging above your bed?"

He laughs. "Not quite. OK, let's see. Our house looks out over Queenscliff Beach. I can see the ocean from my bathroom. Not a bad view when you're having a pee..."

I grab the pen and pencil in my right hand like chopsticks so I can flip between them. When I touch the tip of my 2B to the paper, the lines begin to flow. "What else can you see from your window?"

He thinks for a moment. "A coastal road. A carpark. A tonne of Norfolk Island pines. There's an old Russian lady who lives next door. She's up at the same time every morning to water the flowers on her balcony. No matter how grey the street is, there's always splashy colour outside her window."

"Gosh. How poetic."

He grins. "Ah, but you forget – I'm an artist, too, Sarah. Well, kind of. And for now, anyways."

My hand pauses on the page. "What do you mean?"

He reaches for an apple from the counter. "The acting thing is fun, for now. But who knows if I'll be doing it forever. I even briefly contemplated uni, but you know – a classroom was never my thing. Maybe I'm waiting for the universe to give me a sign. Like, a divine nudge as to what my next move should be."

I snort. "I hear you. Signals from the universe seem to be in short supply these days."

He looks at me curiously as he chews on his apple. "But if I had your skills … it's not like you don't know what you want. You've always wanted to draw. You know that's what you'll end up doing. So what's the problem?"

"I dunno, Daniel," I say, somewhat testily. "Just because I'm good at something, doesn't mean it's the thing I'm supposed to do. And I want…"

"You want what?"

I glance down at the page. The sketchy outline of my character is taking shape, her familiar hair, streaked with blue biro, snaking up from the margins as if blown by an off-page wind machine. Through her windows are shadowy outlines of trees and streets; pieces of Daniel's life, at least, as best as I can picture them.

What do I want? I want to wrap everyone I love in one teeny bundle, and I want to build a wall around my Valley and keep it the same way it's been for the last seventeen years, and I want to wake up every morning in a fog of cinnamon and vanilla, and I want to stop everything from moving until I'm ready for it to move.

"I like my life," I say quietly.

"Everything changes," he says with a shrug. "It's just supposed to."

I look up at him. He's twirling his half-eaten apple around in his fingers, his eyes on me. Maybe it's the sleep-haze, but I realize I was wrong about Daniel's eyes. They're not the same as they were when we were little. Somehow, they're less open than they used to be, and now that I look closely, a few shades darker, too.

He nods his head at my sketchpad. "Can I see?"

I turn the book around. Daniel shakes his head with a crooked smile. "Jesus. A little bit *Hopeless Savages*? Very nice, Alba."

My phone buzzes in the pocket of my skirt. When I fish it out, the close-up of Grady's giant eyeball is flashing on my screen.

Mum just melted a serving spoon on to her best wok. She may have permanently given up on this cooking caper. Think this deserves a celebratory milkshake before we take off. Where are you?

I can't help but smile, knowing exactly what's circling through my bestie's brain. He's annoyed with me, but not annoyed enough to ignore me for more than a few hours. I send him a text back.

Hanging with Daniel. At his place. Give me a min.

I stand up. "I should go. Thanks for the juice. Sorry for waking you. And, you know, for calling you a douchnozzle."

Daniel leaps up. "You're forgiven. So what are you doing today?"

I grab my sketchpad. "Dunno. Everyone else has scarpered, of course. Apparently there's a Christmas Day dance party at the farm. I mean, as opposed to the Christmas Eve dance party, and the random Monday-afternoon dance party."

He laughs. "I guess people are trying to cram in as much as they can before the world bites the dust. But, you know, church was packed last night, too."

I'm in the process of shoving my pencil back into my boot, and I almost jab it right through my ankle. "You went to *church*?"

He leans against the counter. "Sure. Midnight Mass. My folks wanted to see the old place again. And I figured it probably couldn't hurt to repent for my sins and all that."

I hug my sketchpad to my chest. "Daniel, you don't believe any of this, do you? That bozo Ned Zebidiah and his predictions…"

He shrugs. "Do I think the world is going to vanish in a puff of smoke? How should I know? But, Alba, there's always a chance that you could walk out of your house tomorrow and be crushed by falling space debris. Why wouldn't you live every day as if it were your last?"

I swallow. "Gah. You sound like a motivational poster."

He laughs. "Well, I suppose people feel they'd look pretty stupid if they didn't at least hedge their bets. And speaking of bets and hedging – I can't escape tonight. My folks are insisting on a family Christmas dinner. Roast potatoes and tedious conversation, the whole bit. Are you going to this party thing? When can we catch up again?"

My phone vibrates in my hand.

Actually, something's come up. Need to track down my brother. Aunt Molly's denture kisses may've sent Anthony into hiding. Either that or he's founded his own bordello in a tent. Talk l8r.

"Problem?" Daniel asks.

I pocket my phone quickly. "No. No problem. And I think I'll stay in tonight as well. I really just want to hole up in my room and pretend the world hasn't lost its mind outside. Talk to you tomorrow?"

Daniel drags me into another hug. "Sure. Tomorrow. I'm holding you to that, Sarah."

I send Grady a text as I'm walking back down Daniel's drive.

Poor Anthony. This many girls in one spot was never gonna end well for him. No wonder he's been reduced to a drooling, gibbering mess. Like Clouseau that time Mr Grey left his BBQ unsupervised. Call me when you're back?

I make it to the bakery just as the music from the farm crackles to life, and a dozen naked people in Santa hats streak down Main Street to triumphant claps and cheers. I catch a glimpse of the back of Penny-Farthing Man as he pedals into the trees behind the service station for his morning high-rise wee.

I am, most definitely, not checking for a reply from Domenic. Not even when my brain starts to ache, and the silence from my phone feels like it's burning an eyeball-shaped hole inside my pocket.

It's been scorching for so many days now, my aircon is barely making a crack in the wall of heat. I've flicked on my desk fan, aiming the thin puff of air at my neck, but I might as well be sitting inside one of the bakery's ovens for all the good it's doing.

I've lost count of the number of hours I've been twirling in my chair while staring at the computer. I've scanned the roughs from my sketchpad, but I just can't make Daniel's world come to life for me. His trees are too alien, and the composition is all wrong. I have no idea what it says about my skills that I can't capture a real-world street without it looking trippy, like something from a Dr Seuss book.

I waste some time doodling Cinnamon Girl in a Silver Age Wonder Woman outfit, but as her face materializes on my page, I can tell she's not at all happy with me. She plants her hands on her hips, her solid thighs busting out of her star-spangled shorts, and I swear she's glaring at me with contempt.

I don't know what happens to my day. I lose a couple of hours shuffling from my desk to the kitchen for snacks and whatnot, in between doodling Cinnamon Girls in combinations of rockabilly and spandex-superhero costumes, and fielding

Christmas calls from our handful of scattered relatives. I'm not even hungry, though I do snaffle a few slices of chicken pie before Mum disappears to the Corner Arms with Cleo. Before I know it, I look through my window and the sky is all streaky orange and bruised blue.

My mobile has been chirping all day with Merry Christmas messages from my friends. Even Ed sends me an update on his dad's shenanigans; apparently Mr Palmer had one too many Christmas Jägerbombs with some guys from Denmark and almost punched a Merri Man in the face.

Grady doesn't barge through my verandah door mid-afternoon as is customary, and his eyeball doesn't flash on my screen once. I try to tell myself that he's just brooding after our spat, but, thing is, I *know* him. Grady doesn't stay grumpy. Sulking just isn't in his make-up. And hello? I should be the one pissy at him for the lecture, not the other way round.

I'm really not in the mood for a party. But after sprawling on my couch and staring at the same page of *Batgirl* while the noise from the farm becomes louder and messier, I change my mind. I throw on an old polka-dot dress and my Santa hat. I text Tia to check they're still out, before hurrying through the door and into the darkness.

While our visitors are busy turning the Palmers' farm into a stampy dust bowl, a bunch of locals have headed in the opposite direction, to the top of the hill where boulders stand guard over the Valley. The streetlights are non-existent here, and the towering trees give the whole place a distinct lair-of-a-serial-killer vibe. It's almost stranger-free though, and, inspired by nostalgia or simply the need for a time-out, the remnants of our high school seem to have fled here.

Someone has thrown a blanket over the barbed wire fencing, and people are dotted on the other side. A few guys are dancing near the old washing-machine drum that in winter holds a crackly fire. I see Eddie and Caroline and both of Ed's brothers, and a little ways down the road, Tia and Petey are perched on the hood of Pete's dad's car.

I walk, waving at familiar faces and hoping I'm avoiding the roo poo scattered underfoot. If I turned my back on the Valley, this could be any normal Friday night; except for the cacophony of eighties hair metal blasting from the bottom of the hill.

I spot his curly hair and baby face in the moonlight. He's leaning against a tree, his hands motioning madly at a red-headed girl in front of him. Without the trilby, it takes me a few seconds to place her. But I'd be able to spot the eager face and touchy hands from a thousand paces.

It's not *totally* bizarro to see him with a girl. There was this phase in grade four when Grady became inexplicably studly for a few short months, attracting his very own entourage while he hid behind me in the climbing fort. And while he's never been a floozy like his big brother, playing centre on his basketball team has secured Grady a few random snogs, though he's always been vaguely embarrassed sharing his girl stories. And he dated Ellie Knoxbury, co-captain of our high-school netball team, for three whole weeks back in year eleven. Ellie was nice, if a little nondescript. Though, I never did hear her talk about anything other than netball and horses. But Grady spent nineteen days looking fascinated by whatever netbally, horsey knowledge she graced him with. It was weird.

I climb awkwardly over the fencing, and I bounce toward them.

"Hey hey!" I say brightly. "Fancy bumping into you kids here." I wink at Grady and drop my voice to my best husky growl. "You're gonna take that J.C. Penney tie off, and we're gonna have us an old-fashioned man-to-man drinking party, Marlboro."

Grady looks at me blankly. "That line'd be more apt if I was wearing a tie. If I ever wore ties. Maybe I should wear a tie?" he says with a giggle.

Hat-girl gives me a half-hearted wave. "Um, hey there. I'm Jess. And, um ... what?"

"Movie line. *The Long Goodbye.* It's ... old," I say weakly, suddenly feeling shamefully show-offy. I stick out my hand. "I'm Alba. Nice to meet you!"

Jess gives my hand a shake. She smoothes down her hair. "So I guess I'm gonna go check out that other pub," she says lightly. "Catch up later, Dom?"

I watch her walk away with a glance back at Grady, who has never, ever been a *Dom* in his life, and who's still staring at the spot she just vacated. And I feel like the worst kind of rubbishy idiot. I feel—

"Alba?" Grady says.

I drag my eyes back to his brown ones. But really, brown is a descriptor that can in no way capture them. Not quite India ink, but somewhere between Burnt Carmine and Mars Black. And right now, they're uncharacteristically glassy.

I clear my throat. "I was starting to think that you and Mrs Garabaldi were in cahoots, Grady. You been busy stocking up on the tuna and nudie mags you're gonna need come the Rapture? Either that or … you wouldn't have been avoiding me today … right?"

I clear my throat again, not entirely sure why my oesophagus is so squeezy. I punch him in the arm. "You know stories of Aunt Molly shenanigans are the highlight of my Christmas afternoon. And I *know* you wouldn't have ditched me for a girl. Not without giving me every teeny, disgusting detail first. You realize it's the wing-person's duty to offer her unbiased opinion of these things, right?"

"Hmm … what?" he says.

"Jeez. Grady, man. Distracted much? I thought *I* was supposed to be the space cadet of the group. What's the matter with you?"

He takes a loping step toward me. His eyes are

flashing with the manic energy that's particular to little kids and hobos.

I grab him by his T-shirt. "Grady – are you *drunk*?"

"I am not *drunk*, Alba. I have been drinking, yes, but with my height and weight it would take another ... two-point-four drinks for me to be properly drunk. Right now, I am just slightly ... *happy*." He winds one arm around me and grabs my hand with his.

"So you've raided Cleo's stash of cooking sherry? What's going on with you?"

He tilts his head, as if listening to something intently. And then he slows his spinning, adjusting for the ballad that's exploding from the bottom of the hill. I've gotta hand it to him – even drunk, Grady can move.

"Look around, Alba," he says, his voice all booze-infused husky. "Armageddon might be just around the corner. I mean, have you actually let that sink in? In a few days' time, *that* might be it – zero, nothing, zippo left. I'm allowed to be a little bit *not* me, right?"

"Grady, I'm not sure if this counts as being a 'little bit not you'. Besides, you have enough trouble not falling over when you're sober..."

"But this might be one of the last, final parties

at the end of the universe," he says, leaning down so we're eye-to-eye. "I may never have the chance to do a tequila shot off the belly of some hot girl at a frat party."

"Frat party? You are now banned from watching American movies."

He chuckles. "So I was probably going to skip the tequila anyway. But can't I have a few beers with a pretty girl, and dance with my best friend? If I'm going to die, it might as well be while I'm dancing."

I grab him tighter, even as he keeps turning us round and round. Even though I'm still pissy at him, I just can't help it. "Grady. Only you could face the end of the world with a Pinterest slogan."

Laughter rumbles through his chest. "Sarah Jane Albany. Haven't you figured it out by now? I am unflusterable."

"Unflusterable?"

"Yes. He who shall not be flustered. Besides, we may need to repopulate the planet. I figure that has to work a little bit in my favour."

Grady drops my hand and winds both arms languidly around my middle. He's never been all that touchy, but clearly alcohol and possible planetary destruction are loosening him up, because he tightens his arms around me and he doesn't let go.

"Al-ba," he says in a singsong voice. We've slowed down now, our feet tangling, but still, we're moving without falling. It's the strangest thing; I can remember every dorky school dance from when we were little, all rigid arms planted on each other's hips and giggly, out-of-time swaying. In my head, I know there should be some bits linking then and now. But right at this moment, I can't remember the in-between. Only, I think we've always danced this way, neither of us leading nor following.

Grady sighs. He really is more wasted than I thought. I loop my arms around him as his weight tilts me off-balance, my hands landing beneath his shoulders. And then, though I'm vaguely aware that we have stopped moving, somehow the ground continues to tilt. Because beneath his shoulders and his *Space Invaders* T-shirt is the unmistakable shape of proper, solid, boy-muscles. Almost experimentally, I splay my fingers a little. I feel the muscles across his back tense beneath my palms.

"Al-ba," he says again, a distracted, soft whisper this time.

"Um … come on, Domenic. Time to go home."

"Don't first-name me," he mumbles. He rests his cheek on my shoulder. For a moment I think he may have fallen asleep, but I don't want to move to check. I don't want him to fall. I barely even notice that we're not dancing any more. My tingly, numb hands are still idly exploring, like they're all distant and preoccupied.

"Alba," he murmurs, his breath tickling my ear. "Alba… Alba…"

His voice near my ear is barely a whisper now. I don't think I hear him say anything. It was my imagination. Probably my imagination.

But I think I hear him whisper, *"My beautiful Alba."*

He takes a giant breath and stumbles backwards, tripping over his own feet and slamming straight into Eddie.

"Whoa, G-man," Eddie says, grabbing Grady effortlessly with one arm. "Shit, dude. How many chardonnays did you drink?"

Grady makes a sound like *ghamnotfatdrumk*, as he throws an arm around Eddie's tree-trunk middle. "Dude. I know I call you an arsebag, and a butt-monkey, and, you know, sometimes I call you a dick behind your back. But you are awesome, man! I love you, Eddie!" Grady yells in his face.

"Fecking hell, Domenic! Get it together man!" Eddie yells back, though he's half-cracking up as well.

I, on the other hand, am finding this slightly less than amusing. My skin is too warm, and my hands feel miles away from the rest of me. I grab Grady's other arm, and I attempt to pull him off Eddie. "Ed, help me get him back to my place?"

Grady pushes Eddie away and draws himself up to his full height. "No help needed, guys. I'm cool. Really, I don't get drunk ever, well OK, one time before, but I blame Indigo and his stupid face for that, and anyway I'm really OK..." And then he stumbles sideways, and is saved from face-planting into the tree by Eddie, who throws his body right in Grady's path. My bestie – my sensible, responsible, homework-obsessing best friend – face-plants with a surprised grunt into Eddie's chest instead.

"OK. Time to go home," I say firmly. "Francis Edwin – you are responsible for getting him down the hill without a scrape or bruise, or, so help me,

I will be placing you on my list. It's new, and it involves a ninja chop to the Adam's apple. Understood?"

Eddie wraps an arm around Grady and lifts him off the ground. "Jesus. No need to get testy. Whaddya think I was gonna do? Roll him down the hill?"

Grady giggles. "Bowling ball," he mumbles. And then he leans his head against Ed's shoulder and closes his eyes.

"Crap. Eddie..."

"I got it, Alba. Just like steering a wayward calf. Easy as."

Eddie grins at me. I try to smile back, but my lips feel frozen in an expression that I'm sure is both a little bit perplexed, and a whole lot panicked.

Grady looks up, briefly, and his eyes meet mine. Even through the booze-haze, I recognize the look in them: anxious, and sad, like that time when we were seven and he accidentally spilled glue all over my painting of Astro Girl. Back then, it didn't take much to snap him out of a funk; I remember that I held him down and sat on him until he laughed, and all was right with the world again.

Somehow, I doubt the solution will prove to be so easy this time.

Grady closes his eyes, and I turn and stumble blindly toward home.

Granted, the shenanigans of this past week have been a little outside of my area of expertise.

But shepherding my inebriated best friend through the masses of partying strangers – while the band plays a novelty dance song in the background, and Mr Grey attempts to lead a crowd in the YMCA in front of the penis-covered hardware store, and a panel van with the words *Vegans for Jesus* spray-painted on the side spills forth with a half-dozen people in robes handing out pamphlets, and Penny-Farthing Man on my front lawn salutes me with a line of solar Christmas lights threaded around the handlebars of his bike – is a little more than my brain is capable of processing.

Grady waves Eddie off, somehow managing to make it into my backyard and up the verandah steps. He braces his palms on my door and rests his forehead against the glass. Eddie and I hover uncertainly behind him – until Grady's soft snores float beneath the sounds of shouting and laughing and a vuvuzela being enthusiastically honked near my fence.

Eddie rolls his eyes. He swings Grady into a fireman's hold as I haul open my door, and the three of us tumble ungraciously inside.

Eddie dumps Grady on to my bed, his too-long legs dangling uselessly on the floorboards. Ed yanks off Grady's Vans, and then hefts his legs up in one hand and flings them on to the bed like he's tossing a bale of hay.

"That's it – I'm done," Eddie says, dusting his hands emphatically on his jeans. "No way I'm getting anywhere near that boy's pants. You want him in his fecking smalls, you handle it, Alba."

I tug off my Santa hat, and I grab a pillow and jam it under Grady's head. "Ed – thank you. And sorry about the punching you in the throat thing."

He shrugs. "Whatever. I'm not the one who's gonna be cleaning sick off my floor come tomorrow morning."

Grady mutters something under his breath. He rolls on to his stomach, shoving his face between the pillow and my sheets. His shoulders heave in a giant sigh before his breathing settles into a heavy cadence.

I sink on to the floor beside him. "Gah. And I'm

gonna be awake all night making sure he doesn't swallow his own tongue. Good times. Domenic Miles Grady, you are in for one seriously shouty lecture on the evils of alcohol when you sober up."

Eddie scuffs his feet on the floor. Then he squats next to me, all uncomfortable and twitchy. "Hey, Alba? Maybe … take it easy on him. Dude's got some stuff going on."

"Stuff? What stuff? Ed, this is *Grady*! He's the most dependable person I know – jeez, he's like the most dependable person ever *born* – but lately it's as if he's having some sort of giant Infinite Crisis. What's he told you that he's not telling me?"

"Jesus. Grady doesn't talk about serious shit with me, you know that. And I'm not a psychologist, Alba. Bad enough I have to talk my old man down every time the portaloos back up or someone steps in cow shit and threatens to sue." Eddie stands with a sigh. "Look, I gotta go. Think my brother was planning to put the moves on Caroline if I left them alone. Pretty sure Gresham'll be wearing Brian's wang round her neck like a lucky rabbit's foot if he tries. It'd be hilarious. But Mum might be pissed…" Eddie runs a hand along his head. "Just cut Grady a bit of slack. All right?" He leaves before I can answer, the door clicking gently behind him.

I drop my eyes back to the bed. Grady rolls on to his side. He pulls his knees into his chest and bunches his hands under his chin with a soft sigh. He must be totally wiped, cos he only ever sleeps so foetal-positiony when he's exhausted. In the dim light from my lamp, he looks so completely lost that every instinct in my body wants to huddle in beside him with my face squished into his neck, like I used to do when we were four.

I can't remember when it was that we stopped sharing a bed. I don't know why that thought flitters through my head. And I don't know why, the moment it does, my knees do this jelly-dance, like they're no longer concerned with keeping me standing.

I know I could sleep on my couch, or in the lounge, which is marginally cooler than my airless bedroom. But I kick off my shoes and crawl up behind him, resting my head on the edge of his pillow. My face is near the soft curls at the nape of his neck, a hand-span between us that seems suddenly impossible to cross.

I fall into a fitful, restless sleep, with the ghosts of all my stories swirling in my head.

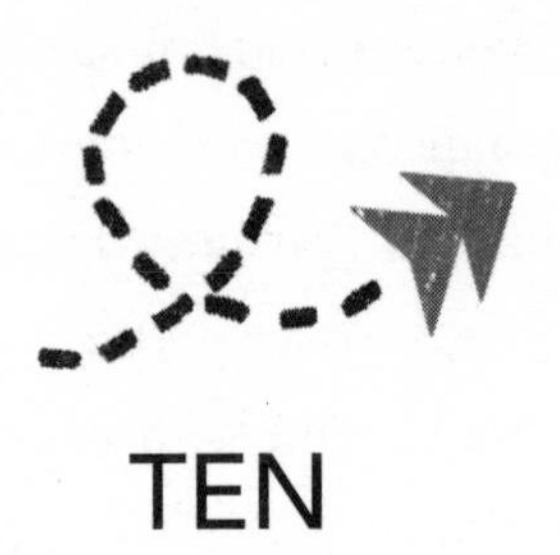

TEN

I know it's not yet properly morning, but the godforsaken never-ending heat is baking my bedroom, and yesterday's dress is sticking to my sweaty back, and without opening my eyes, I can tell it's gonna be a totally rubbish day. Cos I wake up to the foggy realization that it's only five more sleeps till the Rapture, and the *Grease* megamix is blasting from carspeakers near my fence, and Grady is gone.

I check the bathroom, half-expecting him to be sleeping in the tub like the morning after the *Gum Trees* vodka shenanigans. But my bathroom is empty. He's not rifling through the fridges in the kitchen, or scoffing our food in his blue booth. I grab my phone, but before I can dial Grady's number, something freezes my hand. It's like this montagey flashback of the last few days flies through my consciousness;

his stubborn face and totally out-of-character temper and sad, sad eyes. And I feel woozy and nauseated, as if I'm nursing a mother of a hangover myself.

I kinda feel like eating popcorn for breakfast, and moping.

I sort of want to hide under my sheets with a torch and my longbox of *Y: The Last Man* to keep me company.

I'm half in the mood to run to Grady's house and punch him in the head for making me stress.

But maybe it's not Grady I'm stressed at. Not directly, anyway. And maybe punching him in the head isn't exactly going to solve my problems.

I crawl back into bed and send him a text.

Are you dead? Have you woken in an alley with a body at your feet and no memory of the last twenty-four hours? If you are wearing a blood-splattered trench coat – run! Run now! Avoid all dames and broads, and anyone who looks like Orson Welles. Alternatively, you could just mosey back here and watch The Avengers with me. I know it's not Christmassy, but we can festive it up with Santa hats and figgy pudding. OK, I don't know what figgy pudding is. I'll google it. Or maybe you can make me pancakes as payment for dragging your beer-soaked butt halfway across the Valley. I always thought you'd turn out to be more of a port-and-lemonade guy, you know? Kinda like Mrs Garabaldi. Only, less testosteroney. Anyway. Avengers?

OK, admittedly, that takes me a while to type.

And it takes Grady a good forty-five minutes to respond. My phone lights up with that close-up of his eyeball, and a curt message that makes my toes curl.

Not dead. Feel dead. Talk later.

And then nothing. Nada. Complete silence from the only other person on the planet who can talk and text while simultaneously brushing his teeth and juggling small cats.

I fling my phone across the room, only half-aiming for the couch. "OK, Domenic," I hiss. "Be a sulky arsebag! But don't think I'm gonna be chasing you to the end of the earth!"

I stomp into the bathroom and shower under sub-zero water. I sweep my hair into a messy bun, and I layer on my brightest red lipstick. I dig out a black dress from the back of my wardrobe, the one with the pink skulls on the bodice and skirt, cos it totally feels like a skulls-and-blood-lips sort of day.

Mum takes one look at me as I hurtle into the kitchen, and she grimaces.

"Uh-oh. Them's fighting clothes. What's going on?"

I yank my apron from the hook near the sinks. "Nothing's going on. I'm tired. I'm sick of the noise, and this whole town smelling of pit-sweat and car fumes, and falling over drunk-arse morons every time I step out of my house! I want to be in bed with *Best American Comics*, not busting my bits in here serving coffee to people who are waiting to be abducted by aliens and whatnot! And you know what? The only thing I really want to do right now is punch Original Ned Zebidiah in his stupid Fu-Manchu face! *Gah!*" I give up trying to tie the stupid strings of my stupid apron, and I scrunch it into a ball and toss it in the sink. "Has anyone even *seen* Original Ned? For all we know, this whole instalment could've been caused by the dude eating dodgy mushrooms or forgetting to take his lithium—"

"O-*K*," Mum says lightly. She grabs my elbow and steers me into the house, shutting the bakery door behind her. "As much as I enjoy a good dummy-spit, Sarah, the rest of the kitchen might prefer to come to work and not be assaulted by a scene from *Glengarry Glen Ross*." She plonks us both down at the dining table. "You want to tell me what's got you so huffy?"

I drop my head into my hands. "Mum, everything is just getting so … muddled. *Messy*. I'm tired of thinking, and stressing, and not knowing what's happening with … people. With me. I really don't think I can cope with much more of this. I just need everything to go back to the way it was. I need everything to just … stop now."

Mum crosses her arms. "Well. Too bad," she says with a shrug.

I drag my head up. "Jeez. Way to be sympathetic, Angela."

Mum laughs. "What do you want me to say? That you can hole up in your room forever? I'm not booting you out. Stay if you want. We can invest in matching cardigans and spend our nights at the Junction having vaguely racist conversations with the Alberts' aunts. Stay, Sarah, till you're old and incontinent. Or until the mole people return to rule over humanity. *If* that's what you really want."

I hug my knees into my chest and cover my face with my hands. Honestly? Right now, the only thing

I am certain I want is the blissful unconsciousness of sleep. Because if I let myself think about it – really allow myself to imagine living this little life forever – all I feel is that nameless, belly-churning panic again.

I'm merrily sinking into a haze of my own confusion, so it takes a good few minute of staring through my fingers to realize that the light in the lounge is a little … odd. I glance through the window. And, unthinkingly, I float to my feet.

"Mum … look at that."

Mum swivels around and peers out the window as well. "Oh," she says softly.

The vivid cerulean sky of the past few weeks has disappeared. Over the farmland the sky is white, as blank and featureless as winter. It looks like it should be cool, but I head out to the verandah with Mum in my wake and the heat hits me the moment I crack open the door. There are a few people sitting on the hay bales near my back fence, but the atmosphere is weirdly subdued. There's something about the low sky that feels insanely claustrophobic. Almost like this hushed dome has descended over the Valley.

"Maybe a storm's on its way?" Mum says uncertainly.

"Yeah," I say. "Maybe."

But there is none of that ozoney smell of brewing dry lightning in the air, the scary harbinger of bushfires. If anything, it's ... even more unsettling.

I pull Mum inside and close the door quickly. "Mum, do you need me today?"

Mum drags her eyes away from the sky. She sighs. "We'll cope. I'm cutting the menu to staples since now Merindale's basically run out of everything as well. We should be able to churn out enough rolls and vegan brownies to keep the masses from rioting. Go. Do what you need to do, bub."

I skulk back to my room and grab a sketchpad from beneath the piles of dirty clothes. I pull my curtains shut and crawl into bed with a handful of 2Bs. This sketchpad is an old one that I haven't touched in months. Half of it is covered in a rough storyboard, some panels of which eventually found their way into my Cinnamon Girl folio. She's scattered in spirited poses, her face beaming out of the page, back when she still looked cheerful, and hopeful, and not so – well, deranged.

I glance at the sketches that are now littering my bookshelf and walls. Her face is scrunched in expressions that, if she had superpowers, would suggest she might be exploding a planetoid shortly, or vaporising a baddie into his component atoms. Maybe I should give her superpowers. Hey, she's mine, and I can do whatever the hell I want with her. Despite the fact that, across my room, she's insisting on remaining pissy, and antsy, and bored, and annoyed, and something else, too.

I lean against the wall behind my bed with the sketchpad on my knees. My hands fly over the page, a scratchy storyboard in uneven panels. I draw her in giant boots and a kick-arse dress, a snarly frown on her square-jawed face. I draw her as a roaring Goliath, dangling from the side of the Empire State Building, and I draw her as a pocket-sized warrior in a costume just like the Wasp's. I draw her hunched over a bar in a smoky cocktail lounge like one of Grady's noir heroines. I draw her as a clichéd chick superhero, all anatomically stupid pose and giant bazongas, which almost makes my fingers fall off in loathing. I draw her in her warehouse apartment, staring through her windows as the sky explodes in the distance. I draw her soaring, arms stretched, through a wide pale sky, and stomping her way purposelessly across the moon.

Then I toss the sketchpad on to the floor, and I pull on my sleep mask and go back to bed.

It feels like only minutes before I sit up with a start. I tug off my mask and hurry to my window.

The white sky is still bearing down over the farm. A breeze has kicked up, rustling the tents and what remains of the scrappy Thunderdome. I'm sweaty, and my room is boiling, but as I stare out over the field the flesh on my arms becomes all goosepimply.

I rescue my phone from beneath a couch cushion. It's just past lunchtime, and I have only one text. It's not Grady's doe-eye that flashes on my screen, but the puckered selfie of Petey's lips.

Hey Alba. Is Grady with u? We're supposed to be helping Mr Grey move the karaoke machine into the courtyard – he's on a mission to do an Apocalypse Now-themed NYE – but I can't find DG anywhere.

I don't bother responding. I call Grady's number. I'm only a little bit surprised when he doesn't answer.

I wipe away my smudged make-up and scrub

my face till my skin feels raw. I change into cut-offs and Dad's soft blue *Archie* T-shirt that says *I'm with Jughead* on the front. And I scoot through my back door and walk away from Albany's.

I head away from the farm, and the penny-farthing that has gathered a following over the last week; at this moment, a group of shirtless guys are posing in front of the oversized wheel, Christmas hats on their heads and cans of beer in their hands. After the Frida incident, I'd collected the rest of my gnomes and stored them in the space beneath the back verandah. The spots of empty dirt seem wrong somehow, a little gnome graveyard where my ceramic family should be.

I pause at the Eversons' fruit-and-veg. In front of the window is a sun-bleached bench that has lived there for as long as I can remember. I don't know how many hours I've spent on it, drawing and distracting Grady while he's supposed to be working. On a normal Boxing Day, Mr Everson and Mr Garabaldi and Mr Grey would be perched there, side by side, sharing beers and old-man stories. But the bench is occupied by a bunch of strangers, and my three old men are nowhere to be seen.

Without thinking about it, I turn back down Main Street, and head east out of town.

I clear the few caravans and cars on the outskirts of the Valley, and the noise quickly disappears. It's a good half-hour walk down the empty road, but I have this hunch I'm heading in the right direction.

Set back from the road is the primary school that closed a few years before I was born. Now, it's little more than a graffiti-filled building in the middle of an overgrown field, with a weed-infested playground behind it. But it's the closest place that has a proper court, and I know it's where my boy would go when he needs to clear his head.

I hear the thud of a ball against bitumen. I duck beneath the gap in the fencing and pick my way carefully through the grass.

"There you are," I say brightly as I round the building. "I've been looking for you everywhere."

Grady pauses, his back to me. Clouseau lopes across the grass and licks at my ankles. "Everywhere?"

Grady says as he tosses the ball neatly through the rusted hoop. "There's, like, four places I could be. Where exactly did you look?"

I sit down on a bench at the edge of the court and haul Clouseau into my arms. "I dunno. The bakery. The street. *I* am not the detective, Grady."

Grady bounces the ball a couple of times. It hits a nasty-looking thistle growing through the three-point line, and it careens sideways into the grass. He sighs. And he finally turns around. He rubs his palms over his hungover face before he meets my eye.

"So. Either I've developed a particularly offensive skunkification ailment, or you, my friend, have been avoiding me for the past two days. Two days, Domenic. That's, like, five months in dog years." I straighten my spine as my confidence falters. "Not to mention the hard-boiled drinking problem you seemed to have adopted…"

He grimaces. "Yeah. The beer might have been a mistake. If it makes you feel better, it tasted almost as crap on the way back up." He kneads the back of his neck. "And I haven't been avoiding you. I've just been trying to give you 'space'. Isn't that what you said you wanted?"

I gape at him while my brain reels back over our stupid fight. "I said I needed head space, but I didn't mean... Grady, do you even remember the last time you and I went a whole two days without talking?"

He sighs again. He fishes his ball out of the grass, and he comes and sits beside me on the undersized bench. "And do you think that's normal?" he says eventually.

"What do you mean?"

He looks out over the farmland. "I've been thinking about stuff. Stuff that you said, and ... I think you were right. I don't think I've been very fair to you, Alba. It's not my place to talk you into anything." He bumps my shoulder, but his eyes stay focused somewhere in the distance. "I couldn't even talk you into doing Scouts with me when we were kids. And there were toasted marshmallow nights involved. Remember?"

"I would have sucked at all that outdoorsy stuff," I mumble. "But Grady, I didn't mean that I wanted you and me to *not* hang out. That's just the stupidest idea in the universe. Especially now, when time – I didn't mean—"

"The thing is," he says quietly. "Everything you said ... it's stuff I've been thinking about as well." He drops the basketball and rolls it between his feet, slowly, backwards and forwards. "Sometimes your voice is all I can hear in my head, too. Sometimes it's hard to see anything clearly when everything's been so ... great. You know?"

I look down at the bench beside us. It's covered with sketchy graffiti; faded, misspelled reflections from little hands long gone. "Grady ... when did you decide you wanted to be a lawyer? Do you even know why you picked that?"

He scoots off the bench and sits on the ground with his back to me. "Well, when I was a kid I wanted to be Inspector Gadget. You remember that, right?" He runs his fingers over Clouseau's ears. "Not my proudest phase, but – I dunno. I always liked puzzles. I think the world is really unfair, and I like the idea of making it a bit fairer. I would've been a detective, only pretty sure I'd shoot myself in the arse with my own gun." He swallows uncertainly as he glances up at the white sky. "You know why I chose law, Alba. It was because of your dad."

"Dad?"

"Well, yeah. Will always had the best stories. He was always telling me about the cases he studied at law school and the weird people he met at uni. He said it never bothered him that he didn't practise, cos he just loved learning all that stuff. Will was, like, the coolest grown-up I knew."

"I'd forgotten all about that." I stare at the top of his curls in a sudden swoop of shame. "You and Dad. I'd forgotten how close you guys were. I don't know why I never thought about it before, but it's like … you lost two dads. Right?"

"Careless, huh?" he says with a humourless laugh.

I hug my arms tightly around me, even though the heat from the bitumen makes my skin feel like it's liquefying.

"Grady. I miss my dad," I whisper.

He leans his head against my knee. "Yeah, Alba. I miss him, too."

Grady sighs. He swivels away from me and lies down on the hot, cracked ground. And I don't know why, but I have this sudden, insane flashback of us when we were kids. We used to hang out here all the time, watching Anthony and his friends playing basketball, or Daniel ripping up the grass on his bike. And there it is again – for some reason, I can't remember the in-between. In my memory, Grady was a scrawny, boofy-haired kid, and then he was...

He closes his eyes. I remember, once upon a time, Cleo carrying a giggly Grady upside-down by the ankles from here. Now, he towers over his mum, his shoulders way broader than hers.

"Alba, you need to figure out what you want," he says with his eyes still closed. Maybe I've never noticed, but though his voice isn't a gravelly man-voice like Ed's, it's still solid, and sort of deep. "And if staying here is what you really want, then that's just the way it has to be."

Have I really never noticed that a light layer of hair trails down his arms to his wrists, and that his hands are big, and rough from years of basketball and hauling boxes and odd jobs around town? That when he reaches up to run a hand tiredly behind his neck, the muscles in his arms pop – not as chunky as Daniel's, but still, substantial, and so guy-like—

"You were the one who said it," he says softly. "You said we can't do everything together forever. Guess it's taken me a while to get it through my head, but..." He drags himself upright and sits beside me on the bench again. "I think you were right. One way or another … I suppose everything ends."

I focus on the scuffed toe of his Vans. "Domenic. Way to sound dramatic. You know, it's not like you'll be moving to Mars. You'll still visit. You'll text." My throat feels thick, like the words burbling out of it aren't the ones I want or mean. I swallow down a rising panic, but I can't seem to make these impostor words stop. I nudge his shoulder with mine. "I'll see you in the society pages or whatnot, and I'll be all, like, there's the boy I knew from way back when. It's not the end of the world." And then I cover my face with my hands as hysterical laughter bubbles out of my mouth. I stand up quickly. "Look, I need to get back to the bakery. It's all totally fine. I gotta go."

But he grabs my hand before I can move. He looks at it with surprise, like he's not entirely sure how my hand found its way into his. "Alba, I would stay," he says quickly. "I would change everything if you asked—"

I clutch his hand between both of mine, and I hold on as tightly as I can. "No. Grady … you have always been like every secret superhero I know. Just busting to rip off the dork suit and glasses." I take a deep breath, and I smile at him as best as I can. "You weren't meant to stand still. I've always known that."

"But what about you?" he whispers.

"Me? I have no idea what powers I've got hiding underneath. Maybe something cool, like optic-blast eyeballs. Maybe something lame, like fish telepathy or whatever. But I need to find out. On my own. I think it's ... necessary."

Grady is focusing on my hands. The bench is too low for his long legs, but he swivels one knee sideways and pulls me in just a bit closer. "Alba, you know it doesn't matter where you end up. You are going to be brilliant. You're gonna be, like, the next Ramona Fradon or something."

"Hey. You remember who she is? I'm impressed."

"I've learned heaps from you, Sarah Jane Albany." He stares at my hands for a moment longer. And then he turns my palm over, and he kisses me gently on the inside of my wrist. "I'm going to hang around here for a bit. I'll see you later, OK?"

"Sure. Later, Grady."

I walk home, my feet bouncing in time to the heavy bass beat that thuds down the road as I near town. I feel kind of blank. Except, when I pull open my bedroom door, there's that thick, lumpish thing in my throat making it really hard to swallow or breathe.

I know I should use everything that's churning through my head as fodder for my Cinnamon Girl. I should be able to haul out my pencils and translate all my messiness into brilliance on a page.

I bury my face in my green couch, and I bawl my eyes out instead.

ELEVEN

I am not a moper. I've never seen much point in sulking. So – after allowing myself the rest of Boxing Day to wallow in a funk of angst and woe – I leap out of bed at five the next morning, determined to embrace life with new-found optimism. Task one? Drawing my curtains tight against the outside world, and drowning out the noise with the *Wicked* soundtrack cranking through my earbuds.

My phone buzzes with a bazillion messages from my friends – including a handful of missed calls that flash with Daniel's clear blue eyes – but I just don't have time for their nonsense today. I'm occupied with the much more vital tasks of painting my toenails in Wonder Woman cobalt, with red tips and perfectly spaced white stars, and then cataloguing my longboxes of comics into a colour-coded Excel spreadsheet.

In the afternoon, after using up an entire sketchpad moving the furniture in Cinnamon Girl's warehouse, I bolt out of my chair with this sudden desire to bake. I install myself in a corner of Albany's kitchen and churn out batch after batch of lemon-meringue cupcakes with cream cheese frosting and hand-painted fondant daisies. Angie hovers in my vicinity, though she doesn't really say much. She does periodically check in with cups of iced tea. For some reason, she also moves all the knives to the other side of the kitchen.

That night, after battling my crappy internet trying to upload angry sketches to the Hawkeye Initiative, I can't get to sleep. I flip my pillow over and over, trying to keep my face on the cool side, before deciding it's just way too hot to stay in bed. I slip into the bakery and snaffle a glass of icy milk and a leftover slice of apple strudel. Then I pass out on the cool tiles.

When Mum finds me the next morning, I am splayed on my sleeping bag beneath the shelves we use for growing yeast. She stares at me with her vigilant-face on, before making this exasperated sound effect like *argamagah!* And then I am banned from the kitchen for the rest of the day.

The sky is not blue. A blanket hangs over the Valley, and everything is steamy and rank. The news on the telly describes it as an 'unexpected subtropical front'. But the weather is nutsy all over the place. There are floods in places that should be dry, and cold snaps in places that should be warm. Apparently, somewhere in Asia, there was a dust storm in a place that normally has snow. I watch the news from Dad's saggy armchair while eating handfuls of Coco Pops straight out of the box. When the reporter cuts away from the weather report and shuffles his papers nervously in front of him, my chocolate breakfast sort of lodges in my throat. I can't help but notice, before I hastily turn off the TV, that the morning hosts discuss the impending apocalypse with slightly less perkiness than they did a week ago.

I think my room is starting to smell weird. And for some reason, I keep losing my pencils. I'm on to my second pack of 2Bs, and have half-filled a sketchpad with Cinnamon Girl in various Nicola Scott *Wonder Woman* poses, when a couple of sharp raps rattle my verandah door. It's kind of an impressive feat that they manage to sound both pissy and impatient.

I drag my feet over the detritus on my floor and crack open my curtains.

Caroline's disgruntled face peers through the glass. "Oi! Open up! We have three days left on the planet, and unless you have a naked Superman in there, you *need* to get your arse out here."

Reluctantly, I unlock my door. Caroline thrusts a sloshy box of peach wine and a jam-jar glass into my hands.

"Drink," she barks. "Outside your door, there's a van full of Irish boys with really cute accents and super-fine pecs. You should *see* these pecs, Alba."

I take a sip of wine, wincing as the sickly sweetness hits the back of my throat. "Ugh. This tastes like the drink elves would use to torture Satan."

Caroline sits beside me on my bed. "Yeah, well, my parents are rationing their booze. This was all Tia could pinch from her mum's stash." She scoots behind me and tugs pencils out of my bun, one by one. "It was either this or a bottle of Advocaat that expired in 2004."

She hands me a handful of pencils, and half a pretzel stick that has also found its way into my hair. The she sits back and fidgets with her T-shirt, her favourite green one that says *Graduate of the Thelma & Louise Finishing School* on it. "Alba, OK, I promised Tia I wasn't gonna say anything until she got here, but seriously? This is ridiculous. I never pegged you for one of those losers who finds out they're dying and, like, just decides to keep showing up for work at the salami factory or whatever—"

"Caroline, what the hell are you babbling about?"

Caroline takes a mouthful of wine straight from the cask, and she waves a hand in my direction. "You. This whole tortured artist thing you've got going on. Not answering your phone, ignoring your friends – even Mrs Garabaldi's shown up at the Junction for a ginger wine. Three days left, Alba! You don't have time to sulk!"

I thrust my sketchpad at her face. "I am not sulking! I'm working – not that you'd know it by this. Look at it, Caroline. Why can't I get it right? The composition sucks. Her proportions are all wrong. It's way too static, and the panels have no flow… Gah! Look at this one – she looks like her arm is growing out of her boob. And even when I do manage to get her looking OK, no scene I place her in is working."

Caroline glances at the page. "It looks fine to me."

"Fine. *See*? Fine is not good enough!" I collapse

backwards on to my bed. “She should be brilliant. All my comics so far have been brilliant. Cinnamon Girl is the biggest thing I’ve ever tried. And she is turning out to be totally rubbish.”

Caroline twirls a purple strand of ponytail around her fingers. She kicks off her Havaianas and pulls her legs up beneath her. “Look, I don’t know anything about what you do. I think all your stuff is awesome, but, really, what does it matter? It’s going to be irrelevant if the rest of the planet’s nuked into oblivion. And if it’s not – well, it’s not like you’re planning on doing much with your art anyway. Right?”

I sit up and glance at my scribbly page. “That’s not the point.”

Caroline snorts. “Isn’t it?”

She holds my glass between her knees and tops it up with wine. In my sketchpad, Cinnamon Girl is standing alone on the domed roof of the Opera House, hands planted on her hips as she stares out over a watery sunset. I’ve always loved the angles and lines of the Opera House. But I’ve never been to Sydney. I can only replicate it from what I’ve seen in pictures.

I take a giant swig of nasty jam-jar wine just as Tia

pushes through my verandah door. Even in the dark, she looks sort of flustered.

"Where've you been?" Caroline barks. "We said we were going to stick together?"

Tia looks sheepishly at her feet. "Yeah, well, I made plans. I was with Peter. Pete's parents decided to keep the fish-and-chip shop open all night, and his house was empty, so … you know."

"We. Know. What?" Caroline says slowly.

Tia sits at my desk and stares at my stacks of half-catalogued comics. Her face turns red. "You *know*."

Caroline leaps off my bed. She looks at Tia with saucer-eyes. "You *cannot* be for real."

"Are you *serious*?" I squeal. "You and Petey…?"

Tia shrugs. "The world might end. I didn't want to die a virgin."

Caroline stares at her, open-mouthed, as I choke back admittedly hysterical giggles. I suppose if I stopped to think about it, nothing about our current situation would be funny, and yet the thought of Petey and Tia…

"So?" Caroline says eventually. "How did it go?"

Tia grimaces. "OK. Weird. Kind of … bumpy. He accidentally elbowed me in the face, which sort of sucked." She shrugs. "I lost a sock."

"Jesus Christ, Tiahnah!" Caroline bellows, as I lose my battle with laughing. "With *Peter*? There's *literally* thousands of guys here, and you pick the one kid who still wears *South Park* undies and practises ninja moves in his garage?"

"Please tell me he did not try any ninja moves on you?" I say through giggles.

Tia sighs. "I'm not sure Petey really has any moves. Not sure I do either. But it was fine. It was different to what I expected, but really, really … fine."

Caroline kicks at a stray shoe on my floor. "Well … are you all right?" she says sullenly.

Tia lopes across my room and gives her a fierce hug. Strangely, Caroline doesn't attempt to squirm out of it. "Yeah, Caroline. I'm OK. I don't know if Petey's the guy I'm gonna marry or anything, but I like him a lot, and I know he likes me. He's my friend, and hey, that counts for something. There are worse guys to choose than someone who's still going to be your friend the next day."

"Tell me about it," Caroline mutters. Then her face scrunches into a mortified ball.

"Um, excuse me?" I say. "What?"

Tia stares at her. "Caroline Gresham. I am your bestest friend in the whole wide world. Is there something you've forgotten to tell me?"

Caroline scowls. "Not that it's either of your businesses, but … maybe. A little bit. God, it happened, like, months ago. It's completely ancient news, and anyway, excuse me for not sharing *every* detail of my life."

"With *who*?" Tia bleats.

Caroline picks at a thread on her shorts. "Gareth Ridley?"

"Tommy Ridley's *brother*?" I yell. "Isn't he, like, twenty-two or something?"

Tia pokes her arm. "Isn't he your second cousin?"

"By marriage!" Caroline snaps. "And neither of you can judge!" She jabs a finger at Tia. "You, Miss I'm-gonna-jump-the-nearest-doofus-just-in-case-the-world-ends, and—" She points at me, her face turning that special Caroline pissed-off red. "You, I'm-so-comfortable-living-in-la-la-happy-land-with-the-cartoon-birdies-that-I'm-gonna-ignore-the-*obviousness*-staring-me-right-in-the-*face*—"

"No one's judging you, Caroline," Tia says quickly.

"And what does that even mean?" I add, my skin prickling.

"Nothing at all," Tia says, shooting Caroline a death-stare.

Caroline throws her hands in the air. "Seriously, Alba? You *seriously* don't know—"

Tia grabs her arm. "Caroline. Shut. Up," she says, her voice deathly quiet. I think even Caroline seems surprised by the steel in Tia's voice. They stare at each other. And I start to cry. I manage to shake the tear-clouds away long enough to see Caroline and Tia exchange dismayed looks, before both their arms are around me.

"Jesus, Alba. I'm sorry," Caroline mumbles. "Clearly I don't know when to shut my mouth."

"What's the matter with me?" I say through sobs. "Am I, like, the last person on the planet who doesn't know what they're doing?"

Tia rubs my back in slow circles. "Alba – you know, there's this bunch of guys in the post-office carpark who are trying to build an Ark? Lucy Albington's setting up a survivors' centre at the church – she's been on a mission collecting blankets and batteries and stuff all week."

Caroline snorts. "Seriously. There's a bidding war going on to rent out space in the Addlers' feed shed. And I guarantee there isn't a can of Spam left within three hundred kilometres." She gives my shoulder an awkward pat. "Alba, I know you're a little bit … hazy about what comes next. But look outside. I think you're in pretty good company."

I sniffle. "Maybe. Though apparently I am the last virgin left in the Valley."

Caroline snort-laughs. "Ah, I doubt it. You reckon Eddie's got around to touching a girl yet? Somehow, I think the planet spontaneously combusting is more likely." She punches my arm with a wicked grin. "Hey, maybe that's the spark that sets off the end? Eddie touches a boob, and bang! Universe implodes."

Tia glares at her. "Alba, I *think* the point Caroline is trying to make is that it's sucky and scary for everyone. But it's all going to be fine. Apocalypse or not – if *anyone* is going to be OK, it's you. We're here." She smiles at me, and her grey eyes well up but don't spill. "Whatever happens, wherever we are – we'll always be *here*. And we're not going anywhere just yet."

I rescue an old T-shirt from my floor and wipe my face. "Don't you want to hang out with Petey today?

Considering you're all, like, betrothed or whatever now?"

Tia glances fleetingly at Caroline. "Um ... Pete's with Grady. Grady's basketball team is having a 'last days' barbecue at Merindale pool, and, um ... that new friend of his? She was going along too and we ... thought Grady could use some company..."

"Oh," I say. I stare at the shaft of light leeching from beneath my curtains. I look around at the bombshell that is my bedroom; my artwork-covered walls, and my floorboards that have disappeared beneath manky clothes and scrunched sketchpad pages. And all of a sudden, it's like the walls are squishing in on me. All of a sudden, my comfy room is stale and stifling.

"What do you want, Alba?" Caroline says quietly.

I drag myself off my bed and pull aside the curtains. When my eyes adjust to the blinding daylight, I see that the piecemeal fabric Thunderdome is completely gone now, reduced to a carpet of dust-covered rags. In the distance beyond the tents and cars, people are moving like the cells of one uncoordinated organism. I can't tell what song is playing. Yet under the weird pale sky, everyone seems to be dancing. I take a deep breath.

"Right now? I think I want to go out there."

Caroline leaps to her feet with a *whoop*. "About bloody time! Come on. If we hurry, we can catch the vegan truck before they run out of food. Who'd have thought quinoa burgers are actually sort of yum?"

Tia stands up as well. She holds me at arm's length. "Alba, maybe you wanna think about changing first?"

I glance down at my outfit – Grady's *Bronies Before Honies* pyjama T-shirt covered with splatters of yesterday's cupcake mix, and purple velour shorts from our year-nine production of *Labyrinth*.

"My bag lady look not working, Tiahnah?" I say weakly.

Tia gives me a hug. "Alba, if anyone could pull that off, it'd be you. But I'm reading on the internet that shampoo and toothpaste are also really in this year."

I polish off the rest of my wine in one grimacey gulp. "Righto. Give me a minute to get less ... festy." I catch a glimpse of myself in the mirror. And I give my friends a giant smile. "It might take a little bit more than a minute."

Caroline grins. "The clock is ticking, Alba. Stop yammering and move."

In the back of my yard, behind Dad's plum trees, the barbed-wire farm fencing has been surreptitiously cut a little ways in from the corner post. It's fastened with a hinge and clasp, not at all noticeable, unless you know what you're looking for. Grady made the sneaky gate a couple of years ago, when breakfast at the bakery became routine and Eddie decided that he "couldn't be fecked" walking the long way to my house.

Most of the campsite is concentrated in the middle of the north paddock, but some scattered people have set up home between the hay bales near my fence. A tangled couple is snoozing in the shade of a nearby beach umbrella. In the distance past the camp, a haze of dancey-dust lingers in the air.

I walk out into the field with Tia and Caroline following close behind.

"Watch where you step," Caroline says. She's ditched her wine box and is now drinking straight from the silver baggy. "People have been pretty good with the portaloos ... mostly..."

I smooth back my ponytail. "You know, in all the post-apocalyptic comics I've read, no one ever mentions what happens with the toilet situation."

Tia giggles. "Yeah. You have to wonder how people are gonna concentrate on rebuilding the human race or whatever. I'd be totes more worried about who gets the last piece of loo roll."

What's left of the grass crunches beneath my feet as Albany's recedes behind us, and the tent city approaches in front. The noise hits me about three seconds before the smell; I'm only hazarding a guess, but I'm thinking that being trapped inside a greenhouse filled with chook manure and fart would smell something like it. Tia wrinkles her nose, but Caroline marches ahead, grinning like a maniac, right at home among the pong of the unwashed.

I have no idea how, but some vague kind of organization seems to have sprung from the chaos. There are little streets and laneways between the canvas domes, and circles of chairs and beanbags in cheery communal clusters. Rows of cars spill with the bedding and junk of people who clearly could not even be bothered to slap up a tent.

And the people. So many people. More people than I have ever seen in my whole entire life. Bodies stream down to the cyclone fencing that blocks off the Palmers' house and the rest of their farm. We walk past some guys kicking a footy around, and a group of people suspended in serene yoga poses. There's an old guy with a ponytail who reminds me a little of Mr Grey, except this guy is sitting on a pile of empty Jack-and-Coke cans and doing that hiccupy, drunken weeping into the arms of a bored-looking friend. There's a girl twirling a hula hoop around her neck as another girl beats a bongo drum beside her, and, oh – a giant group of naked people covered in body paint who are trying to form a human pyramid.

I have one of my small sketchpads with me, but seriously? There's no way I'd know how to even begin capturing this.

A little way ahead, beneath the Palmers' windmills, a collection of vans and water tankers are gathered. A fleet of Merindale fire trucks and police cars are parked just beyond them. Caroline links her arm through mine and Tia's and pulls us forwards.

Suddenly, I'm surrounded by the smells of sweat and sizzling food. We walk past a blue ambulance that's been converted into *Jimmy Baghdad's Falafel*, and a bright orange van with *Tofu Tupack's Wrap Wagon* graffitied on the side. There's a heap of teeny dust-covered carts selling various fried things. In the shadows of a double-decker vegan burger bus, Mrs Ridley is knitting serenely behind a card table of homemade jams and preserves.

"Where have all these guys come from?" I yell over the noise.

"Dunno," Caroline yells back. "Suppose they figured even the Rapture needs to be catered. We'd be screwed without them though. The grocery store's down to, like, some cans of oven cleaner and a couple of packs of mints." She winks. "Shockingly, condoms were the first thing we ran out of."

We keep walking.

I step over and around groups of people parked on the ground. I manage to crunch a couple of hands, and almost kick this one guy in the face as he's Instagramming his nachos. But no one seems too fussed. In the paddock beyond the boho foodcourt, the dancers are doing their thing; not even the white sky and heat seem to be putting a dent in their spirits. I don't know if there is a handbook for the apocalypse that I've missed. But somehow, everyone seems to have just ... adapted.

"Oh hey," Caroline says. "It's Eric."

"Who the hell is Eric?" I say as Caroline moseys

toward a guy with a Southern Cross constellation tattoo on his chest.

Tia giggles. "Yeah. Caroline's kind of been busy these last few days. It's worse than that time Merindale pool had diving-team tryouts. Remember?" She shakes her head. "Really don't think we can compete with this much boy muscle, Alba."

Tia and I wander to the edge of the foodie area. For a moment I think we're heading to dance, which I am so totally not in the mood for, but at the last moment Tia veers me around to the right. In front of us is a tarp with a *Hairwashing Tent* sign above it. A bunch of semi-clean people are sitting on fruit crates out front.

"Look who it is," she says lightly. "Fancy seeing Indigo here."

Daniel leaps to his feet from the box he was perched on. "Sarah!" he calls out. He bounds toward us. "Thought I was going to have to wait till those dudes finished their Ark before I saw you again," he says as he hugs me. "If we're marched on two-by-two, promise you'll be my plus one." Even though I can't see his face, I can tell that he's grinning.

"Hey. Look at you, getting your earth-sprite on,"

I say as I hug him back. "The girls and I were just looking around, and—"

But when I turn, Tia has vanished.

"I was starting to think I'd done something to piss you off, Sarah Jane. Why didn't you answer my calls? Where have you been?"

"Yeah. Sorry, Daniel. It's been a ... messy few days."

He slips off his sunglasses and squints at me. "Alba, are you OK?"

I shrug. "Hey, aren't people supposed to be all angsty this time of year? Pretty sure a little angst is justified in the face of Armageddon..." My smile falters. I just can't be bothered holding it in place any more. I plonk myself on an empty crate. Daniel sits beside me, seemingly unconcerned about the whirling mass of crazy around us.

"So. Come here often?" I ask. "What are you doing hanging all by yourself?"

"Just checking things out," he says casually. "Avoiding my manager, that sort of thing..." He nods his head at my sketchpad. "You carry that with you everywhere?"

"Pretty much. I probably shouldn't bother these

days though. My comics are a big fat fail at the moment."

Daniel baulks. "Really? Why? It's not like you have a shortage of material." He gestures around him. "Your comics might turn out to be the only surviving record of the last outpost of human civilization."

I glance around. "It's all just too ... much. I don't know where to start."

"Well – how 'bout with that dude?" Daniel points at a sunburned guy standing a little way in front of us. He's wearing nothing but a blue cape and a pair of skimpy, fluoro-pink Speedos. He is waving a half-eaten taco in the air, his cape flapping behind him as he sways to the music.

"Sure. OK. Random taco undies guy. I shall call him ... Avocado Man. And his superpower shall be—"

"The ability to blind his enemies with the glow of his pasty arse-cheeks," Daniel says decisively.

I laugh. Daniel becomes silent as he peers over my shoulder. I cross one leg over the other and prop my sketchpad on my knee. Though I can't hear the comforting sounds of pencil scratches above the noise, the lines still materialize on my page. I draw a simple frame around the figure, and it's like the rough panel somehow manages to keep in check the distractions swirling around him. The edges of my vision become all blurry, with only Avocado Man and his radioactive pink knickers in focus.

My eyes snap away when he is joined by a girl in a denim dress, who grabs him in an embrace and then drags him off through the crowd.

I crack my knuckles. I don't know how long I've been drawing, but I have a half-dozen pages of character sketches, and Daniel has wandered off. I see him standing a little ways away, deep in smiley conversation with a girl in a bikini who feels the need to touch his chest every ten seconds.

I flip open a clean page, and look around again. The air here is slightly less stinky, a combination of jasmine shampoo and wet dog. On the crate beside me, a grey-haired woman in a linen dress is now seated. She's cooling her face with a paper fan, her eyes locked on a copy of *The Alchemist.* I twist around slightly so that I can see her from the corner of my eye, and I keep drawing.

I doubt any of this stuff is going to be much use; not unless Cinnamon Girl finds herself in the middle of Oktoberfest or something. But as a drawing exercise, it's strangely ... liberating. My head still feels way muddled, but for a moment, I forget about trying to capture everything all at once, and I focus on the minutiae instead. The green gumboots on a stubble-faced hair-washing dude, and the matching felt top hats on a couple of boys entwined in a kiss, and the peaceful expression on the face of a woman building some kind of art installation out of falafel wrappers. I draw till a pair of hands clasps my shoulders from behind.

Daniel leans over me. "Sorry. I was talking to you but you weren't answering and then I got ... distracted." He grins. "So. How goes?"

"OK, I think. None of this stuff is gonna win an Eisner. But it's good. Small, but ... good."

He sits on the ground and takes the sketchpad. "I suppose it's a bit like what I do," he says as he flicks through my drawings. "Like, finding a character in a script? OK, I'm not talking about Indigo Lazorio, cos let's face it, dude isn't exactly profound. His entire breakdown might as well have read 'shirtless and dense'. But, you know, in theory ... you just focus on one thing. And you shape the rest from there."

He hands the sketchpad back and turns his face to the sky. We sit in companionable silence, as I furtively open a new page and lay down a few lines in a sketchy profile of Daniel. I rough out the contours of his cheekbone and the shape of his jaw, and I shade the faint birthmark beneath his eye that must be covered with make-up on *Gum Trees*, cos I'd totally forgotten about it until now. I smudge the lines at the back of his neck, where his auburn hair is damp with sweat. I know I'm just mucking around with character studies, but I have this sudden urge to layer Daniel's frame with some background; to draw in his shadows a smiley boy in a *Muppet Babies* beanie and oversized tracksuit, waving a thumbed *Lightning Saga* comic in his hand.

"Alba, can I ask you a question?" he says lazily.

I run my pinkie over the shading of his eyebrow. "OK. Sure. Go."

"You don't have to answer but … what's the deal with you and the guy situation?" He taps my knee with a grin. "I know it must have been a total dead zone after I left, but – are you telling me there isn't a single person here you're keen on?"

"Jeez, Daniel, you make me sound like a monk. I've … dated and stuff."

In fact, the sum total of my Eden Valley romantic history consists of three guys: Alex Chapman, who I kissed on a dare in year seven and who tasted like stale chicken Twisties; Joe-some-guy, a city friend of Tommy Ridley's, who hit on me by recounting the entire sucky plot of the *Green Lantern* movie, and who I kissed in the dark at Anzac Park, partly out of curiosity, partly to make him stop talking; and Brendon Ryder, who I met at one of Grady's basketball games, and who looked exactly like Chase from *Runaways.* We went out for two weeks early this year, but we didn't do much except watch *Ice Road Truckers*, and snog on the Merindale bus. Yes, he was uninspiring, but a brief, and, OK, *hot* distraction, until I got tired of Grady's grumbles that I was 'consorting with the enemy'. Mixed-town relationships are a *big* Valley no-no.

My hands are still on the page. "Honestly? It's … just not something I've spent a lot of time worrying about. Believe me, I've had other things on my mind."

Daniel stands and squishes his butt beside me on the crate. "I'm getting that. But I'm also going to go with this hunch I have that maybe those things … aren't totally unrelated?"

I blink at him. "I don't know. I can't really explain it. The boy-thing, commitment-thing or whatever. But I guess..." I wipe my hands on my knees. "Do you remember when we were in grade five? I went through that whole boho phase? I was listening to lots of Mum's Stone Poneys records and was really obsessed with linen dresses? And it lasted all the way until the rock-chick phase, which, you know, only lasted till I got sick of studded collars and wrecking perfectly decent tights. And then there was the phase when all I wanted to be was Wonder Woman? I used to wear Mum's bra outside my T-shirts?"

Daniel laughs. "And randomly throw your headband at people on the street. I remember. Mrs Garabaldi was pissed. But I don't get what that has to do with—"

"Because when you hook up with someone, don't you sort of just ... stop? Like, you're with a person who's decided they like you one way, but then, what if you're only that way for a little while? And what happens if you're not even sure what you're going to be next? What if you want to dye your hair purple or you get really into the bagpipes or you decide to get a face tattoo—"

"You want a face tattoo?"

"I don't know! But that's my point! It's way too much pressure, choosing someone, having someone else's life and whatnot mashed in with yours, when you don't even know what you're doing with your own stuff and – gah. This probably isn't making sense."

He narrows his eyes, like he's thinking extra hard. "Yeah, OK, so some people will never be able to see beyond the hot guy with a smoking bod and great hair…" He nudges me before becoming semi-serious again. "But someone else might be totally on board with whatever crazy comes next. Cos it's all you, isn't it? Face tattoo and everything." He shrugs. "It's not impossible that someone would get that," he says lightly. "Maybe you just haven't been looking in the right direction."

"Daniel – what happened to you?" I say with a laugh. "You disappeared from the Valley a kid whose most intense conversations involved dissecting *Spider-man*, and you came back some sort of weird mystic guru. Albeit a slightly sleazy one."

He thuds my arm with a boomy laugh. "*Sleazy*? I'm giving you my best stuff here, Sarah. It's actually hurting my brain to be this deep." He wraps an arm around my shoulders. "But what happened to me was … I totally freaked about things changing. You remember? That day Mum told us we were leaving, it was like … I thought my life was over. Then I left, because I didn't have a choice. And I was fine." He squeezes me tightly. "I was more than fine, Sarah Jane. I was awesome."

I close my eyes. My brain feels like it's pushing against my skull, like it just doesn't have room to process everything churning inside it. Somehow, through the noise, I swear I can hear the *thwack* of my own heartbeat, as thunderous as if a comic-book sound-effect were floating right in front of me. With my eyes closed, the sound seems to make everything else around me dim and hushed. Which is why I practically fall off my apple box when the music dies mid-song, and Daniel jumps up quickly.

A collective groan emanates from the people in the field. Daniel glances in their direction. A flash of nerviness passes over his face. "I can't remember, Alba. Are all the power outages you guys have been having here normal?"

I swallow. "We have? I hadn't noticed. I think I may have been a wee bit navel-gazey recently, Daniel."

He pulls me to my feet. "You wanna bail? My folks are having lunch with the Ridleys and my manager's found someone in Merindale to give him a pedicure. I think his biggest worry about the world ending is the effect it's gonna have on his cuticles or something. But – you want to hang out at mine?"

I look around. I have no idea where Tia and Caroline have disappeared to; probably to that secret club where all the other ex-virgins of the Valley hang. I glance up at the bleak, suffocating sky. I step away from Daniel and spin around with a smile.

"Sure, Daniel. Let's get out of here."

TWELVE

Without the background music filling the Valley, Daniel's place is even more depressingly blah than normal. Apart from a single coffee cup on their dining table, the house looks totally unlived in.

"Remind me to bring you a pot plant or one of our plastic Santas," I say as we stumble into the kitchen. "This house looks like the place personality came to die."

Daniel brightens. "That reminds me – I totally forgot last time, but I have a present for you." He bounces over to the sideboard and reappears with a paper bag. "I didn't exactly come prepared. But I do have some stuff I think you'll like. Merry belated Christmas, Alba."

I take the bag from his hands. "Hey! You can't give away your comics! Even though – oh, you have the new

Ms. Marvel, and, no way, the last couple of *Justice Leagues*? I'd been meaning to order them for ages ... OK, this *Earth One* I've got ... the art's ace, but it's like, cheer up emo Superman..." My hand closes around a hardcover book at the back of the pile. On the cover is a picture of a man with way too many white teeth. He's holding a cartoon apple squeezed by a measuring tape. "What's this?"

Daniel takes the book from me. His ears turn scarlet. "Oh ... ah. Well ... this was the book that saved my arse a few years back. You remember how many things Mum tried to get me to lose weight? As desperately as I wanted not to look like that German kid from *Willy Wonka*, your mum's caramel slices always won out. But then I got into this guy's program, and I started running and hitting the weights ... I didn't realize that was in there though." He flips thoughtfully through the book. And then he hands it back to me. "You can have it. You might find it useful, too."

I stare blankly at his cheekboney face. "You're giving me your diet book?"

"It's OK. I normally keep a couple of copies around my house. The one above the fridge comes in real handy when I'm suffering ice-cream withdrawals—"

I'm not entirely sure what my expression is doing. But Daniel stops talking. And his face becomes kind of horrified.

"Oh. No, I didn't mean that you needed ... you look great, Alba, really, but you know, you and I were always the same. It was always the thing we had most in common." He slips the book back into the bag and shoves it into my hands with an uncomfortable laugh. "Do what you want with it. No biggie, right?"

I drop the paper bag on to the counter. "No biggie. I guess ... I just never realized that *that* was the thing we had most in common?" I peer closely at his face. "I never realized it was such a big deal for you. You were always so happy when we were kids. You always seemed like you didn't care what anyone thought."

He grunts, his eyes on his feet. "Yeah, well. Maybe I was a born actor. Some bits of my life here were awesome. And some bits sucked arse. I was never like you, you know. I wasn't a huge fan of me when I was little."

In my head, I guess my memories are a hazy montage, coupled with some frozen, flash-panel highlights. I remember Daniel's squealy, prepubescent voice. I remember weekend afternoons in the gazebo at Anzac Park, me and Daniel face-deep in comics, while Grady played *Mario Golf* on Anthony's old Game Boy. But I'm staring into Daniel's eyes, and, all of a sudden, I'm remembering other stuff, too. I remember the melancholy looks he used to give Grady and his brother as they bounced, shirtless, around the abandoned basketball court. I remember the random excuses he invented to get out of swimming at Merindale pool. I remember all those sleepovers at my house, Daniel hidden beneath oversized jammies, regardless of the weather.

"Did I offend you?" he says quietly.

I shake my head. "No. I just never realized you were unhappy back then. I'm really sorry, Daniel." I give his cheek a fleeting kiss. "I should have noticed."

Daniel smiles. "I wasn't unhappy. Not all the time. You and Grady ... you two made everything OK. You probably don't remember but ... I didn't have anyone until you guys let me in. Not sure I'll ever be able to repay you both for that." His smile falters. "And Alba, sometimes we all suck at noticing what's right in front of our face."

He takes a step toward me. “What happened to you Christmas Day?” he says out of the blue. Like a switch has been flicked, the softness in his face is replaced by that calculating stare I know oh so well. “I looked everywhere for you after dinner. I even hauled my arse to the bakery, but by the time I got there your windows were dark.”

“Oh. Yeah, that. The party got a bit too wild for some of us so Grady crashed at mine and then—”

“Wait. You guys still have sleepovers?”

I suck in a breath at the distinct *whump!* that punches behind my ribs. “Yeah. So?”

“So – you don’t still sleep in the same bed, though. Right?”

I feel my traitorous cheeks flush. “M-mum bought a couch for Grady years ago,” I stammer. “But, hey now, *you* never had a problem sleeping over—”

“I never had a problem sleeping over when we were *six*, Sarah.” He gives me his smug grin. “If you invited me for a ‘sleepover’ now, I might have a few things in mind other than watching *X-Men*, know what I mean?”

God. He even does the sucky little air quotes over the word ‘sleepover’.

"Daniel, don't be stupid. It's not like that with Grady and me. He's like my—"

Daniel holds up a hand. "Sarah, don't take this the wrong way, but if you finish that with 'he's like my brother', I might vomit in my mouth. Jesus. You are the only one imagining siblingy blood between you and Domenic. Trust me on that."

"You're delusional," I snap.

"And you're blind," he says back. "But, Sarah, the End of Days might be here. What does *any* of this stuff matter? If the planet being sucked into a black hole isn't going to give you a shake-up, then nothing I say is gonna make a difference. Is it?"

I jiggle my hands out at my sides, but I can't feel anything in them other than pins and needles. Daniel squares his shoulders. The muscles beneath his T-shirt stretch in that particular boy-way that makes me forget for half a second this whole inexplicable Two-Face thing he seems to have going on. He narrows his eyes, his lips pursed together. There's something oddly familiar in that expression. I just can't put my finger on it—

"You have a *killer* smile. You know that, right?" he says.

Well, actually Daniel, I do. My smile is one of my best features. But probably not a polite thing to admit.

"Thanks," I say, clasping my hands behind my back. "Kind of random, but—"

"And *amazing* lips," he says, his voice suddenly all weird and husky.

Look, I'm cute as, I know this, and it's not like I've ever had a shortage of guys buzzing around. I'm not Eddie, who freaks every time a girl so much as looks in his direction, or Caroline, who's happily smooched dozens of boys, leaving a trail of broken hearts in her wake. Sue me for being sappy, but I haven't kissed that many random guys because I decided I don't *want* to kiss random guys. Kissing is supposed to be no big deal, but really? I just never *liked* being that smooshed together with any old someone. All that mingled breath and lips and stranger tongue – I realize kisses don't ever happen like they do in stories, but I'm not ready to give up on the fantasy.

Which is why, I think, when Daniel Gordon – who got seven votes in that uni web poll of sexy unknown TV stars, and who used to make me laugh so hard in kindergarten that I snorted orange cordial out my nose, twice – leans hesitantly toward me, and his lips come within brushing distance of mine, my lips twitch experimentally back for, like, a millisecond, before my body does this spasmy leap backwards, almost tripping over a kitchen stool. And the words that tumble out of my apparently amazing lips are, "Ew, gross!"

O-*K*. Possibly not my finest moment here.

Daniel takes a hurried step backwards. The scarlet in his ears spills over his cheeks. "Well. Can honestly say I've never received *that* reaction before."

"Daniel, I'm sorry," I choke out. "The gross bit, I mean. That might have been rude."

He laughs. "Rude? Um, that's not the word I would've used. Ego-shattering, maybe. Confusing, for sure..."

I stamp my foot. "Hey! I wasn't asking you to kiss me, Daniel! I mean, hello – what were you thinking? It's *me*. It's as weird as making out with – who's that chick who plays your sister on *Gum Trees*?"

He snorts and laughs and looks exasperated, all at the same time. "Sarah Jane. Firstly, kissing you would be nothing even remotely like kissing a sister. Dunno if you've noticed, but neither of us is six any more. You are one of my oldest friends. Pretty sure we aren't related. There'd be nothing wrong, or weird, about giving it a shot. And secondly, I have *totally* made out with the chick who plays my sister on *Gum Trees*. She has a tongue piercing." He grins. "*So* hot."

I realize, as he has been talking, that I have backed myself against his breakfast bar, a kitchen stool between us like a force field. But he looks less embarrassed now, and more bemused than anything, which just makes me even more pissed. I stomp forwards again till we're toe-to-toe.

"Daniel, after everything I've told you, all the stuff you know is in my head – what makes you think that kissing you would be the answer to *any* of my problems?"

He crosses his arms, his ears becoming pink again. "I don't think I actually said that, Sarah. What I *think* I said was that there would be nothing weird if you wanted to give it a shot. But if kissing me is – well, in your words, so unspeakably *gross* that you'd rather have your tongue gnawed out by a rabid possum – maybe it wouldn't hurt to think about *why* exactly that might be."

I grab my sketchpad. "OK. Thanks for the advice. I'm going to go away now."

"Alba, wait—"

"No really, Daniel, I'm just about done with the smarm. I can't figure out what the hell is going on with you. Sometimes you are the you I remember – the you who I missed like crazy – and sometimes I think you are messing with me for fun. Only, I can't for the life of me figure out why."

He grabs the paper bag of comics, and he walks backwards in front of me as I push toward his door. "Alba, I'm sorry, that was rash and probably … ill-conceived." He stops me with a light hand on my elbow and shoves the books into my limp hands. "But you wanna know what happened to me? What happened was, I figured out that being comfortable isn't always a good thing. And an outside shove was exactly what I needed."

I step outside and turn around, only to find Daniel staring at me pensively, his jaw working back and forth like he's holding back a raft of word spewage.

"Daniel, I'm sorry if I confused you, or whatever. I'll … see you around, OK?"

I walk away before he can answer. Under the white sky, the messy human sounds of the Valley swirl around me. I suppose that snubbing the lips of a gorgeous boy with perfect muscles and piercing eyes – the boy who has always been a missing part of my story – might be considered by some people to be one of the portents of the coming End of Days. Maybe there is something seriously wrong with me.

I slip into my backyard and sit on my steps, my heartbeat drumming a steady, solid beat. Daniel's blushing face floats in front of me, but I can't make myself feel sorry for saying no. Maybe lips, and spectacular abs, are not going to solve any of my problems right now.

And maybe, just maybe, there is nothing wrong with me at all.

THIRTEEN

I open my eyes at 5.22 the next morning to a chorus of gentle singing coming from the farm. In the heat and dark, it's a little like waking in the midst of a shamanic ritual. It is, weirdly, sort of peaceful. I close my eyes, trying to coax my brain into a serene, zen-like state. Until I realize the song drifting into my room is a badly harmonised version of 'Bohemian Rhapsody', at which point I haul arse out of bed.

I get up, I get dressed, and I clean. Armageddon or not, I don't think I can stand living in the middle of my own refuse for another second.

I pull down the Cinnamon Girl scraps from my walls and bookshelf, and I carefully bundle them together in a spare archive box. I lay my sketchpads on top; all but my first one, filled with the rough, hopeful plans for the beginning of her story. I think I might be able to salvage some bits from this one. It may be premature to consider a revised origin or post-*Crisis* story for her, but jeez – it's not like I'm gonna be panned for messing with her mythology just yet.

Beneath my piles of shoes and clothes, last year's school stuff is still scattered. I'd chucked a few things into the bonfire my class had up on the hill after exams, and yet year-twelve debris remains strewn across my room. I gather up the books, and my school diary that's covered in more photos of my friends and me than any actual school business. On the cover is a pic of me, Caroline and Tia; Tia's face peeking up in the background, behind a close-up of my cheek and lips, and Caroline mugging with chocolate brownie mashed in her front teeth. I rip off the cover and balance it on my bookshelf. And then I archive the rest.

The morning sky is streaked the colour of whiskey when I eventually emerge outside. I drag my banana lounge beneath Dad's plum trees, with my pencils scattered around me. I open a clean pad of Bristol board, but instead of drawing straight away, I just hang out, and I watch for a while.

I can't describe the mood as the farm wakes; the best I can capture it on my page is a layered mess of human beings, a bit like *Moses*, this Frida Kahlo painting in one of Mum's art books.

I draw as the sun struggles above the blanket of white. At some point Angie wanders out with a plate of cheese muffins, and she sits beside me in silence as we contemplate my pages. I'm not entirely sure of the storyboard that's emerging. I suppose I just have to trust that my subconscious knows something the rest of my brain is still catching up on. I kinda like this new version of Cinnamon Girl though; her lines are simpler, sort of naive in style, but somehow I think she might be OK with that.

I fall on to my green couch that night and pass out before my head hits the cushions. When I jump up the next morning, I install myself at the edge of my plastic garden and I keep working.

In between, when I feel like a change of perspective, I wander through the secret gate and out into the Palmers' field. I don't head anywhere in particular, just kind of soak up the atmosphere as I meander alone. A non-denominational prayer circle has sprung from the T-shirt rubble of the Thunderdome; as it turns out, not everyone has shown up here just to get tanked. The people who have taken over this spot are quiet, and introspective. I sit under a tree and chat to a couple of Buddhist women who tell me all about impermanence and interconnectedness and stuff. And then someone on stage announces that naked Battleship is about to begin beneath the water tanks, and they take off with cheery waves.

Strangely, as I mosey through the farm, I bump into a bunch of people I know. New faces who have become regulars at the bakery, and a few arsebags I recognise from Merindale, and a handful of friends from school who are still hanging around the Valley, all of whom are embracing the End Times with varying levels of enthusiasm.

I fly a kite. I toss a frisbee. I graciously decline to participate in a nudie dance-off. Once, as I'm weaving through the caravans and cars, I stumble upon an orange-and-blue VW Kombi with fraying purple curtains, and my feet come to a stop.

Thumbing through a magazine in the doorway is dreadlocked bikini girl, one of the visitors who's become a fixture at Albany's. Her name, it turns out, is Lizzy Warren, and she is a second-year graphic-design student in the city. Lizzy lets me sit in the shade of her doorway, happy, she tells me, just to talk to someone who's showered in the past week. We yammer about Marjane Satrapi and Georgia O'Keeffe, and Julie Doucet, who we have, like, irreconcilable opinions on. Apart from Mum, there isn't anyone in the Valley who really gets the stuff that I love. It's kind of nice, if a bit incongruous. I leave with Lizzy's number, and a promise to look her up if I ever do make it to the city. Neither of us points out that this is contingent on the city still existing come midnight tomorrow.

In between, my friends drift in and out of Albany's. Caroline and Tia drag me away from my pencils to hang out at Anzac Park with some random surfer chicks from Perth who they have made friends with. Petey drops by with a parcel of greasy chips and classic TV episodes of *Wonder Woman* loaded on his laptop. He makes himself at home on my bedroom floor while I work up colour-palette options on my Wacom. Even Eddie manages to find an hour free in between chores. He hunkers in my backyard, falling asleep on my banana lounge with a cowboy hat on his face and a mumbled promise to "deck the feck-stick" who sprayed one of his cows blue.

No one discusses the end of the world, or the missing member of our group, leaving my imagination to construct scenarios involving him being abducted by a red-headed siren who looks like a mash-up of Mary Janes from different *Spider-Man*s. But there is an uneasiness to my friends as the clock ticks, a nerviness that, if I were to draw it, would look something like lengthening shadows moving in over their frames.

I wake up late on the final day of the year to the whirl of helicopters hovering overhead and music already playing. The sounds of the Valley are way different this morning. A buzziness filters into my bedroom as I open my eyes, my head filled with that last-day-of-school feeling of excitement and melancholy.

I swipe at the drool puddle that has formed beneath my cheek. I seem to have fallen asleep facedown at my desk. I remember waking up at two in the morning with this crazy urgency that made me leap out of bed and hurry to my bookshelf. I may have been dreaming, but I remembered this sequence of frames in one of my dad's *Gods and Mortals* Wonder Woman books that I just had to find.

I push my chair away from my desk. Around me are the teetering stacks of Dad's and my comics; some of his so thumbed that the pages are barely attached. I never did find the art I was looking for. I got distracted when I stumbled on Dad's copy of *Batman: Year One,* bookmarked a third of the way through with a receipt from the Wasileskis' service station. Dad was always obsessed with this book. I don't know how many times we'd swapped it between us, Dad grilling me about my opinion on the art style and Miller's take on Catwoman and stuff. I hadn't read his copy in ages though, not since I bought my own hardcover a few years back. I always wondered what Dad would have said about the reworked colouring in my edition.

I glance at the clock on my desk. The pink numbers seem to crackle with an intensity way more insistent than normal. I grab a dress from my wardrobe, and I hurry into the shower.

I'm towelling my hair as I slip back into my room, and my elbows are blocking my face, so for all of three seconds I fail to process that Grady is sitting on the armrest of my couch.

He leaps to his feet when he sees me, but then he sort of hovers, like he's not sure what to do next.

I freeze, and I drink in his presence in my room; dishevelled curls and rumpled *Cutty's Boxing Gym* T-shirt and old jeans, and dirty hands, which I know means he's in the middle of work. His face is shadowy with stubble. He looks exhausted.

"Grady. What are you doing here?"

He runs a hand madly through his hair. "I don't know. I was dropping off some boxes but then … I found myself here. I was going to leave. And then I didn't." He falls into my desk chair and buries his face in his hands. "Alba. What's going on with us?"

I toss my towel on to the floor, fizzy frustration sending my voice stratospheric. "What's going on? I dunno, Domenic. You are the one who was all, like, nice knowing you, have a great life and whatnot. And, you know, *you* are the one hankering after the first chick you meet with a city address who gives you the side eye—" I suck in a giant, shaky breath.

"Now you're asking *me* that question?"

Grady's face flushes. "Alba, Jesus, it's not like… I don't know what I'm doing! I was right, I think, about me needing to work through my own stuff, and you were right when you said that you needed to figure things out, but…"

"But what? What, Grady?" I snap.

"But why do we have to do that apart?" he yells.

I fall on to my bed and hug a pillow to my chest. Outside, a shouty song is blasting from the band. Inside, the silence hangs, full of finality. Cold water trickles from my hair and down my back. Part of my brain is yelling at me to speak; the other part knows it's just not ready to say the things it needs to say.

Grady's tired eyes fall on to my desk. I'd tossed Daniel's presents there, and then forgotten about them; right now, his hardcover book is sitting on top of a pile of comics like a cheerful, flab-free trophy.

"What's this?" Grady says. He picks up the book and flips it over, and then he looks up at me blankly. "Alba? Why are you reading a diet book?" he says quietly.

"Um, I'm not. It's not mine. Well, it's mine, but not really. Ah … Daniel gave it to me. I think it's supposed to be inspirational," I say with a really crap attempt at lightness. "Hey, if Indigo's pecs are anything to go by, I'd say it's, like, the Green Lantern Power Ring of diet books."

I swallow, my hands suddenly tingly in a way that has nothing to do with the ominous grandfather-clock sound effect chiming through the PA, and everything to do with the fact that Grady's face has morphed into this expression I've only seen once before, when Anthony backed Cleo's car over the science project Grady had spent months working on. His pupils are so big they're almost blacking out the brown of his eyes.

"Daniel. Did. What?" he says. His voice is scarily expressionless, like Dr Manhattan in *Watchmen*, just before he vaporizes Rorschach.

"Look, Grady, it's just a book," I say hurriedly. "And we were talking about us—"

"Yeah, except there is no *us*, is there, Alba?"

He storms out of my room, slamming the verandah door so hard behind him that the frame of my house shudders.

I consider running after him. But my feet don't want to move in that direction. My eyes linger on

Dad's comics, and the panel of Cinnamon Girl on my screen. She's standing on the steps of Albany's, staring down Main Street at an invisible point on the horizon. I've roughed out the buildings and the sinister penny-farthing in her distance; I realize that though my character is changing with every incarnation, I can draw my town flawlessly without ever needing to leave my room.

I toss aside the pillow and hurry off my bed.

My house smells like fresh laundry and cinnamon sugar. I dig out Mum's photo albums from the top of her wardrobe and carry them into the lounge, sweeping aside our Santas so I can place the albums on the coffee table. I don't know what I'm looking for, but I sit on the floor and flip open the first book. It's one of Mum's junky ones; a few pages are artfully arranged, until she lost interest and just jammed the rest in alongside receipts and takeaway menus.

Mostly, they're pics of Angie in her last bit of high school and her first bit of uni. Mum beams in her school uniform, a gaggle of girls crammed around her with matching high ponytails and cheesy smiles. I see the same faces in a dozen photos; but I know Mum struggles to remember all their names now. My favourite part of this album is the second half: the scattered shots of Mum at uni, when her hair becomes blue, and her lip becomes pierced, and the face alongside hers becomes Cleo's. Sticky-taped inside are concert tickets and flyers to art shows, and in between Mum and Cleo and their bizarro friends, the face of my dad as he drifts into their story.

I reach for a leather-bound green book in the middle of the pile. I haven't looked at this one in ages. There's no rhyme or reason to the order of the pics; there's a scattering of photos of me and Grady, sometimes as awkward prepubescents, sometimes as gappy-toothed little kids. There's an assortment of Eden Valley events, like that one time the Alberts organized a cook-off in Anzac Park, and ended up burning down the gazebo.

And in between, everywhere, like the *Where's Wally?* of Eden Valley, is my dad. A sneaky photo of him sleeping in front of the telly in his green chair with baby me in his arms, and mowing the lawn of the bungalow where we lived when I was a kid, and smooching Mum in front of the new neon sign he'd hung above Albany's trellising. Photos of him and Mr Everson installing the bench in front of the fruit-and-veg, and of him fixing the farm fencing at Cleo's yellow house, and covered in soot and cinders as he helps the Ridleys rebuild their goat shed. There are pages of him with Grady at Merindale basketball courts, and Grady with our family in the *Fantastic Four* costumes Dad insisted we wear for Halloween that one year. And there is that single photo of him atop his stupid ginormous Kawasaki Vulcan, the motorbike blindingly shiny, probably cos it'd been subjected to its bazillionth polish that day.

I drag my eyes up. Dad's favourite green armchair, saggy and faded, still has pride of place in our living room. His law books are still scattered through our shelves. The Cecily Brown print he bought for Mum still hangs over the water stain on the wall, and his face beams down from everywhere, his photos and stuff and *spirit* as ever-present as if he had never gone anywhere.

My dad, tall and broad and solid, his hair the exact same shade as mine, his dark eyes almost the same shape as mine. Always smiley, and goofy and way too loud.

I close the photo album and place it carefully on top of the pile. If my dad were watching me now, I reckon he'd be rolling his eyes at my mushy mawkishness. He'd swat me over the backside with whichever random comic he had in his hand. If he knew the mess that was in my head, he'd probably give me one of his giant, smothery bear hugs, and his favourite piece of faux-dad advice: *Sulking is for sidekicks, Sarah Janey. What would Wonder Woman do?*

I brush away my tears and grab my mobile. The networks have already started jamming, and it takes me three fumbly, panicked tries before I finally get a call to go through. A sonorous voice rumbles through the line.

"Hey, gorgeous. What's up?"

I shoot a glance at the flip clock on the side table. "Heya, Eddie. You busy?"

There is muffled silence, and the purr of what sounds like a tractor being turned off. "Nah. Just trying to move some feed. My old man's busy practising the Harlem Shake in the tool shed with, like, a hundred losers who are filming it for YouTube. Dad looks like he's got his nutsacks caught in a milking machine, and I think he's forgotten we actually run a fecking farm. Anyway. What's going on?"

I refuse to be waylaid, not even by the disquieting mental flash of Mr Palmer and his nether-sacks. "Eddie, I need your help. Can I come round?"

There is a hesitant pause before Eddie replies. "Um, sure? Just you?"

"Yeah, Ed. Just me. I think you might be able to help me with something. I think maybe … you might be the only one who can."

There is conspicuous silence on Ed's end of the line, interrupted by some distant, depressed mooing. "Jesus," Eddie replies. "Alba, has anyone ever told you that you have a … what do they call it? A flair for the fecking dramatic?"

"Eddie – I think that might be a ginormous part of my problem. I'm coming around now. I'll see you in a few, OK?"

I hang up before I have a chance to change my mind. I swap my dress for black jeans and my lucky red gingham shirt, and I tie my damp hair in a knot underneath a red scarf. I look at my face in my mirror, and try to corral my thoughts into a less swoony sort of state. I'm not sure how successful I am, since I can't really feel my hands.

I head shakily toward the door. But at the last moment I spin around, and I grab a random pink post-it sketch of Cinnamon Girl from the top of my archive box. I fold it in half and stick her in the back pocket of my jeans.

If she's gonna be so goddamned difficult, she can suffer right along with me.

I take the road to Eddie's, hoping to speed past the worst of the throngs. But avoiding the masses seems nigh on impossible, cos even the potholed back roads are swirling with bodies. I walk past people dancing in the shade of the gum trees, and people in line to buy corn on the cob from a three-wheeled cart, which might pass the food hygiene standards in medieval Uzbekistan, if the medieval Uzbekistanian food-tester was blind, and tanked. I suppose not everyone interprets the whole you-only-live-once thing with quite the same level of momentousness.

I weave through the sea of bronzed people, past the plethora of exposed side-boob, through the sunscreen tang and sweat and dust. If I could see the mood in the atmosphere, I'm pretty sure it would look like cobalt bolts of lightning, tinged with veins of incandescent ectoplasm, à la the cosmic charge from any comic superhero unleashing her powers. The air is literally vibrating with expectation.

I hurry to the fence that leads to the front yard of the Palmers' house. Eddie is scowling when he unlocks the gate and drags me inside by the hand. He's wearing his battered work jeans and a streaky white vest, his arms covered with grass and sweat. I grab hold of his slick, freckly forearm, and I cling to it for dear life.

"You came the back way?" Eddie says as he steadies me with his hands. "D'you know some sci-fi fan club took it upon themselves to deck out the driveway with solar lights? One of 'em told Dad that they're building a landing strip, just in case. Shit, I think he was only half-joking, too. Alba, I'm telling you, when the Rapture comes, fecking Trekkies are gonna be seriously disappointed."

I untangle myself from his grasp. "Ed – dunno if you've noticed, but the party's started early out there. Are you actually still working?"

Eddie grunts. "The cows aren't waiting for Jesus. Nothing stops here. Even if my old man thinks that getting the sound system sorted is the most important goddamned job in the universe."

Summer sun does interesting things to Ed's skin; his freckles have become so dense in places that they've joined together in orangey splotches, like islands on the map of one pale, muscly landscape. On his right forearm, there's an artful freckle-splodge that, if I squint, looks a bit like the Bat symbol. My eyes zoom in on it; but when I can tell Eddie is getting extra-impatient, I take a deep breath.

"OK, Eddie. Here it is. I'm going to ask you to do something, and I need you not to freak out, cos I'm very close to freaking out myself, and I need you to tell me that it's all going to be fine—"

"Alba – babble much?" Eddie growls. "Get to the point."

I drag my eyes away from his mammoth arms, and I stare up at his face.

"Ed – I need to borrow one of your bikes. No, actually ... I need you to take me for a ride. On a motorbike. And I need you to do it now, before I change my mind."

Eddie blinks at me. I stare back at him; my carefree giant of a friend, with his moon-face and man-voice and body like the side of a barn. His pale green eyes are unreadable. But beneath his freckles, Eddie's face has drained of colour.

"Alba," he says. "You really wanna do this with *me*? I mean, hell. You know ... I'd do anything for you. But I don't think I'm the person you want holding your hand while you have a last-day-on-earth epiphany or some shit—"

I stamp my boot. "Come on, Eddie! You still have those dirt bikes, right?"

"Yeah, we do ... but ... *feck*. Alba. Are you sure? I mean – you know there's a reason why we tried to keep 'em out of sight, right?"

I swallow a sudden grapefruit-sized lump in my throat. Part of me just wants to throw myself on to Eddie's broad chest and bawl. "Ed, I know. I understand what you guys have done for me. And you have no idea how much I love you all for that, but –" I take another deep breath, and hold it for a few seconds before I exhale. "That's why I'm asking you for help. I'm *not* sure, but – I need to do this. It's ... necessary. Will you help me, Ed? Please?"

Eddie stares at me. He dusts his hands on his jeans. "Course," he says quietly. "Just promise you're not having a breakdown or something. My dad and his midlife crisis is more than I can handle at this point. One fecking mental situation at a time."

"Ed, honestly? I think I am having the giant mother of all mental situations. But … I'm not sure that's a bad thing. I may change my mind if I end up as a bloodied smear on the underside of a cow though."

Eddie drapes an arm around my shoulder, and I make a valiant effort not to stumble under his weight. "Alba, these last few days I thought I'd seen every goddamned weirdness in the universe. But this? I reckon if the mer-people from Uranus do blast us off the planet tonight, I'm only gonna be a little bit surprised."

He steers me toward the pebbly path at the back of his house. For once in my life I have zero desire to yammer incessantly. We walk together in nervous silence, toward the tin shack in the shadows of the Palmers' milking shed.

Eddie flicks on the naked bulb as my eyes adjust to the dark. It's strangely cool inside, and the shoutyness from the north paddock seems muffled, too. Shelves of tools and paint tins line the cobwebby walls, but my eyes are drawn instinctively to the three covered silhouettes in the middle of the concrete floor.

Ed brushes aside the spider webs, and he yanks the tarp off a familiar shape.

It's the red Honda that I haven't seen in years. Small, sleek, and less powerful than anything Dad would have really been interested in, but nevertheless – there it is. Two wheels, one seat, keychain of a mini can of Heineken dangling from the ignition, and an aura of smugness that makes me want to kick it right in its stupid steel sprockets.

Eddie wheels the bike to the mouth of the shed, and he swings one leg effortlessly over it. "Howie'll kill me if we take the Bushlander. This one'll have to do."

I know enough about motorbikes to recognize that this seat is in no way built for two people. Eddie scoots his butt backwards as far as he can go, his feet braced on the ground at either side. He looks at me uncertainly.

"Alba, maybe you wanna, I dunno – take it slow? Sit for a bit, get a feel for the seat again—"

"Ed, I don't have time to mess around!" I adjust my headscarf and wince at the pitch that my voice has adopted. I remember the advice of Miss Oxenbury, my kindergarten teacher, and I take it down a couple of octaves. "I figure, it's gotta be like ripping off a bandaid, right? One quick move and all that."

I march toward the bike and swing my leg over in front of Eddie's. I settle into the seat with my back straight and my head held high.

And then I climb off again, and I huddle on the concrete slab with my head on my knees till my breathing doesn't resemble an asthmatic warthog in need of a lung transplant. Eventually, somehow, I push myself upright. Through tear-blurred eyes I see Eddie looking down at me apprehensively. And then, suddenly, the hesitation in his face vanishes.

"Alba, here's the thing. I dunno what you reckon this is going to achieve. Don't get me wrong, I'm all for getting back on the horse, but—" He pats the seat. "But this? You're not gonna be unlocking the secrets of the universe or some shit on here. We'll drive around the south paddock. You might pass out.

You might not. But if you're gonna do it – just fecking do it already! Stop thinking so hard and … go with your gut!" He throws his arms up helplessly. And then he holds a hand out to me.

I stand up again, and I take Ed's hand. This time, when I swing my leg over, I squeeze my eyes shut and grip the handlebars as if somehow I can will my hands into staying put when my body seems determined to escape. I focus on the seat beneath me, and on the brick-wall bulk of Eddie behind me, and his familiar smell of hay and sweat and sugar soap.

Ed leans forwards and places his hands over mine, his shoulders all but caging me in. I allow myself a tiny, shameful sliver of consolation that, if we do crash, Eddie's mass should at least help cushion my fall.

"Alba, you just say the word and I'll pull over. Come to think of it, maybe we should have a signal? Like, if you want me to stop."

"You mean a safe word? Ed, I love you, but I'm just not ready to explore those kind of farm-boy fantasies."

I don't need to turn around to know that Eddie is blushing, right up to the hairline of his shaved head. "Jesus," he mumbles. "You really don't want to put those pictures in my head before we do this thing, Alba."

I still my shaky, sweaty hands and squeeze my eyes closed again. "Sorry, Ed. You know I babble when I'm nervy. I'm ready. I'm warning you though, I might yak."

Behind me, I feel the rumble of his laughter. "Kay. Puke I can deal with. Here we go."

Eddie's fingers tighten gently around my hand. Together, we squeeze the clutch, kick the starter, and with a spluttery cough the motorbike rumbles to life.

I breathe. And I let myself evoke the memory of that very last time I was on a bike, with the icy winter wind burning my cheeks, and the leather-clad arms of my dad around me. The weirdest thing? It doesn't reduce me to a puddle of moosh and tears, as I sort of expected it would. Not even the rattling of the engine that shakes my bones, or the sound that turns my insides to jelly, ever since the day Dad's bike rumbled out of the driveway and never rumbled back.

With a jolt, the ground whips away. Sudden yellow dances behind my eyes as we pull out of the dark. And then there's that whooshy, familiar feeling of abandon and speed.

I guess what I was looking for was that moment of unquestionable *rightness.* In my head, I pictured me standing upright, tall and unwavering, like a burly, less green She-Hulk. I was kinda planning on *whooping* into the sunset as the wind whipped my hair, a triumphant yell that would send the birds scattering from the trees. Seriously, if I ever do draw Cinnamon Girl on the back of a motorcycle, her scarlet hair is gonna be doing all sorts of artful billowing in the breeze.

In reality? I cling to the handlebars, huddled backwards against Eddie, who keeps a tight hold till we hit a smoother surface. Then he loosens his grip and gives me more control of the ride. I lean when he leans, just like I was taught, back when I would have happily spent all my waking hours on the seat of a motorcycle with my dad. My breath comes in sharp gasps, but I don't pass out or puke, which, I have to say, I am mildly proud of.

At some point I manage to talk one eye into opening. We're somewhere on the trail at the back of the Palmers' property, where the thick bushland meets the open pasture. A few cows glance in our direction, but mostly their black-and-white faces seem wholly disinterested in our shenanigans. With my eye open, I realise that we're not exactly fanging it; at the rate Eddie is going, Rosie Addler and Lucy Albington on one of their power walks could probably outpace us.

I force open my other eye. And as Eddie circles past the tree line, I elbow him lightly in the ribs, and I nudge his hands. Eddie seems to understand, cos he pulls his hands away completely and lets me steer us home.

I accelerate. The fading sunlight glints off the Honda, making my vision hazy, and the warm breeze flaps my scarf against my ears. But there is no whooping involved. No screaming into the sunset, or jeez, not even a chorus of exultant music in my head, cos the only song I can hear as we head back toward the shed is a sing-along of 'Love Shack' coming from the north paddock.

I stop the bike, and Eddie kills the engine. I tumble sideways off the seat and press my forehead into the dirt. And I burst out laughing.

Eddie drops hurriedly beside me. "Jesus, Alba, are you all right? Feck, knew I should've got the girls out here first – dammit – do you need tea?"

"Eddie," I manage to say through teary laughter. "I've just put myself through possibly the most traumatic experience of my life. I have stared death in the face, Ed! Like, ruthlessly exorcised my demons and whatnot. And *tea* is the best you can do?"

"Bloody hell!" he shouts. "I don't know!"

I grab Eddie around the waist and pull myself on to my knees. And then I grab his cheeks, and I plant a giant smoochy kiss on to his forehead. Eddie's raspberry-jam freckle-face turns the colour of a beetroot macaron.

"Francis Edwin Palmer. You are the most awesome of all things made of awesomeness. You really are the best person I know. You do know that, right?"

Eddie clears his throat. "Well, Jesus. I didn't do anything. Apart from, y'know, not riding us into a cow. But … are you really all right?"

I fall backwards on to my butt. "Honestly? Ed, I think I'm really, really fine. I just *am*. Who would've thunk it, hey?"

Eddie shuffles into the shade of the shed, and I scoot around beside him. He glances down at me. "So … you find whatever you were looking for?"

I peer up as a few more helicopters circle overhead. I can only imagine what we must look like from above. Through the PA system a voice bellows, "Welcome to the end of the universe, Eden Valley!" and a cheer erupts from the front of the farm.

"Ed, I know this is going to sound super vague, but honestly? I don't know what I'm looking for. You were right about one thing, though – I don't think I'm ever gonna have a lightning-bolt moment. At least, not going twenty kays an hour on the back of a Honda."

"Then what the feck was that about?"

I lean back against the cool shed. "You and I ... we weren't really friends yet, were we, Ed? Back when my dad ..."

"No. But I remember," he says quietly. "I used to see you in your yard, when it was just weeds and that trampoline ..." He clears his throat. "After it happened, I used to see you and Grady sitting out there heaps. You guys never did do much of anything. Except clump together like you were welded that way, looking like life had walloped you both in the gonads. And it's not like I could've missed it, Alba. Jesus, whole town was nutsy about your dad. And G-man and I'd just started hanging out a bit ... he was pretty messed up about it, too. Yeah. I remember. It was shithouse," he says helplessly.

I hug my knees into my chest. "Yeah. It was. And that's the thing, Eddie. I think, despite everything, it was never the fiery crash bit that was the most scary. I think the thing that terrified me most was maybe the … anticipation? Of reliving those things? Of having to feel any of *that* again."

Eddie is silent for a long time. "So what you're saying," he says slowly, "is that you were more freaked out by the idea of freaking out than the actual thing you thought would make you freak out itself? Jesus. That is pretty … angsty. Even for you."

I laugh. "I know it doesn't make sense, but—"

"Nah," he says, shaking his head, "it makes sense. Dunno if you are aware of it, Alba, but you do have this knack for grabbing hold of stuff and hanging on like your life depends on it. You're kinda shit at letting go. With bad stuff … and the rest, too."

I thread my arm through his and rest my head on his sun-warmed shoulder. "Can't I have just one epiphany at a time, Ed? I get that I'm, like, a hoarder of nostalgia and whatnot. But I love this place so much. I love *you* guys. You, and Petey and Tia and Caroline and … I mean, how lucky are we? I know I'll never find friends like you guys again."

Eddie snorts. "Well, I for one am fecking irreplaceable, for sure." He leans his head against mine with a sigh. "You know, you guys – all of you – you're so busy planning and stressing and running around like chooks with no heads. Looking backwards and forwards and everywhere but right in front of your noses—"

"Hey, *I'm* not! I've never wanted to do anything but be right here and now—"

"Uh-huh. *Right.* This from the girl who spends half her life staring out the bakery windows with her head in fantasyland? Shit, if I had a dollar for every time someone used the phrase 'Alba, are you paying attention', I'd be retiring to an island in Hawaii with that chick from last month's *Maxim.*"

I untangle my arm from his. "What are you saying, Eddie?"

Ed crosses his arms. "I'm *saying*, Alba, that you can harp on about being happy all you like. And I'm not saying you're not – just that you have other stuff you want, too. Stuff that's been flapping about in your head ever since I've known you. Stuff that keeps you with one foot right here, and one foot feck knows where in your head. What are you afraid of?" He sighs again. "And the other question would be – why aren't you talking to Grady 'bout all this?"

"Domenic doesn't want to talk to me," I manage to say. "If he wants to be a sook, then so be it. I haven't done anything wrong."

Eddie squints up at the circling helicopters. "Sarah Jane. You are a very cool chick. But seriously?" He taps me gently on the head with one of his sausage fingers. "I think you're too scared to make a call on anything, right, so you just close your eyes and hope everything'll keep drifting along – but somewhere in there I think you know that you flash a smile, and that guy would jump in front of a bullet for you—"

"Eddie, that is *so* unfair – and besides, Grady just isn't that sentimental—"

"No, it's really not unfair. Have you even seen his bedroom?"

"I've been in Grady's room a thousand times."

"Yeah, but, have you actually *seen* his room? Think about it. Feck, Alba ..." He shakes his head. "Trust me. Just look."

I swallow, but my mouth has become Sahara-dry. I stare at the horizon, as if the setting sun might illuminate the answers that feel on the very edge of my consciousness. "Eddie," I whisper. "I know what

I'm doing here. I *like* this version of me. What if … I'm no good at the rest?"

Eddie stands and helps me to my feet. And then he drapes one arm around me in a quick half-hug before he grabs the bike again. "Yeah. But then again – what if you don't have forever to figure it out?"

He turns his back on me and wheels the Honda into the shed, leaving me standing in the muted sunshine with this abrupt sensation of vertigo. It's the strangest thing – scary, sure, and daunting as anything – but not entirely unpleasant. It feels sort of like the Earth is realigning beneath my feet.

"Eddie – thank you," I call out. "For everything. If the world does end, I want you to know, I'm sorry for all those times I called you an arsebag. I'm really, really glad that you were my friend."

Eddie gives me a two-fingered wave. "Feck off," he says with a grin as he shuts the door behind him.

FOURTEEN

I take the main road back to Albany's, the last of the sunlight leaving the Valley as I sprint home. I'm not sure what my face is doing, but whatever expression is on it seems to be working, as people hurry to get out of my way, my boots kicking up beer cans and empty two-minute noodle packs as I run.

I scoot into my bedroom with the tips of my fingers tingling like they've brushed a bakery burner. I grab a new sketchpad and a handful of graphite pencils, and I sit, cross-legged, on my floor. I give myself a minute to catch my breath. And then I place a pencil down, and my hands begin to move.

I sketch out some borderlines, creating a splash panel that takes up almost the entire space. I ditch the warehouse apartment and the industrial furniture, that, now that I think about it, I'm pretty sure I'd unconsciously nicked from *V for Vendetta*.

In their place, I draw the rough line of a blank, hilly horizon. I fill the top half of the panel with a starry sky, a shadowy line of red gum trees standing guard in the distance. In the foreground, I draw my Cinnamon Girl. She is facing away from me, dwarfed by the vastness of the space around her. I draw her without a whole lot of flair; her hands are by her sides, her feet planted lightly apart, the angle of her head tilted upwards with her curls spilling down her back. There are a bazillion details that I want to cram into this picture: a chipped white weatherboard house, and a yellow one that looks like gingerbread, and a family of fading garden gnomes, and a pub with two mad mums in the window, and a motorbike with a beaming, broad-shouldered rider, and a chubby kid in *Toy Story* jammies, and a boy in the background with curly hair and a sweet, shy smile.

I add a few soft contour lines to the fields, and some shading to mark the light of the off-page moon. But I don't add anything more. There's something about the cleanness of the composition that I really like. And the night sky will be an ace space for some lettering, once I figure out what I want it to say.

Instead, I add another panel on the right side of the page; narrow and vertical with a thin, translucent border. I draw Cinnamon Girl close up and in profile here, her waves of hair billowing behind her and bleeding over the edges of the frames. Her face is calmer than I've seen it in a long time; a little smug maybe, but hey, I think that might just be her. I don't add any background – she could be in Paris, or New York, or in a rubble-strewn diner at the end of the world, or stomping purposefully across the moon. I could place her anywhere, or nowhere at all. I spend some time pencilling her solid legs, one foot in front of the other, resolutely marching through her unfilled frame. I smudge a pinkie over the detailing in her giant boots, as her front foot steps forwards and disappears off the page.

I lean my head against the couch, the world coming back into focus. The music from the farm has a fevered, crazy undertone, the sounds of one epic party kicking into gear – potentially, the party to end all parties.

I close my eyes. My body is buzzy, the strangest mix of stomach-churning nerviness, and calm, clear certainty. When I touch my fingers to my lips, I realize that I am smiling.

I jump into a quick shower and slip into my cherry-red sailor dress and Chucks. I shake out my hair. I smooth down my fringe. And I force my feet to walk out of my dim, safe bedroom.

Mum is frowning at her phone at one of the bakery counters. She glances up as I stick my head into the kitchen.

"Hey, Mum, I'm going out. What are you doing tonight?"

Mum waves me over. "Cleo's stuck at work but I'll head to hers as soon as she finishes. You'll meet me there? Really don't want you wandering around on your own tonight, Alba."

"Why? Seriously, Mama, if Thanos is planning on vaporising the planet, I'm better placed than most people here to spot it, don't you reckon?"

Mum rolls her eyes. "Yes, your particular skill set will no doubt come in handy. But regardless, promise you'll find me before midnight. And don't rely on your phone, either." Mum chews hesitantly at her piercing. "You know, Grady was here looking for you a little while ago," she says lightly. "He skulked around the kitchen with a face like the backside of a cow before he took off again. Bub … is everything all right with you two?"

"He came back?" I square my shoulders. "No. It's not all right. Not even a little bit. But Mum, Domenic is insane if he thinks I'm gonna let him just sulk this out. I have things to get off my chest, and he is going to listen to me, even if I have to hogtie him first. The world doesn't get to end before I have a chance to say what I need to say."

Mum smiles. "Good to know." She stands, her smile wavering, and her eyes get all misty as they linger longingly on me.

"Uh-oh. What is it, Angie? You have weepy nostalgia-face."

Mum shakes her head. "It's just, sometimes, I look at you, and you look like him … and when you get all loud and bolshy, you sound just like him…"

"Jeez. Thanks, Mum. Good to know I could be mistaken for a six-foot man who was built like a grizzly bear." I smile at her. "And anyway. You know Dad would probably claim he looks better in a dress than me."

Mum laughs. "Yeah, he was always way too enamoured with those legs of his."

I stalk across the kitchen and wrap Mum in a hug. In the last couple of years, our Dad conversations have usually been reserved for the moments when one of us needs a good, solid bawl. But strangely, I don't feel all that teary. What I feel is that buzzy impatience again, a sense of purpose propelling me forwards.

Mum steps back and grins at me. "You'd better go. You know, that boy of yours might be stubborn as all hell. But he doesn't know how to hold a grudge. And he's never known how to be mad at you, Sarah."

I take a deep breath. "That's what I'm counting on, Mum."

I glance around the kitchen, registering for the first time an unfamiliar sweet smell lingering in the air. A few cooling trays of pastry parcels are sitting on the far countertop.

I untangle myself from Mum's arms. "Hey, Mama? You trying something new? What have you been making?"

Mum glances over her shoulder. "The Eversons keep getting more strawberries than they can store in this heat, and there's only so much jam Donna Ridley can handle. Mr Bridgeman wanted me to whip up something for his dessert menu, and I thought, apple and strawberry tarts aren't fancy, but they're quick, and they'll be good with cider. I never thought I'd say it, but I'm actually *really* sick of making strudel."

Mum looks up. She stops talking. My guess is, because of the panic, which morphs into horror on my face. I gape at the counter again. I can't be sure, but the rows of little pastry rectangles in one tray don't look quite as neat as they should.

"Angela. You didn't leave him alone in here?"

Mum's face drains of colour. "I didn't think – I was so busy – but he would have asked if he thought—"

"Mum! When does Grady ever *ask*? You know he turns into Pac-Man when food's in front of him! He trusts us to keep that stuff out of his reach! He trusts us—"

Mum leaps toward the counter, her hands grabbing for the landline.

But I'm already halfway down my bluestone path at a speed that would make Captain Marvel herself proud, the incongruous dance song blasting from the field like a terrible, pounding lament in my head.

I heave open the front door of the yellow house and barrel inside, almost braining myself after tripping over Clouseau in the doorway.

"Grady! Cleo – Anthony? Is anyone here?"

I stare at the useless mobile in my hand, doubled over as I try to catch my breath. The entire house is flooded with light. Grady is always flicking the lights off after his mum; no way he would have left the house like this. I run down the hallway, past Anthony's bombshell bedroom, and the hallway cupboard with the broken door that Grady's in the middle of fixing.

I throw open his bedroom door. My eyes scan his unmade bed and Clouseau's chewed doggy basket and the blue bookshelves, stacked with novels and lined with basketball trophies. One wall is covered with the New York canvas he bought on one of our city trips last year. Above his desk is the giant pinboard he's had since forever, thick with random things. It's been here for so long that I've never bothered looking at it closely, but Eddie's gravel voice is suddenly bouncing in my head, so I stumble toward it and let my eyes run over the junk.

Grady seems to have no order for the stuff on here, just bits pinned on top of bits. There's funny dog memes printed from the net, and our year-twelve graduation flyer with a half-circle coffee stain. There's a few photos of Clouseau, and a black-and-white pic of Anthony from Merindale's paper that time he won the basketball club meat raffle. There's articles of the stuff Grady finds interesting enough to keep, and some law-school flyers from the uni sessions he's been trekking out to all year.

On the far right of the pinboard is a badge we picked up at Melbourne Uni open day earlier this year; a white disc with *I ♥ Maths* on it, which, for some reason, Grady seemed to find hilarious. Beneath that, peeking out from behind a Threadless receipt, is a tiny piece of green ribbon, twisted into a loop and secured with a pin.

I peer closer at the scrap. It's familiar, in a brain-tingly way. I unpin it from the board and run it between my fingers. And then I remember.

It's a bow from this dress I wore to Lucy and George Albington's wedding when I was in grade six. I remember, cos Grady and I snuck out of the reception at the school hall to climb the new equipment in the playground. I remember, because I got the dress caught on the slide, and a giggly Grady had to cut me loose with a steak knife.

I stare at the slip in my hand. The distant music thumps through my feet, but I can't move, and I can't breathe.

I keep staring at the pinboard, at the stuff he has saved, and it's like one of those magic-eye pictures coming into focus, fragments merging to form a clear image. There's a fading postcard from the year-nine art show at Merindale, the very first nervy time I displayed one of my drawings. There's the lanyard with my old bus pass, carefully held in place with a silver pin. There's an unused pair of movie tickets, the comedy we never actually saw on our ill-fated Valentine's dare-date. And in between Grady's detritus are bits of my art; some nothing more than doodles on Albany's napkins or scraps torn from the margins of his school notebooks. There's half a seventh-birthday card with my inexpert drawing of a Labrador puppy, and a carefully flattened piece of sketchbook with a skeleton of superhero Pete, and a beer coaster duck-hat from all those years ago at the Junction pub.

I turn around. In the shelf of his nightstand sits the Paddington bear with the missing nose that I gave him for his birthday when we were five, and beneath his lamp, the tacky Big Banana snow-globe I bought for him on that road trip when we were eleven. Sitting carefully atop a basketball trophy is the teeny plastic Bambi I won from a machine in the city a few years ago; I tossed it at him, assuming he'd just bin it, because really, no one needs a plastic Bambi.

And stuck on a skewy angle on the side of his desk lamp is a giant pink post-it: a sketch of Grady with a chalk outline, and my all-caps comic-book lettering: *STRAWBERRY BIOHAZARD. HANDS OFF D.G.*

And I realize that my tears are bordering on the hysterical, but I draw upon whatever fraction of control I still have left, and run out of his room again.

Main Street is chaos. I push through the crowds, past the Taco Truck, and Mrs Garabaldi's homemade barricades that are now covered with multiple penises in assorted sizes. And then I skid to a dead stop, my pathway blocked, my blood throbbing so hard I swear I can see it burbling behind my eyes.

My nemesis, the penny-farthing, is wedged right in my path.

"Get your stupid dumb-arse hipster poser bike out of my way, arsebag!" I yell. Bike-man looks down at me blankly.

"Chill out, little lady," he says. "You're messing with the vibe."

"Feck. *Off!*" I scream, except I don't say *feck*, and I kick his stupid oversized tyre for emphasis as I hurl myself over the footpath barricades and tear past him. I think I detect some alarmed looks, but I don't stop to think about them.

Because all I can think about is Grady.

Grady, who slept in my bed for weeks when his dad left, curled against me like a puppy, his face damp with tears. Grady, who camped in my room for months after my dad died, awkward and insomnia-plagued but right there beside me whenever I woke from a nightmare. Grady, who moved out of the house he was born in when me and Mum moved in, but who was only ever happy that I co-opted the bedroom that was once his. Grady, who took me to *South Pacific* for my birthday in year eleven, even though he looked like he was being waterboarded for most of it, and who trekked with me to every comic store in every corner of the city, even though he's never really been into comics. Grady, whose face gets all glimmery when he looks at my art and who waits for hours while I draw without getting antsy or bored. Grady, who would do anything not to see me cry.

Dr Lucas's office appears before me. Across the road, the Corner Arms is spewing forth a mess of sweaty people in sparkly wigs and matching bathing suits. In a distant corner of my brain, I have this flash of them stranded in a post-apocalyptic wasteland, huddled together in a baffled mass with nothing but pints of cider and noisemakers in hand.

I barrel into the doctor's building. Even though it's way past office hours, the tiny waiting room is choked with sunburned people. A St John's Ambulance man is holding an ice pack over the head of a groaning guy who has an inflatable frog floatie clasped around his waist. I'm not even going to ask.

Cleo is behind the reception desk. She stands hurriedly when I push aside a woman in a kaftan and stumble toward her.

"Where is he? Where's Grady?" I gasp. I can't catch my breath.

Cleo's eyes are wide. "He's gone," she says quietly.

I close my eyes. In my head, I'm floating in a bouncy castle. Maybe I am experiencing a dissociative episode or whatnot, but out of all the places I could check out to, I'm not sure why my subconscious has picked this one. Suddenly, I realize where I am. It's Merindale show, and I'm six years old. It's getting dark, and the show is closing, and I have no idea where my parents are, but I can't seem to make myself care. I can hear Grady calling me; he's stuck somewhere outside, and his voice is getting frantic, but I'm having way too much fun bouncing around in here. And anyway, I know he'll wait as long as he needs to. I can take as much time as I like, cos even though he's mad, there's just no way he'd go anywhere without me.

The earth is shifting, the ground tumbling beneath me. So it takes me several moments to process that Cleo didn't seem too fazed that her youngest son has passed into the great beyond. Cleo seemed to have been flipping through a copy of *Craft Weekly*, and eating a licorice whip.

I drift to the reception desk. "Cleo? Answer me carefully. Grady. Has. Gone. Where?"

She shakes her head. "Beats me. He took off like his bum was on fire about half an hour ago. My guess is he's home, though judging by the mood he was in when he tore out of here, who knows?"

"You mean he's OK?"

Cleo snorts. "Well, he's vying with Mrs Garabaldi for the title of craziest cranky pants in the Valley. But apart from a bruised ego and a sore head, he's fine."

"Jesus Christ! Cleo! Be specific!" I yell. And then I burst into tears.

Cleo hurries around the desk. "Alba, honey, what on Earth is going on with you two? Domenic has been moping around the house like the world's already ended, and tonight, my eldest son hauls my baby in here, apparently after dragging him out of an actual *fight*. In his entire life, Domenic has barely raised his voice. And now I find myself playing mother to a character from *Sons of Anarchy*. Help me out here?"

She rubs my back until my hitchy sobs peter out. I grab a handful of tissues from the counter and blow my nose. When my eyes clear enough for me to look at Cleo, she's watching me with that mum-look of knowing sympathy, and I'm pretty sure she doesn't need an answer.

"Cleo, I have to go," I say through sniffles. "When you see my mum—"

"I'll tell her you've been waylaid. Vital End of Days stuff," she says with a grin. "Angie'll understand. Hey, if we don't make it to tomorrow, you're probably safe from a bollocking anyway."

I give her a hug. "Thanks, Second Mama. Sorry for the hysterics. For what it's worth, I think you'll kick arse in a dystopian future. Like Sarah Connor, or Tank Girl."

"Really? Always pictured myself more Tina Turner in *Mad Max*," Cleo says as she steers me gently out the door. "It's the outfit," she yells as I scoot away into the glowstick-lit crowds. "I'd totally rock that chain-mail suit!"

I check his house, where the lights are still blazing, and Albany's, where Mum is belting out a cheery Smashing Pumpkins song in the bathroom. I stick my head in at the Junction, where a beaming Mr Grey is bustling at the door in a T-shirt that says *Charlie Don't Surf* on it. The atmosphere is heavy with this frenzied eagerness as I hurry through my streets, like, everyone is determined to prove to everyone else that they are having a really *really* amazing time. But every now and then I pass some people – a couple, or a group of friends, or this dad with a gaggle of kids – who are huddled together in their own private bubbles, cocooned in their little worlds against the mess and madness. Every so often, I pass someone glancing surreptitiously up at the sky.

I suppose my friends will be somewhere in the middle of the Palmers' farm by now. A part of my brain whispers at me that I should be down there with them, that without Tia and Caroline and Petey and Ed, I'm all unanchored and adrift.

I take the road past the garage, and I quicken my pace.

I turn around briefly to face the Valley. The view from the top of the hill is epic; so much light and colour, one rolling sea of people-energy. A laser clock is beaming numbers on to the screen behind the stage – a thirteen-minute-and-thirty-one-second countdown, visible even from way up here. The clock fizzles into a school of laser fish that shimmies into the darkness, before splashing back on the screen again. I think I saw something like that on the last

Grammy Awards. At some point, Mr Palmer is *really* gonna have some explaining to do.

I keep moving. It's quieter up here, and calmer. There are people chilling on picnic blankets, locals and strangers just taking in the view. A handful of kids are running around with sparklers, oblivious to the expectancy around them. I scan my eyes over them as I hustle past, but honestly? I think I know where I'm headed. The face I'm looking for might as well have a neon Bat Signal flashing right above it. Pretty sure I could find it anywhere in the dark.

He's sitting beneath a tree in his grey jeans and flying squirrel T-shirt and worn Vans that really need to be replaced one of these days. He's staring, unfocused, over the Valley, as he scuffs a stick absent-mindedly in the dirt. His curls seem to be more lifeless than normal. And on his right cheek, the telltale bruisey sign of boy-stupidity.

He sees me as I step out of the shadows, and he stands up quickly. But he doesn't meet my eye.

"Well. There you are." I clear my throat. "Here I am, worried sick, while you've been gallivanting around town with your no-good pals, getting up to mischief…" I take a deep breath. "Wanna tell me what happened?"

He's looking somewhere to the left of my face. "Nothing happened," he says sullenly. "I went looking for Daniel. Obviously, my reflexes suck arse."

I baulk. "*Daniel* hit you?"

Grady winces as he touches the raw spot on his cheekbone. "Naw. His manager did."

"His manager! Jesus."

"Yeah. He said, and I quote, 'there's no way some punk from hicksville is messing up my star client's money maker.' I think even Gordon seemed surprised at the dodge cliché. Not as surprised as me and my face, but—"

"Grady, are you completely stupid! What the hell were you thinking?"

He finally snaps his eyes to me. "What was I thinking? I was thinking, Alba, that Daniel Gordon is a moronic butt-monkey who deserves several punches to the testicles. I was thinking that if I didn't smack the smug right off his arsebag face, I was going to bust a blood vessel. He had no right to even *dare* give that book to you."

I stamp my foot in the dirt. It's juvenile, I know,

but sue me, I'm pissed. "Domenic," I growl. "I'm *fine.* You really thought I was going to freak out and, like, develop an eating disorder or something? Have you *met* me?"

He runs his hand frantically across the back of his neck. "No. I guess not. You're smarter than he is, though that's not saying much. But Alba, you have to know, you are amazing and Daniel Gordon's eyesight is worse than his shit acting if he can't see that. You are perfect and beautiful and—"

"You think I'm beautiful?" I say. It's possibly not the most important thing I should be focusing on, but a butterfly army is on manoeuvres in my belly, and my brain zooms in on that one thing cos it has no idea what else to say.

Grady's cheeks flush. "You don't know that?"

"Well, yeah, but I didn't think … you saw me that way. You never said you thought that about me?"

He looks at me for the longest time, as a guy wearing a novelty pirate hat yells something unintelligible in our direction before falling into the bushes.

"Yes, I did," Grady says quietly. "So many times. When we were ten, at that stupid school barn dance … you were wearing a red dress and your first pair of heels

… and when we were fourteen, and you dressed up as a pumpkin for Anthony's Halloween party, and you got annoyed because the other girls were dressed as sexy cats and stuff but I told you that you made a really beautiful pumpkin … and last year, when we went to Comic Con and you wore that thing with the lace … but you were more interested in meeting the lady who writes *Batgirl…*"

"I don't remember," I whisper.

And Grady makes this sound, which is something like, *gahrhaah*!

"Do you remember *anything*?" he yelps. "Do you remember grade-five camp? You had chicken pox, and I ended up in hospital cos I ate a bunch of strawberries just so I could stay home, too. Do you remember year-nine holidays? Dad wanted me with him, but I faked frigging *appendicitis* so I didn't have to go. Do you remember this year, when I spent *six frigging hours* in one day on the train, when I should have just stayed the night in the city with Dad—"

"Grady, I don't understand—"

"I know you don't," he says helplessly. "You never have. You don't understand why I haven't been able to sleep properly in weeks – not since you told me you were thinking about staying here. You've never understood ... that I can't go anywhere where you aren't, Alba. You've never understood that I can't stand being away from you, even for a weekend. Not even for a day." He squeezes his eyes shut. "You just don't *get* that I am so hopelessly in love with you that the thought of moving away, of not seeing you every day, makes me feel like someone is yanking out an arm, or – wait, let me put it in words you *actually* understand, Sarah ... like I'm that *X-Men* chick, you know, the weather one with the hair, when that guy does that thing and zaps all her powers—"

"You first-named me," I whisper. "You first-named me *now*?"

He covers his face with his hands. And then he looks up at me, and his face is so sad that my stupid tears spill over again.

"Alba ... I have loved you for *seventeen years.* If it takes that long to get over you – do you know how old I'm gonna be? I'll be living with a thousand dogs and collecting spoons or whatever guy losers do ... because I've tried and tried to want someone else, but you are the only person in the whole world who I *know* I belong with. And I know you can't care about any of that, because you're too busy kissing Daniel cheese-head Gordon—"

"Wait. Grady. You think I kissed Daniel?"

He shrugs, still refusing to look at me. "He pretty much said as much. He's been needling me and hinting at … stuff with you, ever since he and his stupid abs came back to town. And I know how you two were when we were kids … I'm not an idiot…" He kicks at a stray streamer floating past. "Why wouldn't you kiss him?"

"Why? Because, *Domenic*, you know I don't kiss just anyone – despite plenty of offers over the years, and not just from Daniel fecking Gordon, either." Grady looks up with a start, cos I rarely swear, but whatever. I'm on a roll, my hands all shaky and energized.

"I told you I was done with randoms – the only person I'm ever going to bother kissing is the person I am madly in love with. Sue me for being sentimental, but I'm still holding on to that. Even if the world is ending. Even if Daniel Gordon is the last guy in it. And even if he does have a spectacular six-pack."

Grady scowls. "I've heard enough about his dumb-arse six-pack. Jesus, that guy is a moron, and a giant sleaze, and hello, one of your gnomes has more personality—"

"God, why are you so obsessed with Daniel! It almost sounds like *you* wanna kiss him! And why would *I* kiss him if he's such a moron?"

"Why wouldn't you!" he yells back.

"What *possible* reason would I have for kissing Daniel, when the person I love more than anybody else in the world is standing right in front of me?"

I take a step backwards. He's still scowling at his feet, because my boy may be smart, and great at lots of things, but quick on the uptake he is not. I can practically see the moment my words sink into his stupid beautiful curly head.

He looks up slowly, and his eyes meet mine.

I take a deep breath, suddenly more nervous than I've been in my whole entire life. But I give him my best, most dazzling smile, cos despite everything, I know it works better than any words.

"Hey, Grady?"

"Yeah, Alba?" he whispers.

"If you don't kiss me now, I might change my mind about smooching Daniel Gordon. Hell, leave me standing here for much longer, and Eddie's gonna start looking like a viable alternative—"

He covers the space between us in one frantic bound, and he grabs my face in his hands. He stares down at me, his eyes travelling over mine – and then he freezes again. Funny thing is, I know exactly why. I know we are entering completely unchartered territory here, an alternate-universe, *Infinite Crisis* us. Ending one story and starting another that neither of us knows the rules for.

But still. Jeez. I have to do everything around here.

So I stand on my toes, and I kiss him.

If the universe worked the way it's supposed to, then this is the moment fireworks should have exploded over the fields. At the very least, the song from the stage should have changed to something more romantic than 'The Final Countdown', which is a totally rubbish song that I only know cos it features on Cleo's Zumba playlist.

But none of those things happen. Instead, the sounds in the gully seem to slowly disappear. The music, and voices, and pirate-hat-man's puking, fade into the background.

Grady's hands are immobile, his lips unresponsive for a few slow seconds. Then his entire body seems to just *dissolve*, with the teeniest of gasps against my lips. His arms wind around me, and my hands curve around him and our lips shyly find their way. His kiss is soft and strange and perfect; an undiscovered, full-colour volume of this person I've loved my whole life.

Eventually, somehow, I drag my lips away. His eyes in the darkness are all shiny and wide, and he's looking at me with that dazed, adoring thing again, a brand-new look of his that turns my insides to moosh and jelly.

I giggle. "This is weird."

Grady tucks my hair behind my ears, and he's smiling like an idiot, but he shakes his head defiantly. "No. It isn't," he murmurs as his lips softly brush the side of my neck.

"No. It really isn't," I manage to reply. My brain is occupied by his lips, and by my hands, which have found their way beneath his T-shirt to the warm skin on his stomach, and all my brain can process is *ooh, boy-muscles!* and that they're another part of him I don't know yet, but that they feel *really* nice under my hands. "You have abs. I didn't know that," I say distractedly.

"Sarah ... do you have any idea what that feels like?" he whispers.

I drag my hands away from his belly and loop

them around him instead. "Don't call me that, Grady. It isn't my name. I mean, it is, but it's not *me*. You know why everyone calls me Alba, right?"

He grins. "It was my fault, wasn't it?"

"Yes, it was your fault, doofus! Like, hello, two-year-old Domenic, learn to pronounce *Albany*, it's really not that hard—"

He leans toward me again. But through the haze, I realize that the music has stopped. The people around us are on their feet. The night sky is suddenly hushed and still.

I think we may have missed something significant.

Counting. There was counting.

When I glance over my shoulder, the flashing fish numbers on the stage are blank.

I glance back at Grady. He looks at me, and his eyes widen.

There is a pause in the universe, what feels like a frozen moment when the bodies in Eden Valley are holding their breath. I could swear I felt the breeze kick up a notch; that weird midnight summer wind that raises the hairs on the back of my neck.

I clutch on to the front of his T-shirt. He pulls me

toward him, all warm muscle and tension, his arms securely around me. The two of us seem to be sharing one partial, held breath. The silence hangs above us, thick and tangible.

Who knows what form that whole life-flashing-before-your-eyes thing is supposed to take. Surely mine *has* to be a flipbook of splashy comic panels, like the credits of any Marvel movie. But right now, I'm not being hammered by visions of all the pieces of my life that have gone before. I'm looking out over the swarm of people, this tiny world within my Valley, and the expanse of dark endlessness beyond it. I feel Grady's arms around me, and all the possibilities that they contain. And all I can think is, *not yet not yet not yet not yet—*

Pretty sure I detect a faint, collective groan of disappointment.

And then the gully erupts into rapturous, euphoric cheers. An orchestra of car horns honk in unison, and above them an off-key 'Auld Lang Syne' drifts up toward us, rambling and discordant, like a thousand people in different dimensions playing the kazoo.

Grady's hands loosen their grip. They trace the

line of my spine, and the curve of my hips, then he touches my cheek with trembly fingers. "Alba … can I please kiss you again now? You know, I've kinda been waiting to kiss you my whole life."

I swim back through the dreamlike fog, leaving behind a vision of Grady and me entwined for all eternity like one of those ash-potted couples from Pompeii.

I place my fingers on his lips. "Wait. Answer one thing for me."

"What?" he says, his eyes all glazey.

"If I did decide to stay here, would you still leave?"

His jaw tightens. "Alba, that's not fair. Especially not now."

"Domenic Miles Grady. Answer the question. Take me out of your decision—"

He laughs. "Not possible. That was never an option. Not since that first time Cleo dumped me in your playpen."

"Gah! Would you stop being such a slushy romantic! Answer the question."

He closes his eyes, his big hands framing my face. "I don't want to. I don't know how I can. But … I think I'd have to," he whispers. "It doesn't have to mean anything, Alba," he adds quickly. "We'll figure it out, if that's what you really want, some way to make it all work—"

I run my hands through his curls until he opens his eyes again. "Domenic – right answer," I say. I ignore the confused look on his face as I pull him toward me, cos it's been, like, thirty seconds, which is way too long to spend not kissing him.

He kisses me back for the longest time, and then he nuzzles into my neck and mumbles, "I love you. So, so much. But don't first-name me, Alba."

"Righto," I mumble back. "No first names. And I might have forgotten to mention this, Grady, but I love you, too."

Grady takes a tiny step away from me, his hands trailing down my arms until he can link his fingers between mine. His face is glowing and happy and more beautiful than I think I've ever seen it. And then he glances over my shoulder, and he says, "Aw, crap."

I turn around to see Eddie, Tia and Pete gaping at us from the darkness of the tree line.

Eddie snorts. "Well. That was gross."

Pete blinks at us. "Yeah. Like watching your cousins go at it."

Tia's face looks just like that time she saw a pair of cherry-red Louboutins on eBay. She pumps her fists into the air with a giant *whoop* and bellows, "Caroline! Hurry! They did it! You owe me money!"

Caroline shuffles her way up the road from somewhere behind them. She looks at us with this amused glint in her eye, and then takes a long swig from the plastic cup in her hand. "Ah. I thought it was something important."

Grady wraps his arms around me from behind and rests his chin on my shoulder. "This is important, Caroline. This is mind-blowingly, earth-shatteringly important."

I can feel those hysterical giggles bubbling up again. "This is, like, the most important thing in the history of the universe."

Caroline rolls her eyes. "It's really not. Seriously thought I was going to win that bet. But thank Christ you two stopped acting like morons."

Eddie punches her in the arm, causing her to stumble sideways and spill half her beer. "My money was always on the G-man. I knew he wouldn't turn out to be such a fecking wimp." He holds up his hand for a high-five. "Dude. Nice one."

I can't see the expression on Grady's face behind me. But whatever it is makes Eddie drop his hand to his side with a start.

Tia is still gaping at us. She bolts across the hill and throws her arms around me and Grady at the same time. "I cannot believe this! I mean, this is so great! Seriously, we were contemplating locking you both up in Ed's shed and leaving you there till you saw sense, but Pete was worried we'd get arrested."

"Yeah," Eddie says. "And now I guess I'll have to watch you two suck face every thirty seconds as well. Caroline, s'pose you and me'll be hooking up next?"

Caroline chugs the rest of her beer in one gulp. "Eddie, if you value your testicles, you will never breathe that sentence again."

"Fair enough," Eddie says. "But feck, guys – you couldn't have sorted this out sooner? We just missed the biggest thing that's ever gonna happen to any of us cos we were searching all over this godforsaken hole for your sorry arses. I missed my old man trying to crowd-surf off the stage. Apparently he's home with an icepack on his nads. And am I at home laughing and pointing? Apparently not."

"Ed, you're gonna have plenty more chances to witness your dad's nad-breaking," Pete says with a grin. "I saw him on YouTube. What was he wearing? A mankini?"

Caroline throws her cup at Pete's head. "Dude! Inappropriate! Don't talk about your friends' dad's junk."

I curl my fingers through Grady's and pull his arms more tightly around me. He buries his face in my hair, silent laughter rumbling through him.

"OK enough!" I yelp. "I love you guys, so don't take this personally, but seriously? You all need to kind of – get lost now."

Caroline rolls her eyes. Eddie gives Pete a punch in the arm. But they're all grinning like idiots.

Caroline grabs Tia by the elbow and Petey by the back of his T-shirt. "We'll be at the Junction when you're ready to find us. Happy new year, guys," she says with a wink as she drags a still-smiling Tia away by the arm.

Eddie looks at us for a moment longer, and then he gives us his two-fingered wave. "World didn't end, in case you were wondering," he calls over his shoulder, as I turn around, and Grady's lips meet mine, and the rest of the universe just melts away.

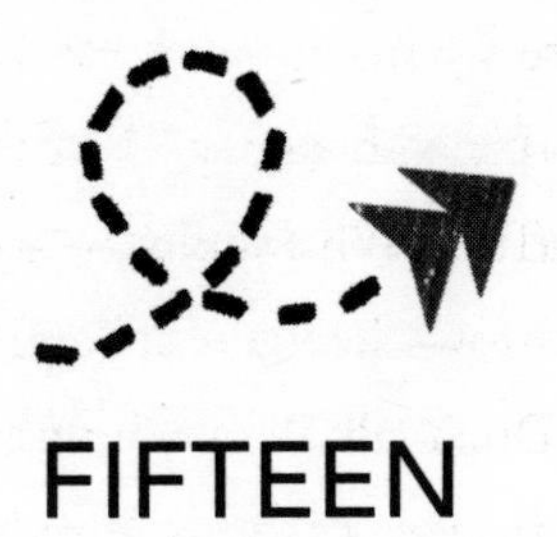

FIFTEEN

I have no idea what time zone the Rapture was supposed to be in. It's possible that somewhere in the world, a bunch of Amazonian tribespeople or French goat herders are staring at a boiling sky and feeling pretty stupid for bothering to do their laundry or whatnot today. But I doubt it. Somehow – despite the shenanigans of the past two weeks – I think everyone always suspected that we were going to be just fine.

We arrive home to find that all of our plastic flamingos have disappeared, and some random dude is passed out on my banana lounge, wrapped like a ham with our glowing paper lanterns, pornographic Sharpie doodles covering his face.

Honestly? At this point, I'm mostly just over the amateur graffiti porn.

Grady and I find ourselves on my green couch, in a tangle of arms and legs and kisses and stories, and fits of giggles that keep engulfing us out of the blue. At some point while our lips are smooshed together, I open my eyes to find that his are wide open too, and he's looking at me like he's not entirely convinced I'm real. Once, in the middle of a particularly awesome kiss, he pinches me lightly on the arm, and he shakes his head incredulously. "Just checking," he says with a grin.

Grady was right about one thing. It's weird, but not weird. If anything, it's just a bit perplexing – like, this plate of delicious apple strudel has been staring us in the face, and we've been choosing the quinoa or something. Grady cracks up laughing when I tell him this, even though I thought it was a pretty decent metaphor. I suppose it's like so many things; the angst about doing way more terrifying than the actual leap.

The sun rises. The birds do their thing. Cleo and Angie stumble into the kitchen, where Grady and I have dragged ourselves for breakfast. I am perched on a counter, and Grady is standing in front of me. We're smooching beside a frypan of burning pancakes and so, I think, have reasonable grounds for taking several seconds to realize that our mums are in the doorway. Most normal parents would probably have the decency to act embarrassed or something, but *nooo* – our mothers shriek as if they've discovered the ghost of Kurt Cobain hiding in the Garabaldis' basement. Mum gets all misty-eyed, and Cleo envelops Grady in a hug with congratulatory back-slaps that make his sheepish face turn the colour of a strawberry tart.

Apart from all that? New Year's Day proves to be pretty uneventful.

Eventually, when the sun has risen on the weary crowds, Grady decides he needs to go home to change, and I decide that spending the night in the same clothes is probably not a habit I should adopt as a signature statement.

An hour or so later, I'm waiting on Albany's verandah for him to come back. I've laid out a plate of yesterday's food, but my appetite has evaporated. After some deliberation, I'd texted Daniel. I know that his family have decided to leave today. But however stubborn my boys may be, I'm not letting Daniel go anywhere without at least trying to patch things up between us first.

I'm sitting half-asleep on our stairs, doodling

sketches on my black Chucks, when I see it. Across the road at the Wasileskis' service station – that shiny bald head, and a flash of a Fu Manchu.

"Oi!" I yell, bolting across the litter-strewn road. "Original Ned – Alvin Smith!"

He turns around, already grimacing. "I have no statement," he says hurriedly.

"You're seriously just going to sneak out?" I say breathlessly. "It's not like a fart in a lift, Ned! You can't just skulk away and pretend it wasn't you!"

He looks frantically down the road, but the few people wandering around seem lost in a haze of their own hangovers. "What do you want from me?" he whines.

Up close, Original Ned is a good few inches shorter than me. I plant my hands on my hips and frown down at him. "How about, like, an explanation? Come on, man! What in the actual hell?"

He fishes a handkerchief out of his pocket and honks his nose. He glances past Albany's and the circus that is the Palmers' farm. And then he sighs.

"They were going to cancel my show," he says quietly. "I thought maybe I'd get a couple more fans … I never expected any of this."

"Ned. Really. This whole thing ... was just your big plan to boost ratings?"

He shrugs. "Something like that."

"*Dude!* Your show sits between the midnight prayer hour and home videos of Lebanese weddings. Did you ever think of just – I dunno – getting a real job?"

He gives me a sheepish smile. "But it worked, didn't it? Maybe a smidge better than I expected, but ... I just got tired of being small. You know? Honestly, I didn't think more than a few people would pay attention. I never understood that whole Twitter business."

Ned looks at me uncertainly. I'm not sure I can make sense of my warring instincts – to give his shiny head a sympathy pat, or to punch the Fu Manchu right off his fake-tanned face.

"Is that it? Can I leave now?" he says wearily.

I cross my arms. "No. One last question, Alvin. Why *here*? Did you just spin around and point at a map?"

"Ah. Not exactly..." And then he straightens, like the weight of the world has lifted from his shoulders. "I sold a house once in Merindale Creek. Did you know I used to work in real estate? Crap job, boring as hell, but I remember passing through this town. It was … nice. Friendly and peaceful." He nods his head at Albany's. "Dunno if you've eaten there, but they make a really fabulous apple strudel. I always wanted to come back for one of those."

I stare at him. "Apple. Fecking. Strudel," I say. And then I burst out laughing.

Original Ned smoothes down his moustache. "Well. Sorry 'bout all this. You know, I didn't even know my show was on YouTube. One of the work experience kids must have put it up there. But I'm thinking I'll look at a web series or something next. Who knew the internet was where it's all happening, hey?"

I'm still laughing when he saunters to his caravan and chugs away down Main Street, a cloud of confetti and party-popper streamers swirling merrily in his wake.

It's strangely mild this morning. A breeze whispers through the trees, and for the first time in weeks, my skin doesn't feel like it's melting. From Albany's verandah, the wandering people seemed chilled, too. I think I can finally appreciate the vibe here; this communal feeling of having survived something major. Even if that major-something was remarkably idiotic.

None of which explains the nerviness that churns through my belly when Daniel's manager's car pulls up in front of Albany's.

Daniel walks languidly toward the bakery and peers through the verandah railings. "Sarah Jane. Happy new year." He takes the stairs and leans back against a table. "I'd give you a kiss, but not sure my ego can hack being shot down again." He looks at me through his eyelashes, thumbs hooked in the pockets of his jeans. I can't for the life of me decipher his expression. "So. Guess this is goodbye. Again," he says.

I leap down from my table. "You're leaving right now?"

He glances briefly at the plate of food. "Yeah. I've got a photo shoot lined up tomorrow. Some 'isn't it great we didn't die in a fiery asteroid explosion' thing for a website. It's lame. But publicity, right?"

"Sure," I reply vaguely. "Anything for your fans."

He rocks back on his heels. "Listen, Alba, there's something I need to say, and you're probably not gonna want to hear me, but I think it's important that you do—"

Grady takes the stairs two at a time and lands beside me with a thud. His familiar smell of soap and shampoo and the fleeting, loaded smile he flicks in my direction temporarily renders me all fuzzy and unfocused. "Hey," he says faintly at Daniel.

"Hey," Daniel replies. "So … come to kiss me goodbye, Grady? I'm flattered."

"I'm not here for you," Grady says evenly. "The only reason I'm here is because Alba asked. I think I've accepted the fact that you and I left anything we had in common behind us when we were ten, Daniel."

Daniel sighs. He rubs his eyes tiredly. "So what, you want to have another go at me? Domenic, I know we've missed some years, but I've known you for a long time and I've never seen you that worked up. You even *bothered* analysing why?" He shakes his head. "Besides, you need to work on your duck and weave. My manager had drunk half a bottle of Bundaberg, and he has a lazy eye, and he *still* managed to land one while you stood there like one of those hypnotized goats—"

"Daniel, shut it! God, are you auditioning for the role of generic henchman? Once upon a time, you were actually a really decent guy!" I reach over, unthinkingly, for Grady. He covers my hand with both of his and pulls my arm toward him. "Where did that boy go?"

Daniel's eyes widen. They dart back and forth between Grady and me. And his face dissolves into a slow smile. But it's not his condescending smile, or his smug smile. Daniel Gordon is looking at Grady and me, and his smile seems really, genuinely … warm. And, inexplicably, relieved.

"*Jesus*! You two took your time. Thought I was going to have to put the moves on Grady next. I almost resorted to randomly taking my shirt off – always seems to work for Indigo."

I gape at Daniel. He waggles an eyebrow at me. And the itchy thing that's been irritating my brain since that night at the Junction becomes suddenly, patently clear.

"Are you *serious*?" I squeal. "This whole time…?"

Daniel giggles, an ancient, maniacal sound of his that I remember way too well. "Well, it's true that I like brunettes. OK, having a crack at kissing you was probably a rash move, but I was seriously running out of ideas."

"You were … *running out of ideas*? Daniel – you manipulative arsebag!" I yell. "What would you have done if I'd kissed you back? What the hell made you think I wouldn't? Hello – have you *seen* you?"

Grady makes a kind of snorting, grunting sound at my side.

The colour rises in Daniel's face. "Yeah. I didn't actually think that far ahead. Though, if you actually *did* wanna kiss me, Sarah, I probably wouldn't have said no. I meant it when I said you have awesome lips, and, you know, I am a guy." He grins sheepishly at us. "Alba, you and I might have been tight once upon a time – but it was always supposed to be you and Grady. Everyone knew that. *I* knew you both knew that, somewhere in those stubborn-arse heads of yours. I'm just glad you guys finally figured it out, too."

"I just … cannot believe you thought you could play us like that!" I say, though I can't help but laugh a little bit, too.

Daniel bows, the cheese-eating grin back on his face. "Yeah, well, remember this performance when I'm accepting my first Oscar," he says with a wink.

"And they say I'm a sucky actor. Honestly, what do they expect? You know the guy who plays my dad is stoned half the time? Try emoting to that."

Grady is gaping, fish-like, in his direction. "Dude. Your manager punched me in the face," he bleats.

Daniel grimaces. "Yeah. Sorry 'bout that. But to be fair, you *were* planning on smashing my face in first. And, you know, he's an arse, but he's actually a pretty decent manager. Whaddya gonna do? It's a weird business."

"But Daniel … *why*?" I say.

Daniel smiles, but it's far away, and tinged with sadness. "I really did miss you guys like crazy when I left. You have no idea. Try being plucked out of the only place you've ever called home and thrown into a city school with, like, a thousand people. And when you looked like I did back then…" The tips of his ears turn pink. "I've got some great mates now. But I've never found friends like I had when I was a kid. I guess … it always made me happy to think that you two were still together." He chuckles. "And your friends were getting sick of your will-they-won't-they antics. Not even a soap opera can stretch that storyline out for seventeen years. You should've heard the verbal tsunami they unleashed on me that first day in the grocery store. Why do you think I volunteered to give you both a prod? Have to say, it was the funnest job I've had in a while."

"They did what!" I yelp.

He waves a dismissive hand. "Relax. They love you guys. And they figured an outside shove might work where their best hints had failed miserably." He gives us a wicked smile. "Remind your friend Caroline she owes me twenty bucks. And anyway – consider it payback. Red Bull drinking game? I'm hurt, Alba. My abs have to be worth at least two shots."

Daniel laughs at my blazing face, his muscly arms folding me into a hug. "Keep in touch, OK? Look me up if you ever make it out my way. I'll show you round. There's a couple of comic-book stores I think you'll love."

"Daniel, you are an arse," I say as I hug him back. "Find me on Facebook. Don't ... disappear again, OK?"

He kisses the top of my head, and then he tugs gently on the end of my hair. "Promise. You know, you really are brilliant, Alba. Go forth and be even brillianter."

Daniel holds out a hand to Grady. Grady shakes it, his face still bewildered. "Yeah … see ya?" he says vaguely.

"You're welcome, dude," Daniel says, punching Grady in the arm with a boomy laugh.

Daniel contemplates the plate of baked deliciousness with a thoughtful tilt of his head. And then he grabs a couple of salted caramel slices, and walks away with a backwards wave.

Grady stares in Daniel's wake until I wrap my arms around him. He shakes his head, then drapes an arm around my shoulder and hugs me back.

"Whaddya know?" I say. "Seems like the entire universe was conspiring against us. Or for us. What do you call that, Grady? A destinyish conspiracy?"

"Fate-ally meddling?" he says with a grin. "And I dunno. I think it just worked out handy for me that you have good taste. I still think Dan would've taken a shot if you gave him half a chance."

I give his side a pinch. "It's nice to know I have options. I could *so* be a telly WAG."

Grady rolls his eyes, and he spins me around so I'm pressed tightly against him. "Alba, you have as much chance of becoming a generic wife-or-girlfriend as I have of winning a Superman look-alike contest."

"Aw, don't be so hard on yourself. You have muscle. Add some spandex, and you'd at least place. Maybe in the junior division. I could so draw you like that."

"Woman, seriously? Sometimes, you can be really mean," he says as he leans down to kiss me.

We watch as Daniel ambles toward his waiting car, his manager giving us the death stare. Daniel pauses with his hand on the door. He glances briefly at Albany's, his face set in a contemplative half-smile. Then he shoves a caramel slice into his mouth and climbs into the car, and, just like that, he is gone.

Well. I *did* say it's not what you think.

Life goes on. The crowds depart soon after New Year's, taking with them most of our road signs, the Eversons' bench, and all of the penis-covered boards from the hardware store. The only hint that Penny-Farthing Man ever existed is a rusted bicycle bell left balanced on Albany's verandah railing. I store the bell between the mementos on my bookshelf; it's nice to have something tangible that keeps him from becoming just another character in my comics.

The clean-up lasts a while. We never do find Frida, my gnome, though sometime in January, an envelope arrives at Albany's. It's stamped from Morocco, and contains a single photo printed on copy paper. And there is Frida, looking haughty as she poses with a lopsided fez on her head, a blurry, colourful market in the background. I'm happy for her. I think everyone deserves to see the world at least once.

Tia and Petey fumble along in their sweetly inept bubble – until the day Tia receives an acceptance letter from the Wane Institute of Design in Sydney. Tia does this bug-eyed thing as she flips through the welcome pack, which I can only describe as the look of someone falling madly in love. Poor Petey never stood a chance. After some weeks of awkwardness, involving many tear-fests at the fish-and-chip shop, and way too much poetry, they settle into a timid, tentative friendship.

Pete still has no idea what he wants to do with his life. But he surprises everyone by getting into a Bachelor of Arts in Newcastle. He gets way excited about studying philosophy and learning to surf, and makes plans to meet up with Tia in Sydney for mid-year holidays, which Tia seems genuinely pleased by. Who knows what will happen there?

Eddie decides to give year twelve a go, resolving to get through the year without making any teachers cry. It lasts all of a month, until this one class where Ed cheerfully declares that "Macbeth's a pussy" and the vein on Mr Baxter's temple explodes, and Eddie decides that the classroom isn't for him after all. But he doesn't go back to the farm. Instead, he starts training at the garage with Anthony and all those guys. Ed texts me a selfie on his first day, looking handsome and so *grown-up* in his overalls. Even Caroline is forced to admit that, as life decisions go, Francis Edwin Palmer could have done a lot worse.

Caroline continues as she always has, on a one-way path straight out of town. She's a little deflated when our visitors clear out, until she snags a temp job in Sydney, and bullies her parents into fronting the rest of the cash for her car. She refuses to let me throw her a going-away party, and simply drives off one quiet night, leaving a giant gap in the Valley where her surly, purple-haired presence should be. But she texts, like, every day, and fills our Facebook feeds with photos of cute guys from the hostel where she's landed. I express-post her a box of treats from Albany's. I like to think that the smiley faces in her texts are just a teeny bit smilier when she receives them.

As predicted, *A Home Among the Gum Trees* is cancelled a few weeks into the new year, disappearing with zero fanfare. But Daniel does keep in contact;

last we heard, he was heading to Korea to shoot a commercial for seaweed ice-cream. Call me crazy, but I have this feeling that Daniel Gordon has the potential to be huge in Korea.

Original Ned Zebidiah is booted off community television, presumably for giving the station that broadcasts *Naked Table Tennis* a bad name. The next time he rears his head, he has reverted to his God-given moniker of Alvin Smith, and is hosting a show on YouTube called *Card Tricks and Cooking*. Alvin does card tricks. And Frank makes soup. It is, weirdly, entertaining.

And Grady and me? We spend the summer like we have every other since we were born. Together. We're still us, only now there's an awful lot of kissing involved. Like, *a lot* a lot of kissing, and, well, let's just say our sleepovers become – ahem – more *experimental* than they used to be. Grady discovers a temporary cure for his insomnia when he spoons behind me, napping with his knees tucked behind mine while I read on his iPad. I don't know how I ever lived without this; downloading comics has *totally* revolutionized my life. And eventually other stuff happens between us, too, which is strange and wonderful and something I am so *not* discussing any further.

Grady gets into law with marks to spare, as we all knew he would. Though he's sombre when he receives the news; he doesn't happy-dance like I expected he would, but he does hug me tightly, and he doesn't let go for ages. I know he's nervous and eager and wistful, too. I see it in his face as we hang out with our friends at Anzac Park, and as we squish into our table for Thai Thursdays at the Junction, and as we walk hand-in-hand through the streets that have been our home for forever. I can tell he's absorbing every detail as if his eyes are seeing the Valley for the very first time.

The approaching end of summer makes me randomly teary as well; the awareness of something slipping through my fingers that no amount of wishing can preserve. I can't help but feel like a giant piece of my heart is breaking, knowing this part of my life I've loved so much is coming to an end.

But honestly? I'm also freakishly excited about the fine arts course I've been accepted into. I think I might even dabble in some animation stuff as well. Who knows? I guess I have to trust that my gut knows what it's doing. For now, I'm just buzzed to be heading into the big wide unknown.

As it turns out, nothing in my box of Cinnamon Girl sketches really goes to waste. I'm able to create a pretty wicked folio of her development, demonstrating the hell out of the 'engagement in drawing' requirement that'll be needed in my first-semester class. Her new comic is not what I was expecting. At the moment, she exists in dozens of black-and-white panels, the only colour, a splash of red-and-blue ink in her hair. I'm not sure who, or what, I can compare her to. She is neither a superhero, nor an ordinary girl. I think she's going to kick arse, regardless of where her story goes.

Grady has a bunch of prep stuff to do before uni, and he finally relents and decides to spend some time with his dad. But I want to stick around till Paulette's cousin, our new waitress, starts at the bakery. So he goes ahead without me. The morning he leaves is muggy and overcast, a blanket covering Eden Valley that makes the fields even more vibrant than normal. He pulls up at Albany's in an ancient Holden EK Special that Anthony had secretly been restoring for him, its back seats packed with boxes, my computer and Wacom nestled safely under bubble wrap.

I know that Angie and Cleo have been counting down the days with cheerful stoicism. But on the morning Grady is due to go, they both totally lose it; our mothers reduced to tearful messes by the time Anthony tugs them inside so that Grady can say a proper goodbye to me, and a huggy, prolonged goodbye to Clouseau.

Two weeks is the longest we have ever been apart, but hey, no one is dying. And it's kinda nice to have Eden Valley all to myself and my mums for just a little while.

After endlessly debating online ads, we finally just tossed a coin to pick a share-house in Northcote, an old place with peeling blue paint and a jungle-dense yard. Grady says the photos on the net don't do the house justice, cos inside it's huge, with high ceilings and amazing light in the bedroom that will be ours. Our housemates' odd bits of furniture give the place an op-shop-meets-music-store vibe but, at least via Skype, I love it. We'll be sharing with two first-year uni students who've just moved in together, some musician chick and her film-student boyfriend. They seem to have adopted Grady like an orphaned puppy, and I think he might be slightly in love with both of them, the way he gushes. I'm nervy; they sound way too cool for me. But Grady insists I'll like them. I suppose it can't hurt to try.

I have no idea when my story started. Maybe it was the first time Dad sat beside me with a stack of *Wonder Woman* comics, reverential and hushed, while I flipped, spellbound, through the pages. Maybe it started the moment Cleo dragged my mum out of a uni party and let Angie sleep it off in her car – a story that, according to Mum, I'm not even supposed to know. Or maybe it was the first time I picked up a pencil. Was it the time Cleo dumped a screaming Grady in my playpen and he fell asleep squished up beside me, or was it a lifetime later, the very first time I kissed him?

Maybe my story will start when I leave here. I suppose it's possible that it hasn't started yet. But honestly? I think it's more likely it started eons before I was born.

I may have said that stories can have a multitude of false starts. But now that I think about it, I'm not sure there's any such thing. It's sort of like the best comics

– frames burst into one another, and colours bleed between lines, and the richness of a universe is only fully graspable when you understand the prequels and crossovers and spin-offs and stuff. Like the superhero stories that veer through a thousand different incarnations, with no beginning or end. It's possible that this is a rubbish metaphor. My point is, most stories can only start when you place yourself in them.

And I think I'm ready, finally, to draw myself in mine.

ACKNOWLEGEMENTS

As always, thank you to the incredible team at Hardie Grant Egmont for their tireless dedication, feedback, enthusiasm, encouragement, coffees, wines and Skype sessions – Karri Hedge, Niki Horin, Kate O'Donnell, Marisa Pintado and Hilary Rogers – superheroes, each and every one.

And, as always, a giant thank you to my beta reader, Sophie Splatt, for your insightful advice, diverting sloth emails, and for letting me pick your brain about the minutiae of rural life. Extra thanks also to Sandra and Graeme Splatt for letting me hang out on the farm, and for fielding random questions about motorbikes and canola.

To my always-excellent writing group – Jo Horsburgh, Benjamin Laird, Neen McKenzie, Simon Mitchell, Ilka Tampke and Jacinda Woodhead

– I couldn't ask for a greater group of writing-and-occasionally-beer-drinking buddies.

Thanks and hugs to my family and friends for your support over the past year; my lovely cousins for listening to me prattle endlessly about comic books; and to Lucy and Ben for keeping me fed when I spent all my money on *Spider-Man*s.

Special thanks to the fabulous staff at All Star Comics, Comics 'R' Us, Evil Empire Comics and Minotaur – cheers and thanks for the chats, and the helpful assistance and suggestions.

And lastly, a very special thank you to the lovely, amazing, passionate and all round wonderful young readers who I've had the pleasure of encountering on my travels – your enthusiasm, emails and letters, and general awesomeness have heartened even the most difficult of writing days.

Author photo © Julie Renouf

Melissa Keil is a writer, children's books editor and compulsive book-buyer. She has lived in Minnesota, London and the Middle East, and currently resides in her home town of Melbourne. Her first young adult novel, *Life in Outer Space*, was the inaugural winner of Hardie Grant Egmont's Ampersand Prize, awarded annually to the best manuscript by a debut author.

Say hello at www.melissakeil.com
or www.facebook.com/MissMisch77
or find her on Twitter @MissMisch77

WHO IS MELISSA KEIL?

We asked Melissa some questions about herself and her writing.

Hi, Melissa. Which books influenced you when you were writing *The Incredible Adventures of Cinnamon Girl*?

Hi there! I actually try not to read much fiction in the genre I'm writing while working on my first draft – I'm always too worried about unintentionally absorbing other people's ideas! But I did read a whole heap of comic books and graphic novels while writing *Cinnamon Girl* – I loved being inside Alba's head, and reading the books she enjoyed really helped me see the world through her eyes. Some of my favourites were *Ghost World*, *Friends with Boys*, *Anya's Ghost*, as well as a heap of superhero comics like *Captain Marvel*, *Runaways*, *Ms Marvel* and, of course, all things Wonder Woman.

Who was your favourite character to write?

I love all my characters equally (I'm supposed to say that, aren't I?), but I did have a lot of fun writing Eddie. His deep, booming voice was so clear in my head that it felt like he was sitting beside me, with all his swear words and dirty innuendos. I have a thing for apparent 'tough guys' who are just big sweet softies on the inside.

If the book were to become a film, which actors would you like to see in the roles of Alba and Grady?

You know, I spend a lot of time gathering visuals for all of my characters while I'm writing – their home environments, their clothes, the posters on their walls – I have folders of pictures of exactly what I'm imagining for all of those details. But I really struggle to find real-world equivalents for my characters. I think it's partly because the vision I have of them is so clear in my head that no one who actually exists is ever quite right. I'm sure there's a perfect unknown Alba and Grady out there somewhere though!

What made you want to become an author?

Like most authors, I've been a book nerd for as long as I can remember. I've always been happiest with my head in a story; telling my own stories is a pretty natural extension of that.

Where do you write?

I mostly write at my desk at home, but occasionally venture out with my laptop when I feel like a change of scenery. When the weather is nice I love writing in my backyard with my dog Hugo snoozing beside me (though I do find I'm easily distracted by birds and shiny things). If I'm working on a scene set in a particular place, I'll try and visit, and do a bit of writing on location, which is always fun. I live in the city, but spent a bit of time out in the country while I was working on this book, which helped enormously with creating Eden Valley.

If you could be any book character, who would you be?

If I could only choose one character? I'd have to be Arthur Dent from *The Hitchhiker's Guide to the Galaxy* (btw, my favourite book ever). The idea of travelling the universe while living permanently in pyjamas is pretty appealing.

Finally, what would be your favourite treat from Alba's mum's bakery?

Oh, definitely their famous apple strudel! I spent many nights dreaming about strudel while I was writing this book.

Love
LIES &
Lemon
Pies
KATY CANNON

KATY CANNON
Secrets,
SCHEMES
&
Sewing
Machines

SAIL. SALVAGE. SURVIVE.

eBook available